GIRL JACKED

A DETECTIVE JACK STRATTON NOVEL

CHRISTOPHER GREYSON

GREYSON MEDIA

Novels featuring Jack Stratton in order:

AND THEN SHE WAS GONE
GIRL JACKED
JACK KNIFED
JACKS ARE WILD
JACK AND THE GIANT KILLER
DATA JACK
JACK OF HEARTS
JACK FROST

Also by Christopher Greyson:

PURE OF HEART

THE GIRL WHO LIVED

ISBN: 1-68399-020-X
ISBN-13: 978-1-68399-020-8

CONTENTS

1

NOTHING MORE

Two women anxiously waited on the hard, wooden bench of the Fairfield police station. Haddie Williams and her much younger friend—one of her many foster children over the years—looked down the hall toward its opposite end, seeking news, not sure they wanted to hear it.

At last, a lanky police detective with a downcast face ambled toward them. As he handed the old woman a copy of the missing person report, he said, in a monotone, "I'm sorry, ma'am, but there's nothing more we can do."

The words hit Haddie like a punch in the chest. The old woman stood, though her body shook. Years of hard work had worn her down until she was frail and bent, but that wasn't the reason she trembled. Right now, her soul ached. She looked up—her brown eyes pleading her case. "I raised that little girl since she was five. I know her. She'd never leave without telling me."

The detective's gaze wandered down the hallway as he scratched at the base of his jaw. "Well… you know, she's in college. She's over twenty-one. Kids grow up and want to lead their own lives. We get reports like this all the time." He escorted them to the front door of the police station. "Give her a week or two and she'll come home, probably looking for money. They always do." He patted the old woman on the back.

Haddie's maternal hackles rose. "I've raised twenty-seven foster children, including my friend here." She glanced at the young woman next to her. "I know my Michelle. She never missed one day at school or got into any trouble. She studied hard and helped around the house. She'd never leave without letting me know." Her companion nodded her head vigorously in agreement, setting her ponytail bobbing.

"Yes, ma'am. You let us know when you hear from her." As he held the door open, the world-weary policeman's expression made it clear that whatever compassion or drive had led him to join the police force had long since ebbed away and he wasn't going to help.

The wind blew cold and bitter around the corner of the building. Haddie shivered as the door clicked shut behind her. It could have closed with a thunderous boom and it wouldn't have sounded any more final.

At the top of the steps she lifted her face to the darkening winter sky. The thought of Michelle out there, alone, afraid…

Her ebony hands balled into fists. "You need to go get Jack," she said.

"But Aunt Haddie, he—"

Haddie clutched the young woman's arm with one hand and the cold metal railing with the other. Almost to herself, she whispered, "Jack will find Michelle."

"But… he hasn't been back to visit since he left the Army."

Haddie's chin quivered, but her eyes were unwavering. "Something's happened to Michelle. I'm sure of it. And Jack will find her."

The young woman's green eyes hardened. "Are you sure he'll help us? Why hasn't he come back since…" Her voice trailed off.

Haddie closed her eyes and shivered a little. "He blames himself for what happened. But I know Jack. He'll help. He'll bring Michelle back."

The young woman fastened the top button of Haddie's jacket. "Let me get you home."

"You promise to go?" Haddie squeezed her hand. "You have to promise me. And trust Jack."

The young woman nodded.

Haddie looked up again at the sky. "Better hurry. It looks like rain."

2

THE BOAR'S BUTT

"Jack?" The female police dispatcher's voice crackled over the radio.

"Copy."

"We've got a ten-ten in progress at the Boar's Butt."

Jack always laughed at the offbeat name. Calling the Boar's Butt a restaurant was a stretch. It served a few different types of pizza. If you asked for an appetizer, the waitress pushed a bowl of popcorn closer to you. They served beer, hard liquor, and cheap wine out of a can for the rare drinker who dared to ask. Said establishment was a local bar and pizza joint that mainly catered to a regular crowd of rowdy guys and featured often in ten-ten calls.

"Any other info?" The adrenaline began to pump as Jack swung the cruiser around and hit the lights.

"Bartender called it in. No other details. Backup's going to be delayed. What's your ETA?"

"Ten minutes."

"Ten-four, Officer Stratton."

Jack grinned. He never got tired of hearing those words, *Officer Stratton*. He'd survived a tour of duty in Iraq, struggled with money through college, entered the police academy, landed his first job here in Darrington—all pretty much as planned. He was the low man on the totem pole, and routinely assigned the graveyard shift, but he didn't care. He was living his dream, doing the thing he loved—being an officer of the law. It was the only good part of his life he had left.

Jack's smile grew as the cruiser's speed increased. He glanced at the dashboard clock: 11:35 p.m. There wasn't another car on the road, no nightlife or excitement at this hour as he raced through the sleepy backwater of Darrington. He gripped the steering wheel and settled back into the seat; the leather creaked happily as he took the corners. He felt alive.

The other cops knew Jack had practically claimed the new, refitted Charger as his own. V8 Hemi engine, 368 horsepower, 395 pounds of torque roaring to life every time he went out on patrol.

And to Jack, the car *did* belong to him, which was why he'd almost gotten into a fistfight with another officer, Billy Murphy, when someone saw Murphy doing doughnuts with it in a deserted parking lot. Billy Murphy was a beneficiary of clear nepotism—his father-in-law was the county commissioner. No matter how many times Murphy screwed up, nothing changed. So, getting one up on Murphy every time he drove this baby only made it more enjoyable.

Jack cut down a side road that ran straight for a mile, telephone poles whizzing by. When he pinned the gas pedal to the floor, the Hemi purred with pleasure. A rush of adrenaline surged through him as he relished his momentary freedom. Keeping his hands slightly loose on the wheel, Jack made only minor corrections. But all too soon he neared the end of the street and had to slow down.

He killed the lights and rolled into the bar's parking lot. He was already in enough hot water with Sheriff Collins, so he decided to angle the Charger pointing toward the woods rather than the front of the bar. *No need for the dash cam footage to end up on the boss's desk.*

There were fewer than a dozen cars and trucks parked outside. Jack scanned them quickly. Two stood out: an old Chevy Super Sport and an enormous red Timberline work truck. Jack had pulled the Chevy over a number of times and the guy who owned it also owned quite an attitude. He fancied himself a tough guy and a ladies' man. Jack didn't think he was either.

The Timberline truck meant he'd find lumberjacks inside. After a dangerous tour of duty overseas, Jack had seen some tough guys, but a lumberjack made his shortlist of guys he *didn't* want to fight.

He grabbed a backup set of cuffs and jumped out, instinctively snagging his hat before locking the door. His instincts were now honed to a sharp edge by the academy. Something as simple as a hat could be used for crowd control—from the gold shield on top to the trick of angling your head to hide your eyes.

He ran his fingers through his dark-brown hair. Sensing something in the air, he pulled his hat down a little lower than usual.

It's a fight. Crowd control: investigate, intimidate, dissipate.

Climbing the steps that led to the outside deck of the rundown bar, he made sure not to touch the thick railing made out of two-inch rusted plumbing pipe screwed into the porch; it would turn the palm of your hand rusty-orange the instant you touched it. He held the large wooden door open for a young couple hurrying out.

"Thank you, Officer." The man looked nervously over his shoulder back into the bar and prodded his girlfriend to move faster. She flashed a smile at Jack that must have lingered a little too long, because the boyfriend hustled her down the steps, glaring at Jack.

Jack hid a smile. He was used to the unwanted attention, though he played down his looks as much as possible. All he knew was that he'd never had to work too hard to attract the ladies—though keeping their attention, as he was well aware, was not so easy.

The entire restaurant was a single large open area with a kitchen at the back. Opposite the door was a long serving bar with a dozen stools. Booths lined the other walls. Next to them were five large tables, each covered with a red-and-white-checkered vinyl tablecloth. Jammed into a corner beside two pinball machines was a jukebox. The smell of pizza and beer filled the air. The brown floor had been painted so many times it was hard to tell it was wood.

Jack could see the problem the moment he walked in. No one could miss the three drunken lumberjacks standing next to the jukebox, laughing. None of the men stood less than six feet, and one was a giant of a man—three hundred pounds easy.

Figures. Paul Bunyans. Wonderful.

The jukebox was playing Dwight Yoakam's "Little Sister." Jack cracked his neck and rolled his shoulders. At six-one and a hundred ninety-five pounds, he could easily intimidate most guys, but that wouldn't work with these three.

The bartender, a fat guy with a beer belly, hustled over to Jack. He looked pale. "I didn't serve them. They showed up stewed. They said they ain't leaving without a drink."

Jack nodded.

"These same guys were here last season. They smashed the place up when the owner kicked them out."

"You want to press charges?"

"No!" The guy wiped his brow with a stained dish rag. "I just want them out of here."

"Okay, thanks."

Jack looked around at the other people in the room. Some stared at him blankly. Others just peeked up. A few even smiled. The one emotion they all seemed to share was hope. Jack felt the weight of the badge on his chest. *They expect me to handle it. That's what cops do. We come and bring the peace.*

The three men stopped laughing and turned to look at Jack. The biggest one held a nine-inch hunting knife. As an uncomfortable silence settled in, the bartender moved away.

Backup is going to be delayed, Jack cautioned himself.

"Hello, Officer," the drunken goliath with the knife hollered out. "We're just playing darts!" He looked at his buddies. "But they didn't have any, so we had to use our own." He laughed and launched his blade across the room at the tattered dartboard. When it hit with a thump, the three men cheered wildly.

"Are you here for a game?" mocked one of the other men—Chevy Super Sport.

Jack saw two knives sticking out of the board and scanned the hands of the lumberjacks. Empty.

He looked around the tightly packed room full of innocent bystanders. He had to get the troublemakers outside. "Can I have your attention?" Jack's voice was calm as he held up his hands. He didn't have to shout. Everyone was already looking at him. "Would the owner of a red pickup truck please come to the front of the building?"

"Why?" sneered the third lumberjack, the smallest of the three.

Jack lowered his arms. "Because his truck is on fire."

The lumberjacks looked at one another in bewilderment and then scrambled for the front door. The smallest man reached it first and yanked it open, but the giant pushed him aside. Then the Chevy owner charged through, leaving the small guy holding the door.

Perfect.

As the last man stepped outside, Jack moved like lightning. He slapped one of the handcuffs over the man's wrist and the other through the door handle.

As the second guy started down the deck stairs, Jack yelled, "Watch your step!"

In his drunken stupor, the man panicked and grabbed for the railing. Jack dashed up behind the pudgy one and handcuffed his fat wrist to the railing.

Two down—one to go.

The giant had stopped in the middle of the parking lot. He looked at his truck, and his face scrunched up. "My truck's fine." He turned to Jack. "There's no fire!" Confusion quickly turned to anger when he saw his friends in cuffs; he crouched and prepared to charge. "You stopped my dart game," he slurred. "I'm gonna stomp you!" He rushed forward.

Jack stepped to the right and grabbed the hulking man by his collar and belt.

This is gonna hurt.

Jack pulled the guy against his leg, twisted his body, and pivoted his hip, leveraging the three-hundred-pound lummox right off his feet. Both men groaned as the guy's feet went straight up and Jack strained, pushing him toward the pinnacle of the flip, then stepped aside. His adrenaline rush, pushed into overdrive, caused everything to slow. The man seemed to hang in the air like a basketball player whose slam dunk had gone terribly wrong.

The giant landed flat on his back with a thud and an explosive groan that blasted all the air from his lungs.

As the lumberjack opened and closed his mouth like a fish out of water, Jack flexed his shoulders, took a step forward, and leaned over. "I'm sorry, sir. It seems you tripped."

The lumberjack winced.

"You're going to leave now, and everything will be fine." He waved his hand like Obi-Wan Kenobi. "But if you give me any lip, I'll take the three of you in right now."

The large man nodded, and Jack gave him a hand to get to his feet. He tried to look menacing as he walked over to the other lumberjacks, who had silently watched the scene unfold.

"We'll go. Sorry. We'll go now," the tough guy, who no longer looked so tough, babbled.

Total surrender. Cool. Jack allowed himself a little smirk, set him free, and the man hurried over to his friend, who was still panting and gasping with his hands on his knees.

The last lumberjack stood cuffed to the door. Jack crossed his arms and furrowed his brow.

"Sorry," the man muttered sheepishly as he looked at his feet.

Take out the big guy and the little ones fall into line.

"How many drinks have you had?" Jack asked as he unlocked the cuffs.

"Two, sir."

"You're designated driver. Got it?"

"Yes. Thank you, Officer."

The two smaller men helped their giant friend to the truck just as another police car, its lights flashing, skidded to a stop in the parking lot. All three lumberjacks looked nervously back at Jack. He waved them on as Officer Kendra Darcey jumped out of her cruiser, her shotgun at the ready.

He gave her a quick nod. "Everything's under control." Both of them watched the red truck pull slowly out of the parking lot.

Kendra frowned. "I missed it?" The twenty-four-year-old rookie was an all-round athlete and an adrenaline junkie.

He tilted his head. "If I had known you were on tonight, I'd have left one for you."

"Yeah, right," she said with a smile, resting the shotgun on her hip. "If you're all set, then I'll let *you* handle the paperwork."

Jack walked down the stairs and leaned in close. "I was hoping you'd volunteer to fill out the forms for the both of us?"

As she smiled, her blue eyes sparkled and the four-inch scar that ran from the corner of her chin to her eyebrow stood out. Only a few people knew how she'd gotten it, and Jack was one of them. While on a walk with her enormous, high-strung German shepherd, the dog spotted a coyote and bolted after it. The retractable leash snapped and caught her in the face, and the rope burn never healed quite right.

But that wasn't the kind of story that earned a rookie cop respect. She told Jack she got it in a fight with four guys during a bust, but he knew it was a lie right away. He called her on it, but he also gave her a way to tweak the truth and make it sound cool: She got hurt training a K-9 unit. They became good friends after that.

Kendra laughed and set her blond ponytail bobbing. "Don't go flashing those baby browns at me, Jack. I'm not one of your girlfriends."

Jack knew she was teasing him. They were friends, and Jack wanted to keep it that way. Friends could all too easily change into something more, and he'd had enough problems with ex-girlfriends to know he didn't need one at work.

He asked, "You riding solo?"

She lifted her chin. "Collins thinks I can handle things by myself now."

Jack raised an eyebrow. "Really?"

She blushed. "And... Don called in sick."

"Don't rush solo. Maybe we can team up again soon." Jack winked and headed up the steps. "I have to go back in and talk to the bartender. Thanks for the backup."

"I'll watch your backside anytime," she purred, heading to her cruiser.

Jack wrapped up the interview in the bar quickly. It was easy, because no one wanted to pursue it any further and no arrests simplified things. As he walked back to his cruiser, he made a mental note to buy some extra-large handcuffs.

At the station, he muddled through the monotonous paperwork. When he finally allowed himself to glance up at the clock, he was glad to see he'd be home before 2:00 a.m. He finished his shift and headed to his car, whistling "Little Sister."

But if he had known what was waiting for him at home, he wouldn't have been whistling.

3

YOU SUCK

Jack stopped short in the doorway of his apartment. Gina, his on-again-off-again girlfriend, stood in the middle of Jack's crappy living room. Four-and-a-half-inch heels, tiny miniskirt, silk top showing off her cleavage, fake fur jacket hugging her waist, shiny ruby-red lips—that was Gina. All topped off by a mane of blond hair that would make any eighties sitcom actress envious. She could have been the cover girl on a hot-rod magazine, but just for now—until she got her big break, or whatever—she was working at the beauty salon two blocks down.

She let him take a good look at her, then threw her head back and yelled, "You suck!" followed by bursting into fake tears and storming out. The echoes from the slammed door rippled along the paper-thin walls.

Jack tossed his keys on the kitchen counter.

Anniversary, birthday, some promise... He ran down the list of possible screw-ups he could have made, but he drew a blank. He hadn't been on a bender for a long time, so it wasn't that. He wasn't cheating on her. *A lie? You have to talk for that to happen, and talking's not exactly our specialty.*

He replayed the events of the last two minutes in his head. No bags. Pocketbook, but no suitcases. She might be back.

He shrugged and walked over to the refrigerator. His reflection brought him up short.

Stupid mirror. Who puts a mirror on a refrigerator? Gina had said it would help her stay skinny. His brown eyes darkened.

"Way to go, Jack. You sure know how to pick 'em."

Miles, too many miles, all of them hard. He was twenty-six, but felt older. After he got back from Iraq, he'd tried a round robin of vices to kill the pain: drinking, smoking, women like Gina, women completely unlike Gina... Nothing worked; the pain remained, a dull ache. He couldn't remember eating a vegetable in the last month or the last time he'd gotten a good night's sleep. His once happy life had spiraled out of control.

No shock that he looked rough, but Gina dug that type of guy, the "dangerous" type. She'd stormed out a few times before, but each time she'd returned. And when she did... she was wild. Jack's smile broadened into a full grin. They'd trashed the bedroom the last time.

But his smile evaporated when he looked in the fridge. Unless he was in the mood for a few drops left in a bottle of spiced rum and some crusty mounds where something had spilled long ago, he was going hungry. Gina wasn't much for keeping a well-stocked kitchen, and he wasn't much for keeping the rum bottle full.

He was debating going out for takeout when he saw the front door was still open. Wouldn't be the first time it had rebounded, especially after one of Gina's tantrums.

"Stupid lock," he muttered. No way would he ask the landlady to get it fixed again. She'd been mad enough the last time it got broken.

Jack trudged over to the door. Whether or not from excessive slamming by the resident diva, now you had to jiggle the handle for the latch to engage. He fiddled with the knob and pushed at the latch until it popped back out. Yawning, he shut the door, turned around, and then—shrieked.

"You squeal like a baby, Jack," said the young woman standing in his living room.

Jack's mouth fell open. He'd seen a lot in his life and had thought he was beyond instant shock, but all his training went out the window as he gawked at the pretty young woman standing smack-dab in the middle of his living room, wearing nothing but a towel.

She moved closer. "You've got nothing to eat—"

"What the hell are you doing in my apartment? Get out!" Jack grabbed the young woman by the arm, pushed her out the front door into the hallway, and slammed the door behind her.

She knows my name?

A moment later, BANG! BANG! BANG! He could actually see the door shaking, and the walls along with it.

She must be slamming her whole body against the door.

Jack panicked when he thought about what would happen if someone found a half-naked woman outside his apartment, so he yanked the door open and she charged headlong into the living room, tripping and sprawling across the floor.

Jack heard feet stomping up the stairs.

Oh, no, just what I don't need.

He peeked into the hallway, and sure enough, his landlady was sailing down the corridor in her extraordinarily large plaid flannel nightgown, her face flushed bright red. He ducked back inside and locked the door. But a few seconds later, the heavy footsteps came to a stop just outside his door.

Knock. Knock. Knock.

Behind him, the young woman scrambled to her feet and adjusted the towel around her torso. "You jerk," she growled, and shoved both hands into his chest. Caught off-guard, Jack staggered back and crashed into the door.

"Mr. Stratton, what is going on? Was that a girl in the hallway?"

"What's your problem, Jack?" the young woman demanded. *Wait, I've seen her before.* She shot him an angry glare.

"That's it, Mr. Stratton. I've had it with you! And your wild antics! I'm evicting you this time! You'll hear about this…" The landlady's threats faded down the hall.

Jack waited until he could no longer pretend to be listening to Mrs. Stevens stomping back to her troll's lair on the first floor. As he tried to choose among the questions he wanted to ask the interloper—*Who are you? What's your problem? Where have I seen you before?* —he tried to keep his gaze on her face and block his view of… everything else. Her shoulder-length brown hair was dripping wet, but it was her piercing eyes that finally grabbed his full attention: emerald-green, flecked with gold.

Jack blinked and focused. "Who are you and why are you in my apartment?"

She adjusted the towel, her eyes darting to the floor and her voice softening. "You don't remember me?"

"No. Should I?" He had a feeling he definitely should.

"I'm Chandler's sister."

Jack was confused. "Michelle's his sister."

"Yeah. So am I." Her hands tightened into fists.

Jack opened and then closed his mouth. There was always a steady stream of kids in and out of Aunt Haddie's foster home. Most stayed for only a few weeks, but one girl lived there for a few years. Aunt Haddie had taken her in long after Jack had moved out and been adopted. She'd worn her hair in a ponytail on top of her head and was always following Michelle and Chandler around whenever Jack came for a visit. And… yes, now he remembered. Chandler had insisted she had a crush on him.

She must have been twelve or thirteen then. That would make her almost twenty now.

"… Replacement?" Jack said her nickname out loud as he tried to reconcile his memories of her with the curvy young woman who stood before him.

"Yes."

He could hear Chandler: "Leave it to my Aunt Haddie. We're the only poor black family that goes and adopts a white kid."

Chandler's gone. The pleasant recollection faded as the memory that still stabbed him in the heart took its place and he swallowed down the bile in his throat. He'd spent the last six years trying so hard not to remember. Not to remember the war. Not to remember all the death he saw. Not to remember anything—including his friend.

"Sorry. I—didn't recognize you," Jack said.

"Whatever. I need to talk to you."

"Listen, I stayed away for a reason. You can't just barge in here and—take a shower! *What are you doing here?*"

"Aunt Haddie sent me."

Jack's heart thumped. "Why? What's wrong?"

"Hold on." She clutched the towel. "I need to get dressed and my clothes are soaked from the rain. Do you have a clothes dryer?"

"No. There's a laundromat around the corner."

"Are you kidding me? I'm in a towel."

He could see that. "Wait a second." Jack walked past her into his bedroom. On the right side of the closet, which Gina had coopted entirely, were all the outfits she complained didn't fit her anymore. He grabbed a green-and-white dress, marched back into the living room, and held it out to Replacement awkwardly. "Here. It might be a little big."

She took the dress, hardly giving it a glance. "Thanks. Can I change in there?" She nodded toward the bedroom.

"Sure, be my guest," said a haggard, sleepy Jack. She went into the bedroom and shut the door behind her.

With a massive headache about to crest, he rubbed his temples as more memories came flooding back in. He and Chandler—his best friend since the day Jack arrived at Aunt Haddie's, aged seven—had been about to graduate from high school, just a summer away from enlisting…

Another disturbing memory surfaced—a woman had been murdered. Jack and Chandler found her body, out by Hamilton Park; they helped solve the case. Such a strange time, so many hormones… his first "real" girlfriend, Kelly…

Suddenly he remembered he and Chandler running out of Haddie's kitchen door and Replacement crashing into him on the back porch. She dropped her groceries and they bumped heads when he went to pick up the bag... He felt the bump on his forehead; saw her huge, star-struck eyes staring at him. She was called Replacement because...

Jack's heart thumped again. She had been an abused kid when Aunt Haddie took her in—night terrors, painfully shy, the whole nine yards. Jack had to break her door down one night when she locked it and was screaming in her sleep. Michelle sat up with her all night, rocking her, singing to her.

Chandler had named her. She was supposed to be *his* replacement, if ever he wasn't there to take care of Haddie and Michelle. The nickname stuck.

Something must be terribly wrong. Jack put his head in his hands. Aunt Haddie? She wasn't his real aunt, or anybody's real aunt for that matter, but everybody called her that. Haddie took him in as a child, after he'd been preyed upon, neglected, abandoned, and she healed him—loved him back to health with great cooking, life lessons, faith, and hugs.

He could always conjure up the big black woman's bright smile and knowing, young-old eyes, but now they wouldn't come to him. He hadn't seen Haddie in years.

He jumped up anxiously and went to the bedroom door. He was just about to knock when it opened and Replacement stood there, hands on hips. She still looked peeved, but at least she was decent. The dress was a little long for her petite, five-foot-four frame, but it fit her slender figure well. Looked better on her than on Gina, actually.

Before he could get a word out, she said sternly, "Aunt Haddie needs your help."

He knew he should have gone to see her. He'd been back and in the area for over six months now, but he always hesitated. His memories of Chandler were too raw.

Jack held up his hands. "Yes, of course, I'll try, if I can." He only owed Aunt Haddie everything, after all. Maybe she needed money.

"It's about Michelle..."

Oh, no. Replacement's knee bounced and her eyes restlessly searched the room behind him.

"Michelle is gone. She's missing."

Jack felt like he'd been kicked in the gut. "What?"

"She's gone!"

"What do you mean, gone?"

"We haven't heard from her in over two weeks. She got accepted at White Rocks Eastern College, and then..." She sputtered like an engine that was revved too high. "... I tried going up there, but when we went to the police..." Her eyes welled up with tears. "They said..."

Jack's heart was pounding, but he forced himself to slow down and breathe. "Wait a second. Michelle has to be, what, twenty-four? And she's in college?"

"She got a work scholarship. It was her first year. She always wanted to go before, but she couldn't afford it." She sniffled. "She didn't come home and... we went to the po—police station—"

"It's okay. Take a breath." He pushed a box of tissues toward her on the coffee table. "I'm sorry I gave you a hard time."

He let Replacement blow her nose and calm down a little. "What day was she supposed to come home?"

"Four days before Christmas."

"Okay. You went to the police. What did they tell you?"

"They said she transferred to Western Tech out in California and just left. But she wouldn't do that. She wouldn't just—*go*." Replacement threw her hands up. "She had just started at White Rocks and she had a full scholarship. Why would she leave?"

"Did she ever talk about transferring?"

"No. And she didn't transfer. After Chandler died, do you think she'd just take off to the other side of the country without telling Aunt Haddie? Do you honestly think *Michelle* would just leave and not tell *her*?" Her voice trembled.

Chandler and Michelle, biological brother and sister, were at Haddie's when he first arrived, and after he left, the siblings had remained with Haddie, because they were never adopted.

Jack sometimes felt guilty that he'd been adopted and they weren't. Part of it was because they were black and he was white, but the other reason they were always passed over for adoption was that they refused to let anyone separate them.

To Michelle and Chandler, family was everything. Replacement was right. Michelle would never leave Haddie in the dark.

"I didn't realize she lived nearby."

"That's because you cut us off."

She was right. He'd had nothing to do with them lately. Guilt had driven a wedge between him and Michelle and even Haddie. He couldn't face them. How could he possibly go back home to Aunt Haddie without Chandler? Jack had failed him, failed all of them.

I should have…

He couldn't think about that now. He pushed back his feelings and walked toward the kitchen. "What can I do?"

He meant to sound eager to help, but she took it the wrong way. "I don't know; you're the cop." A pair of blazing green eyes ripped into him. "Aunt Haddie still thinks of you as family, and you were Chandler's best friend, for whatever that's worth."

He knew he deserved that, but Jack was a new cop. Rookies didn't get missing person cases; they were the gophers for the detectives who did.

"Who's handling the case?"

"Aunt Haddie filed a missing person report in the Fairfield County Sheriff's Department. The detective there said they would ask someone over here to look into her last known address. They said his name's Gavin… Devin…"

"Davenport," Jack said.

Replacement nodded.

Joe Davenport was an older detective in Darrington with not many years to go until he retired. Joe wasn't a bad guy, but at this point in his career, Jack thought he was coasting to the finish line—or the fishing line, more like it.

Still, a missing person case involving the university… he must have given it a solid going-over. "If Joe looked into this—"

"I knew it. I *knew* it. You don't care!" Replacement marched over and jabbed her finger in Jack's face. "You don't give a flying—"

"Just shut up for a minute. Now, you listen—"

"Listen to what?"

Jack leaned in, but he hardly knew what he was doing—this woman, with her smoldering scorn, ticked him off more than Gina could with an hour of screeching. Jack couldn't believe it when she stuck her head forward, even closer to his.

"Well, what?" Her lips quivered, not out of fear, but with fury. They stared at each other, nose to nose, like two prizefighters waiting for the bell.

Jack closed his eyes for a second, but he could still feel her glaring at him. "I need to think. It's two in the morning, the university is closed, and I just got home after a very long day. My turn for a shower." He called out sarcastically over his shoulder, "Make yourself at home."

Although Jack wanted to, he forced himself *not* to slam the door.

4

DRAMA QUEEN

Jack stood under the shower, lost in the sensations of each muscle as it relaxed and thanked him. There was nothing he loved better than a long, hot shower, and the giant hot-water tank was the best thing about the grungy apartment. Steam filled the small bathroom, creating a mini sauna, but it finally started to run cold. He stood in the refreshing cascade for a minute before getting out.

He stared into the fogged mirror, but nothing stared back. Maybe that was his real reflection. Misty. Shifting. Empty.

"You suck. You jerk!" Gina's and Replacement's words rang in his ears.

He ran his fingers through his hair and absentmindedly grabbed a pair of shorts and a shirt from the hamper. He hated putting on dirty clothes, but he'd only worn them around the house yesterday, and considering there was a girl in the living room, it beat going around in a towel.

Jack was worried. He knew Michelle wasn't the type to run off. She'd never leave Aunt Haddie. He hoped she just went out to California to check it out, considering a transfer. Maybe she had a boyfriend and decided to take a little trip between classes. Or...

Think about something else... anything else.

Jack knew pain and misery too well. He'd had a lifetime of it, way more than his fair share. Thinking that someone else, especially Michelle, might be in danger right now tore him up inside.

As he methodically got dressed, brushed his teeth, and got ready to face Replacement again, his thoughts zigzagged between his landlady—he'd never seen Mrs. Stevens *this* mad—and Gina. She'd show up tomorrow and get all her stuff. After that... gone. Too many fights. Jack wondered why he hadn't kicked her out and sent her packing a long time ago.

I never can. They all leave—but I never do.

Jack's mind wandered back to Kelly. He cut her off, too, but she didn't give up on him. She wrote to him every day. She waited for him to come back from Iraq. But when he saw her at the airport... He couldn't even talk to her. Everything had changed. She was the same. The town was the same. His 1978 Chevy Impala was the same. But Jack wasn't.

He remembered looking right into her eyes and knowing she didn't know him anymore. He wasn't the same man. She'd walked away, and he'd let her.

Jack didn't know how much fight was left in him anymore. He lingered at the bedroom door, not wanting to go back into the living room. But of course, he couldn't stay in the bathroom forever.

The second he stepped out, Replacement was right back in his face. She must have been pacing outside the door. "What the heck were you doing in there?"

The twenty minutes he'd spent chilling out in the shower didn't seem to have calmed her down at all. Her whole body vibrated. "I have to let Aunt Haddie know. Are you going to help or not?"

Jack hesitated.

"I knew it! I told her you didn't care. If you cared about us, you'd have come back already." She moved forward until he could feel her breath on his face. "I saw the letters with those worthless excuses—after Iraq, you had to go straight on to college. You couldn't come for a visit? Not one holiday or summer? Yeah, right."

Her hands balled into fists. "You've probably never even paid your respects at Chandler's grave. And then to find out you moved an hour away months ago, and you still haven't visited or even called? That's low. Really low."

Jack couldn't control the snarl that came out. "Listen, I'll help you look for Michelle, but if you say another word about Aunt Haddie or Chandler—"

Jack was cut off when the front door swung wide open and Gina sashayed in, carrying a couple of bags and a drink from the local convenience store. When she saw Replacement, her eyes went wide and she dropped the bags and cup. Soda flew everywhere.

After an awkward pause, her glare shifted from face to face. "You're still here?" Gina shook a bright-red fingernail at Replacement. "You—you—little slut! That's my dress!"

Before Jack could explain, Gina took three strides and slapped Replacement across the face.

Replacement swung immediately, fast and hard, but Jack scooped her into his arms just in time and the punch swished by Gina's face. Even though the blow didn't connect, Gina squealed and protectively covered her cheek, staggering backward.

Jack knew Gina. Total drama queen. Even the thought of something happening to her face was enough to terrify her. He'd almost called 911 one time when he heard her screaming, only to find out it was over a broken nail.

"I let her borrow—" Jack tried to explain, but she cut him off.

"How dare you!" Gina shouted. "That's it. Over. I mean it." Her red lips twisted into a sneer. "You're pathetic. Poor, poor baby. You're so sad. Poor Jack has mommy issues…"

That's it. Jack had had enough. Gina had just turned that corner when love and lust turned to hate and disgust. She was hitting below the belt, and he wasn't one to just sit there and take it.

Replacement, restrained in Jack's arms, clearly wanted another chance to pound Gina. So Jack released her.

She sprang forward. Gina shrieked and ran for the door, no match in her high heels for the Replacement bullet train, but then Replacement slipped on the spilled soda and had to catch herself on the doorframe.

"Wench!" Replacement shouted at the top of her lungs as Gina fled down the hallway.

For a little thing, she sure is loud. Jack dashed over, yanked Replacement back into the apartment, and shut the door. *Wench?* Had to be one of Michelle's words. Some of her insults were a little Shakespearean.

"What's wrong with you? Be quiet." Jack grabbed Replacement by the shoulders and spun her around. "It's nearly three in the morning. My landlady is gonna evict me. First you sneak into my apartment—"

"I didn't sneak," she snapped as she tried to adjust Gina's dress.

Jack's finely tuned BS detector went off. "Gina let you in?"

"No… but she found me here."

That explained some things, but not others. "Why would you break into my apartment and take a shower?" Jack looked at her with one eyebrow raised.

"The apartment wasn't locked, and I waited for hours in your stupid stairwell, freezing, because it was raining like a monsoon. And I didn't think you'd mind…" She tapered off.

"Mind? I don't even know you."

Her expression was sad for a brief second. Then she shook her head and returned to glaring. "Well thanks a lot, you jerk."

Jack backpedaled furiously. "What I meant is, you've changed so much and… you were really young, and—"

"Whatever." She held up her hand again and looked away.

"I do remember you."

She still wouldn't look at him. On the floor by the spilled soda, he noticed the bags of food Gina had left in her haste to leave. He picked up a loaf of bread and some sliced chicken. "Hungry?"

No reaction.

He shrugged and went to make sandwiches. He gave her one, then went and sat on his old green couch and looked over at the mess.

Replacement took a massive bite of her sandwich. "You're not going after her?"

"She'll go to her friend's house. Whoever that is. I've got a hunch we're done. At least I hope so."

"Good move." Replacement moved to sit next to him. He didn't argue, just took a bite of his sandwich. "She didn't seem like your type."

Jack nodded.

"A little wacko."

"Ya think?" Jack muttered.

He watched Replacement from the corner of his eye. She still had the same impish grin as when she was young. It had been so long since he'd last seen her, and so many things had changed since then.

She hadn't told him her real name. Maybe she didn't like it for some reason, and he wasn't about to ask her about it, and spoil their temporary truce. They ate their late-night living-room picnic in silence. It was funny that it didn't feel awkward.

When the sandwiches were devoured, Jack got up and suppressed a groan. His back was still a little sore from flipping the lumberjack, but maybe he could sleep now. He threw the paper plates into the trash and looked at the clock—2:57 a.m. Outside, the clattering sleet had changed to soft snow.

"You got a ride home, or do you want to crash here? We'll go out to the university in the morning."

Replacement's face lit up as if she'd hit the lottery. "The couch is fine!" She bounced up and down.

Grinning to himself, Jack went into his bedroom and shut the door.

* * *

He lay in bed for almost an hour, unable to sleep.

If Michelle isn't in California, this isn't going to be good. The police will have already checked the hospitals… and the morgue.

He closed his eyes and breathed deeply, trying to force those thoughts from his head.

Think about something else. Something good.

It wasn't hard for Jack to remember. He thought about this memory often.

Michelle was twelve; Jack was already living with the Strattons. While other kids were playing and having fun during summer break, Michelle was hard at work babysitting—wiping snot and changing diapers. As the weeks passed, Chandler and Jack tried to guess what she was going to buy with the pile of money. The boys had gone from guessing a doll, to a dollhouse, to finally thinking that she probably had enough money for a pony. All she would say was, "I'm saving it for something special. Something I've always wanted."

Near the end of that summer, Jack came for a sleep over. Chandler was forlornly sitting outside waiting for him. The house was dark except for a few candles lit here and there. Chandler said he didn't want to go inside yet.

"What's going on?" Jack asked.

Chandler said Aunt Haddie's hours were cut back at work and she didn't have enough money for the electric bill.

It was strange that night, and very dark, after Jack snuffed out the candle in his old room at Haddie's. He hadn't worried about money and food for a long time, since before Haddie, when that was *all* he thought about—and keeping warm; when he waited for his mom and her druggie friends to fall asleep so he could look for a half-eaten sandwich.

The next morning at breakfast, Haddie was quiet; Chandler was almost completely shut down, barely talking; Jack could hardly keep his eyes open. But Michelle didn't seem troubled. She looked excited as she announced, "I had an idea last night that we should look for extra change around the house."

Chandler yawned. "A little change won't pay the bills."

Michelle eyed her older brother. "You never know how God provides."

They started to search around the house, behind furniture, under the couch cushions—all over. But they found only a few stray pennies.

"Aunt Haddie, maybe you should check through your old handbags in the closet," Michelle suggested. The thing about Haddie was, her faith was strong. She put her chin down and limped rapidly down the hall.

Jack and Chandler stared at Michelle, but she just crossed her arms and hummed a little tune. A few minutes later, they heard Aunt Haddie yell, "Hallelujah! Thank you, Lord! Thank you, Jesus!" and she flew out of the bedroom waving a wad of cash. Michelle simply smiled. Jack would never forget Aunt Haddie leaping around the kitchen, and all four of them dancing around the table.

After that, whenever Haddie called Michelle her special angel, everyone knew why.

It was a sweet memory, one of Jack's favorites, but it did nothing to stop his worrying or help him get to sleep. With a groan, he pulled the covers back, grabbed his sweatpants, and headed to the kitchen.

Quietly stepping around the sleeping form on the couch, he could see that the place was spotless. No spilled soda. Replacement had cleaned up. Not only the soda, but all his usual mess, too, and a glance into the kitchen confirmed his suspicions—dishes washed, potholders hung up, dish towels folded. Just like Haddie had taught them.

Asleep, clutching a thin blanket, Michelle's fierce little defender looked even smaller. It bothered him that he couldn't remember her real name. *What did Aunt Haddie call her?*

He went back into his bedroom and grabbed the comforter from his bed. Gina had thought his old army-green blanket was too scraggly, so she'd gone shopping one weekend and picked this out for him. He shook his head. It looked ridiculous—purple and white with pink flowers—but it was incredibly warm, so Jack put up with it, displaying the plain purple underside.

He returned to the couch and gently laid the comforter over Replacement, with the flowery side on top. Her eyes fluttered open. "Thank you," she whispered.

"You're welcome."

He watched her snuggle into the warmth. He wanted to walk away, but he knew he'd never get any sleep unless he got it off his chest.

"Seriously, why are you so angry with me?"

Replacement slowly opened her eyes. "Do you really need to ask?"

He'd regretted the question as soon as it left his mouth, but still he nodded.

"When you and Chandler turned eighteen and went off to Iraq, everything changed at Aunt Haddie's. Before then, if there was a problem, Chandler always fixed it. If stuff broke or something went wrong, he was there, like Superman. And if he couldn't fix it, he'd call *you*." Her eyes searched his face. "Do you get it?"

Jack shrugged. "He's Superman. I get that. But—"

"If something happened that Chandler couldn't handle, you'd show up and take care of it. Chandler would just pick up the phone, and you'd come, and everything would be okay. To me, you were like… I used to call you Batman."

Jack's shoulders slumped. He couldn't tell her, or anyone, what happened in Iraq. *What the hell does she want me to say? She doesn't get it. Chandler really was like Superman, but I'm no Batman. I was like stupid Jimmy Olsen following him around.*

"So when Chandler died, I kept thinking you'd come back and fix everything."

He waited silently, unable to defend himself.

Her eyes conveyed her hurt. "But you didn't come back. You didn't even try." Her voice cracked. She rolled over and burrowed into the comforter.

Jack swallowed. "I'm sorry." *For so many things.*

The comforter moved up and down as she nodded.

Jack walked back into the bedroom, shut the door, and closed his eyes.

I'm no hero. I'm the guy who killed Superman.

5

FISH OUT OF WATER

IRAQ
Six Years Ago

Jack adjusted his assault rifle and looked back across the dimly lit room at Chandler and the two other soldiers next to him. When Chandler lifted his huge machine gun and nodded, one of the other soldiers moved to stand behind Jack and to the left.

Jack pushed the door open, and his gun snapped up. His visual sweep showed a square interior with open cabinets against one wall and a table and chairs against the other. Rubbish littered the floor.

Empty.

In the middle of the back wall was another door. Jack held up his hand and made two quick gestures forward. He slipped silently into the room and picked his way over the trash-strewn floor.

One more room.

Jack reached the second door and stood off to the side. He held up his hand and closed it into a fist. He looked back at Chandler, who nodded. Jack pushed the door open. The room was filled with canisters and gray sacks.

They'd been briefed on phosphorus bombs.

"OUT! MOVE!"

The four soldiers sprinted back through the rooms they'd just cleared. Chandler's huge gun slowed him down.

Jack dropped behind his friend. "Chandler, run!"

"I am!"

"Lose the gun!"

Chandler tossed it aside. In under a minute, they made it to the front room, where the other two soldiers were frantically shoving against the door.

"It's jammed!"

"MOVE," Jack commanded, and even Chandler got out of the way.

Jack lowered his shoulder and hit the door as hard as he could. The door cracked, but it didn't open.

Everyone started yelling. "Do something! We're all gonna die!"

Chandler called out, "Out of my way!" and charged across the room. When he rammed the door, it moved the wall itself, and the wooden frame and chunks of concrete—with the door still attached—fell forward. As soon as it landed in the dirt, the four soldiers scrambled out and ran.

Jack remembered looking back in terrified fascination, his hearing completely gone. Through the hole where the door had been, like dragon's breath, flames were shooting out. The fire was so hot it flicked blue and white before wrapping together into red and yellow streams that floated skyward.

He ran until he saw Chandler, and flopped down on the ground beside him.

"Thanks." Jack couldn't hear his own voice, but Chandler nodded.

The other soldiers joined them, and the four men watched the flames consume the place where they had last stood.

Jack finally said, "You have to get faster, bro."

"Oh yeah? Why don't you get bigger?"

They laughed.

Chandler pushed at Jack's shoulder. Jack pushed back. Chandler pushed harder.

"Wake up," Chandler said in a high girl's voice.

Jack looked down, puzzled. The hand. Tiny, white, with a little silver ring. Not Chandler's.

"What?" Jack's eyes opened.

Replacement pushed him again. "Get up!"

Dazed, Jack scooted away to the far side of the bed. "What's the matter with you?"

"Me? You're the bum." Replacement leaned in close. "How late are you going to sleep? I thought you said—"

"Go away."

"When are we going—"

Jack groaned.

"—to do something about Michelle? Do you always—"

"SHUT UP!" he barked right in her face.

The full-blast roar would have made any soldier stand at attention. But it didn't seem to affect Replacement. She just smiled.

Jack shook his head. *She's Chandler's sister, all right.*

"Let me clean up, and then we can go," he muttered.

"We?" Her face lit up.

He held up his hand. "Don't say another word. Not a peep, or you don't go."

Replacement shrugged and pretended to lock her lips.

He'd have loved a cup of coffee but doubted there was any in the house. It didn't matter anyway, because there was zero chance of there being any milk, and he hated it black. Splashing water in his face was the next-best thing to caffeine.

As he shaved, he started to plan. Normally, his first step would be to go to the investigator here in Darrington. But if he went to see Davenport, Sheriff Collins would have to be informed—which would lead to the inevitable disclosure that Michelle had been Jack's foster sister. Departmental policy was to treat anything involving a family member as a conflict of interest, so he wouldn't be allowed anywhere near the investigation. The longer he stayed off the radar screen, the better. And if he did get caught, he had a Get Out of Jail Free card he intended to play with by-the-book Collins: technically, Michelle wasn't a relative.

He also didn't want Collins to think he was grandstanding. Sheriff Collins was part of the reason why Jack took the job with the Darrington County Sheriff's Department in the first place—he thought he'd work well with the former Air Force captain. But it hadn't gone that way.

During his first month on the job, Jack had stuck his nose in and solved a John Doe case. A hiker had found a partially decomposed body in the woods. Animals had eaten most of it and the head was missing, so dental records couldn't be used. The case had been assigned to Detective Flynn, but Flynn hadn't followed through on the only real clue they had, the tattoo on the guy's arm—crossed swords over a four-leaf clover. Nothing on it in the police database, so Jack, on his own, checked one local tattoo parlor after another until he came up with the name of the guy, a local with a drug problem.

Instead of promoting him, Collins wrote Jack up, placed him on late-night traffic detail for ninety days, and blasted him up, down, and sideways about grandstanding.

Collins didn't get it, though. Jack didn't care who got the credit—he just wanted to help. Still, he'd learned a lesson about working with Collins, and didn't want to make the same mistake again—especially on this case.

He finished shaving and decided he'd start by checking at Michelle's last address. He selected a navy-blue casual pullover that was a little loose. If he was dealing with college kids, he wanted to appear approachable.

He thought about the gun in the safe, decided against it. He carried himself differently when he was packing; people seemed to sense he was a cop; he didn't want that today.

And he didn't need it. He'd been practicing martial arts since he was twelve. Twelve was when he confided in a friend about his birth mother. The story burned through the school like wildfire. *His mom's a hooker!* Jack got into three fights that day. Lost every one. The school counselor chalked it up to "kids can be cruel," and said Jack would just have to learn to deal with it. But Jack's adoptive father, Ted, had the far more practical and helpful approach: he signed Jack up for karate, and Jack took to it like breathing.

He snapped himself back, angry that he had gone down the rabbit hole again. *Okay, no gun. What else do I need?* His mental checklists were becoming as scattered as his life. The soldier he was six years ago would have beaten the snot out of him for being so sloppy now.

"Ready?" he called, opening the bedroom door.

Replacement was already waiting by the front door, bursting with questions. "Where are we going? Where do we start? Are we—?"

"Replacement, this is what I need you to do today: SHUT UP."

Her face fell.

Immediately, Jack felt bad. "I'm sorry. It's just, I have a job to do, and I can't have you screw it up."

She raised herself up on her toes and leaned in toward him. "I won't screw it up."

"If you get in someone's face like you just got in mine, you will."

Maybe he needed to dial it down a little. Most kids brought up in foster homes were like feral cats. Social graces were far down on the list of skills kids learned in broken homes—and survival was at the top. Still, she had had long exposure to Aunt Haddie, and he could expect some manners even from this feral cat.

He softened his voice and posture. "Do me a favor?"

She nodded, warily.

"It looks like we have a truce going, right?"

"Just because you said you'd help." Still scowling.

He hid a smile. "Can you try to follow my lead?"

Her head rose. "Like we're in it together?" Before Jack could stop that train of thought, it had already left the station. "Hell, yeah. Let's go."

This, he felt, was his first mistake of the morning.

His second mistake was exiting by the front. As they passed his landlady's door, Mrs. Stevens sprang like a lion, her red hair standing on end, like she'd waited all night at that door to spring her trap. And Jack had walked right into it.

"Mrs. Stevens… I wanted to stop by and apologize about…" She was so blotchy and crazy-looking that Jack forgot what he was going to say. He just held his hands open and out as if he were handling a hostage situation.

Mrs. Stevens's eyes grew even larger. "You weren't stopping."

"I was going out to get you a little *something* so I could apologize *properly*." He emphasized the words, hoping that her mental image of a bribe would calm her down. Jack dreaded moving, and right now there was a high probability that his landlady would throw him out, so it was worth the groveling, though he hated for Replacement to see him doing it.

"How could you possibly apologize for everything you've done to me?" Laying it on pretty thick. All that was missing was the back of her hand held theatrically to her forehead and a Victorian swoon. "Your lease is extremely specific about the level of noise. Last night…"

She's quoting the lease—that's bad. He'd have to play on her emotions, but he didn't have time to think it through. "I'm just so sorry. You see… this girl… she's the sister of my friend who has passed. His younger sister…"

Mrs. Stevens's eyes narrowed and her fat lips pursed into a puffy line, but Jack kept talking.

"And she's stunted emotionally and a little… off. I just want to get her to a place that would take care of her—"

"What about the other one?" Mrs. Stevens tapped her foot.

"The other—"

"Girl." He didn't know how Mrs. Stevens could even say the word; her lips were pressed together so tightly.

"The other girl is my… my… cousin." He regretted the lie as soon as it passed his lips.

"Crap," Replacement said behind him. "Sorry, crap. Sorry, pretty lady." Her head twitched and her arms and legs were jerking spasmodically. Even though Jack knew it was an act, it was unnerving. "Crap. Son-of-a—"

"There, there. It's okay." Jack wrapped an arm around her and pulled her close. He honestly needed her to stop before he broke out laughing.

Mrs. Stevens stepped back and clutched her robe to her chest. "Is she dangerous?" Her eyes were wide with fear.

"No, no. She's harmless." His voice was reassuring as he hustled Replacement down the hallway. "I just need to get her meds refilled right away."

Jack didn't turn back, but he could feel the landlady's eyes on them as he hustled them out the front door.

"What was that?" Jack snapped, angry at himself for lying. "Are you trying to get me kicked out?"

Replacement made a goofy face. "You said follow your lead."

"Shutting up would have been following my lead."

"You made me sound nuts, so I went with it. Where did you come up with that anyway? And your cousin?" She stuck out her chest. "You thought she was gonna believe Miss Silicone is your cousin?"

"If you wanted to act unbalanced, how about trying to come off harmless and not like some twitchy psycho?"

"I called her pretty." She shrugged as if that should cover everything.

Movement at a second-floor window caught his eye. Mrs. Stevens had pulled the curtain back to look down at them from the upstairs hall.

"Okay, act *a little* out of it—she's watching."

Replacement went back to her fish-out-of-water dance. This time she toned it way down, though they still got some odd looks from passersby. As the reluctant Batman led his self-appointed Robin, twitching and cussing, to the car, he couldn't help but smile.

* * *

"You still have the same car?" she asked with a sour expression. "This car is—"

Jack's look shut her right up. "Never criticize a guy's car."

His thumb caressed the place on the steering wheel where the stitching was coming loose. Okay, the semi-refurbished blue 1978 Chevy Impala had an improbable number of miles on it. Jack and the car were twins in that regard, but to tell the truth, the Impala was running better than he was right now.

"Yeah. Same car. Sit still. You're making me nervous."

After that, she rolled the window down—daring him to point out that it was winter cold outside, but he didn't take the bait—and kept quiet a lot longer than he'd have thought possible.

A few miles later, she shivered, frowned, and rolled the window up. "Where are we going?"

"White Rocks. First stop is Michelle's apartment, then we'll go to the university."

"Why don't you find out what the cops have?"

Jack kept his eyes on the road. He didn't want to explain that his by-the-book boss would go crazy and tell him to step aside, let Fairfield PD and Joe Davenport handle it. No way was Jack going to sit by and let Slow Davenport set the pace on this investigation.

"We'll start at her apartment. Do you have the address?"

"Yeah, but I was there once already and they didn't know nothing." Replacement tapped her knuckles against the car door in frustration.

"Didn't know *anything*."

"Sorry, teach. I'm just visiting the college, not enrolling today." She crossed her arms.

Jack chuckled. "Good one."

She smiled, put her hands behind her head, and stretched her legs out on the dashboard. *Nice legs.*

"We'll start looking at her apartment. And I'll *quietly* call over to Fairfield's Sheriff's Department and see what they have."

"Do you think she's all right?"

Jack tightened his grip on the wheel. "Yeah. I hope."

Replacement looked out the window and remained silent for the rest of the ride except for the occasional "turn left" or "turn right." Michelle's last known address was in an upscale apartment complex, close to the university, in a trendy part of town.

Jack took in the vibe—people with jobs in IT, graphic design... He tried to guess a few more, based on the cars in the lot. Lawyers?

"How could Michelle afford to live here, plus school?"

"She got a full scholarship." Replacement's voice rang with pride. "Free everything."

"Really, what for?"

"For computers. She's super smart. She had to work part-time at the psychology center, but she could take all her classes for free."

Jack drove past the apartment. His car would stick out in this neighborhood. A block later, he swung into a parking space and shut off the engine.

"Just keep quiet, okay?"

Replacement again pantomimed a key locking her mouth and flashed him a grin.

Jack frowned. That smile said she was going to do what she wanted in the long run. Replacement had the body of a woman but she still acted immature. He'd learned—from a variety of teachers—that a person could get stuck in time after a tragic event. Aunt Haddie had mentioned that something happened to Replacement when she was younger. She didn't share the details, all she said was—"... *that little angel has been through Hell.*" If something really bad had happened to Michelle... he was afraid his new partner here might be traumatized.

Best to keep it as professional as possible. Realizing he should have asked before, he fired off questions as they walked toward the apartment. Did Michelle have a roommate? Boyfriend? Was she in a sorority? Did she talk about friends?

Replacement fired the answers right back. Yes, roommate. No boyfriend. No sorority. And no, she didn't really mention friends."

They arrived at the apartment building, and Replacement pointed to 2B. "That one. Missy Lorton."

Jack scanned all the apartment tags, and it was the only one with just one name—Lorton. And it was typed on fancy tan paper that was slightly darker than the others.

"You're sure this is the one, right?"

"It was different when I came out before."

Another rock dropped in his stomach.

"It said Lorton and Carter before."

Someone doesn't think Michelle is coming back.

Jack pressed the buzzer. Someone buzzed them in without asking who it was. There was an elevator, but Jack always preferred stairs, if there weren't too many. Jack's foot hadn't hit the top step when the door to 2B swung open. A short, plump girl stepped out of the doorway.

"Took you long enough..." She looked up and her whine trailed off. She took a step back.

Jack knew he'd better pick the right smile. Confident, friendly, but not over the top. "Ms. Lorton?" Her pudgy face barely hid her disgust as she pulled the door back and tried to slam it shut. "No solicitors."

But Jack stuck his foot out just in time—and his foot paid the price of acting as a doorstop. He tried to hold his smile and not clench his teeth in pain. "Miss, we're looking for Michelle Carter. I'm her foster brother."

"She transferred to a different school." Missy stepped back from the door.

Jack grabbed Replacement with his left hand and encouraged her forward so Missy could see he was with a girl, hoping that might soften her up. "Do you know what school she transferred to?"

"Western Tech. Look, I have to meet someone." She started to close the door again.

Jack held up a hand. "Okay, listen, *Missy*. We haven't been able to get in touch with Michelle. When did she leave?"

Missy rolled her eyes. "Two weeks ago. I had a night class. When I came back, she was gone. I tried calling her, but she doesn't answer. Or my texts or emails," she finished up with a last flourish of her hand.

Replacement stepped forward. "What about her stuff?"

"She took it." Missy shrugged. Then she seemed to brighten. "Hey, tell her she owes me for half of last month's rent cuz she left with no notice. Which is against the lease, and it's also low-class. Just like her!"

Jack grabbed Replacement around the waist just as she lunged at the portly girl. Missy fell backward and rolled, squealing, into the kitchen. While Replacement hurled a string of extremely salty obscenities, Missy moaned and struggled to sit up.

"Get out! Tell Michelle she's a backbiting thief!"

"Thank you! We'll be going now."

Jack lifted Replacement and carried her down half the stairs, till she stopped struggling, but he didn't let go. When they got to the car, he yanked her door open. *"In."*

He pulled out of the parking spot with an angry screech of tires. "What's the matter with you?"

"Aw, c'mon, didn't ya hear what she said about Michelle?"

"Still, you can't just take potshots at people who tick you off. What would Aunt Haddie say?"

Her voice was strangely small now. "Michelle didn't go anywhere. That means someone stole her stuff. Probably Miss Piggy." She looked devastated.

"Look, all I ask—and I'm begging, okay—this could be serious, so we've gotta be serious. I can't help if I have to get you out of trouble all the time." He waited, until she nodded acknowledgment. "And if you get *me* in trouble, we're all screwed. Understand? I don't know how Aunt Haddie would put it."

She mumbled, "Jeopardized?"

"Yeah, well, that takes too long to say, but screwed is my word for it."

She propped her head on her hand and leaned against the frosty window. They rode in silence.

What did she think would happen? Once I started looking, Michelle would suddenly appear? I show up and everything is fixed because I'm a superhero?

This is reality, and reality sucks.

6

YOU WILL KNOW PAIN

White Rocks was a closed campus, and everyone entering had to go through the gate. Jack stopped at the manned security booth.

"Morning. Where you headed?" asked the young security guard.

Jack flipped open his wallet and flashed his badge. "Campus police station."

"Yes, sir." The guard buzzed the gate open and waved them through.

Jack had responded to the White Rocks campus police station quite a few times. Usually it was noise complaints and drunks. Sometimes he got overtime doing traffic duty for events. They called it campus police, but it was only a couple of rungs up the ladder from high school hall monitor. The "force" consisted of less than ten guys and two gals, who were either just out of high school or already retired.

A nice, quiet group—perfect for White Rocks Eastern University, an old, private institution with fewer than five thousand undergraduates and graduate students. Although small, it was the source of a very large portion of the county's tax base—a fact Sheriff Collins never let anyone forget.

It was with this fact in mind—and his desire to stay under Collins's radar—that Jack seriously considered locking Replacement in the car.

She must have read his mind. "I won't say anything." The fight had gone out of her, and she seemed downcast.

"You want to wait here?" he asked hopefully.

"No. I wanna come in."

Great. "Okay. I'd appreciate it if you didn't say anything."

The security office was a small building, only a few rooms. They walked up the cement ramp and could see the large main desk through the windows.

A woman with an immense hairdo greeted them before the little bell over the door even finished ringing. "Why, good morning to the both of you," she chirped. "How may I be of help today?" It was hard to tell how old she was, considering the layers of makeup, but the smile seemed genuine.

"Good morning to you, too. I'm looking for the…" He searched for the right word but drew a blank. Sometimes security people tried to match police titles, and would get their feelings hurt when you used the wrong one. At the mall in town, they referred to each other as "officers," and loved it when he did, too.

"Registration office?" the woman finished, trying to help him out.

"Um, no. I'm looking for the person covering right now." Jack figured the generic phrase would pay off.

"Certainly." She pushed back in her chair, away from her computer, and wheeled it over to the phone. She dialed, and after a short pause, a phone rang in one of the offices. "Neil, there's a nice couple here to see you."

A second later, an older man, in one of the whitest shirts Jack had ever seen, stuck his head out of the office and gestured to them. "Sure, c'mon in."

"Okay. I'm going to run and get a bite," the woman announced. "Do you want anything?"

"Where are you going?" Neil asked.

"Debbie Sue's. Want your usual?"

"Sure. Thanks, May. You kids all set, or can May pick you up something?"

Jack was hungry, but he didn't want to take the time. "Thanks, we're all set." Shooting Replacement a *No, you can't have a muffin* look, Jack walked over and shook Neil's hand.

"Jack Stratton. I just have a couple of questions, and we'll be out of your way."

"Neil Waters." Neil held the office door open. "Come on in."

"I'll wait out here." Replacement's sad face was back.

Jack nodded approvingly, while Neil's inner monologue, if he was having one, seemed to tell him not to question the nice young couple's regrettable decisions not to have a muffin or come in together. Which was just fine with Jack.

Neil's office was as clean as his shirt. *Everything in its place and a place for everything.* Neil gestured to a comfortable chair as he moved behind the desk. "What did you say your name was again?" Neil ran his fingers through hair almost as white as his shirt.

"Jack. Jack Stratton."

"Now I remember. You helped with traffic during the alumni benefit." Neil folded his hands, leaned back in his chair, and smiled.

Great... he remembers that I'm a cop. Nod. Don't alarm him. "I'm here... as a family friend of a student. Michelle Carter."

Neil nodded. "You still haven't been able to get in touch with her?"

Jack shook his head.

"That's too bad." Neil straightened up in his chair, and Jack could see him gather his thoughts. "We talked to her roommate, and she told us that Michelle transferred to Western Technical University out in California. I called Western Tech myself and spoke to the registrar. Nice group out there. Anyway, they said that Michelle had transferred there. It's all in the computer."

"Did they say she's there now? Has anyone seen her or confirmed that she got out there?"

"They couldn't recall her specifically. Everything is electronic now anyway."

"Do they have an address for her?"

"No. According to her transfer records, she planned to live off-campus. It could be she just hasn't gotten housing yet. She hadn't started classes, but she was good to go."

Neil was trying hard to express reassurance with his body language, but maybe he needed a few more acting lessons.

"She hasn't started classes? Did they say why?"

"Well, classes haven't started. They're between semesters now. Maybe she just took a little time to herself, and she'll check in?" Neil leaned in and put his arms down on the desk. "Kids do that. She might be blowing off steam. These heavy schedules are murder on these students."

Jack stood up and handed Neil his card. "Yeah... thank you, Neil. I appreciate it."

Neil shook Jack's hand, and they walked back out to the lobby, where Replacement was sitting with her hands folded in her lap.

Jack looked back at Neil. "One more question: can you tell me where the psychology center is?"

Neil's smile faded. "Neuropsychology. It's in the old nature center, just outside campus. I checked with them too—Michelle quit."

"I'll just see if anyone's heard from her," Jack said.

Neil straightened his tie. "Okay. I'll write you directions. There's a couple of visitor spaces at the front of the lot. Be sure to use those. I can give you a pass to hang up in your car." He cleared his throat. "I was planning on following up with them this week. To be thorough."

"Thanks," Jack said again, hiding a whiff of sarcasm. "I appreciate the help."

Ten minutes later, as light snow began to fall, he drove past an old open gate at the top of a hill and pulled into a small, empty parking lot.

The large, two-story, circular structure looked as though it was constructed in the 1960s. The quiet but important-looking lettering on the modern sign at the front of the building announced that they had arrived at the White Rocks Eastern University Neuropsychology Center.

Replacement's face contorted. "I already checked here. They said she transferred, but that's crap."

"I'm just covering all the bases. Wanna come in?"

Replacement shook her head and turned her face away.

Jack got out of the car and headed for the entrance. A student walking out held the large glass door for him.

Inside, a gray carpet with black and red flecks covered the floor. Light oak staircases with clear-plastic-and-metal railings led up on both the left and right. Jack liked the look: modern, but with a natural feel. The place even smelled new.

A young, bored-looking girl sat behind the big reception desk. She looked up from her phone. "Good morning. Can I help you?"

"I'm looking for someone who works here. Michelle Carter."

"Do you know what department she's in?" The girl's finger traced down a phone directory.

"Computers."

The girl drummed her fingers on her mouse. "Michelle?"

"Yes."

"Oh, yeah. I think she works for Dr. Franklin." She walked over to the door behind the counter on the right and gave a light knock.

"Come in," a man's voice called.

The girl opened the door, revealing a spacious office, where Dr. Franklin sat behind his large wooden desk: in his early fifties, tall, with sandy brown hair that was on the long side but pulled back into a short ponytail. Tweed jacket, jeans, and round wire glasses finished off the professor look.

"Do you need something, Carrie?" Franklin said, leaning back in his chair.

"This man is looking for Michelle Carter. The computer girl."

"Black, tall, slender?"

Carrie nodded.

"She's not under me. She works for Dr. Hahn."

"Sorry to bother you." Carrie turned to walk out. Dr. Franklin's eyes followed her with a leer that wouldn't have been appropriate at a singles' club, let alone, Jack would have thought, in the hallowed halls of neuropsychology.

"Thanks," Jack said on his way out, again opting for the safest part of *Thanks for nothing.*

There was no answer to Carrie's knock on the second door. She looked a little harassed but she bravely smiled at Jack and said, "One sec," then scissored efficiently over to the reception desk and picked up the phone.

"Brendan? Is Dr. Hahn in? No." She smiled apologetically up at Jack and shook her head.

"Who's Brendan?" Jack asked.

She covered the receiver with her hand. "Dr. Hahn's assistant."

"Can I talk to him?"

She spoke back into the phone. "Do you have a second? A gentleman is out here." Her shoulders relaxed. "Thanks." She hung up. "He'll be right down."

A minute later, a young man walked down the staircase to the left. He was tall, just over six feet, with blond hair and blue eyes. He wore khaki pants and a white shirt. He waved and then shook Jack's outstretched hand. "Brendan Phillips."

Manicured hair, muscular, handsome, and preppy—a combination that reeked of privilege and always rubbed Jack the wrong way.

"Jack Stratton. I'm trying to get in touch with my foster sister. Michelle Carter."

"Michelle? I thought she transferred out."

"That's what I'm trying to figure out," Jack said. "She didn't say anything about it to her family, and no one's heard from her for two weeks."

Brendan held up his hands. "Wait a second. She didn't tell her family she was transferring either?"

"Either?" Jack asked.

"Michelle didn't give us any notice. She just sent an email saying she was quitting and going to school in California. I never would have expected it from her. She was always very professional."

"Did you know her?"

"Not personally. She reported to Dr. Hahn and I'm his assistant. It's part of my graduate work. It sounded like she was offered an amazing opportunity and had to jump on it. I mean, she should have given some type of heads-up, but you gotta do what you gotta do."

"So you haven't heard from her since?"

"No. I emailed her but she hasn't written back. I figured she just felt bad about leaving so quickly. Hahn was really mad." A bell rang and students started to stream down both staircases. Brendan glanced at his phone. "I'm sorry, I have a class to get to. Um, is Michelle all right? I didn't really know her, but it seemed out of character. She was a really hard worker."

At last, someone who seemed genuinely concerned. Jack took out a business card. "I'm looking into it. If you hear back from her, please let me know."

Jack jumped into a stream of about a hundred students out to the parking lot. When he got in the car, Replacement said, without looking up, "They just said she transferred, right?"

"Yeah." Jack started the engine.

"It's not true." Replacement's breath made the corner of the window fog.

They pulled out of the parking lot as a campus police car was coming in. Jack couldn't see the driver's face, but from the white hair and whiter shirt, he was thinking Neil Waters.

Looks like he's being thorough now.

Both were thoughtful as they left the university behind them, looking to hit a diner for the long-deferred muffin and coffee on the way out of town.

She finished classes and headed out west? Just took all her stuff and didn't tell anybody? That's something I'd do. Not Michelle.

"Did Michelle have a car?" Jack asked.

"Yeah. A blue Honda Civic. I told the brainiac detective, and he said he'd put an alert out for it."

Stupid. I should have asked her about it first. I'll have to run it when I get home.

"Should we check with all the hospitals and police stations between here and California?" Replacement said. "Just in case? But I know she didn't go out there."

Jack opened his window and let a blast of cold air sweep into the car. It was a good idea but naive. A monumental interstate search like that would keep even a well-run police database busy for weeks.

"When did Michelle decide to go to college? She was a lot older than the usual freshman."

"So what? I told you, she always wanted to go to college. She loved computers, school, and learning. She just couldn't afford it. She was saving up for it, and then she got that scholarship." Replacement looked at her feet and shook her head. "She was so happy when she found out."

"Where did she work before college?" Aunt Haddie always made the kids work if they were still with her in high school.

"McDermott Insurance. She did computer security. She taught me."

"What do you do for work?"

Replacement shrugged. "I have some… computer jobs. A little website stuff now and then. I'm sort of on call. Michelle said I should get some certification, so I took an online security class. Michelle…"

Replacement's knuckles hammered on the door panel in frustration. Jack tried not to watch out of the corner of his eye as she welled up. She looked up at the ceiling of the car and the tears began to fall.

Jack pretended to concentrate on driving, thinking back to one of his first criminal justice classes, Psychology of the Victim. The instructor's words haunted him now.

"When a crime is committed, who is the victim?"

Hands shot up all over the room, along with one brave voice. "A person who suffers harm or death from another person or from some adverse act."

"And, using that definition, who is the victim in a missing person case?"

"The missing person?"

"Wrong." The teacher brought both hands crashing down on the podium. "What about the mother? What the poor little brother? The uncle, father, sister, teacher, lover?" He fired down the list; his words hung in the air, suspended on the silent response to his question.

"And… if the *victim* is one who suffers harm or death from another person or from some adverse act, what about *you*? Do you think a law enforcement officer doesn't lose any sleep wondering what happened? Do you think you won't pore over the facts again and again and re-interview all the shell-shocked people who have no idea what happened?

"'Where is our loved one?' they ask. They've turned to you for help, but you have no answer. You look at them with pity, but you turn the accusatory question inward, on yourself: Why can't I find them? And then your wife or husband grows tired of asking, 'What are you thinking about?' Your little child asks, 'If I got taken, would you find me?' and you want to reassure them and say, "I'll never let anybody hurt you.' But you know that's a false promise."

The professor's final words hammered in his brain. "For those of you who want to wear the badge of a police officer, you must know this: *You will be a victim. And you will know pain.*"

* * *

The exit to downtown disappeared behind them on the highway.

"Where are we going?" Replacement asked forlornly.

"I'm taking you home. You still live in Fairfield, right?" Jack assumed she would remain close to the town where she had grown up with Haddie, and she didn't contradict him.

"Aren't we going to keep looking?"

"*I'm* going to look. And you can't come back to my place."

Replacement pouted.

"Look, my landlady's ticked off. My girlfriend's off-the-rails crazy, I only got a few hours' sleep, and I'm tired."

"But—"

"And I'm working tonight. I'm taking you home." He felt bad—she'd been right. All the official responses had been useless—but he needed to get some rest before his shift. "Look, my head's too overloaded to ask the right questions now. You're going home. That's it. Where is it?"

"Marshall Ave."

That ended all conversation for the remainder of the forty-five-minute ride to Fairfield. When they crested the last hill, just before the small town came into view, Jack felt the closest to happy he'd been all day.

Jack's hometown. It wasn't where he was born or where he'd spent his first seven years, but it was his home, with Haddie and Chandler and Michelle.

It hadn't changed much since he'd last been there, and it hadn't changed much since the seventies, when a large influx of artists came to round out the population of paper workers, loggers, retirees, and outdoors types who had earlier gravitated to the beautiful area nestled in the hills.

Jack didn't know whether Haddie couldn't have children of her own, but he did know she was married once. Alton was his name, and the only picture she had of him was a wedding picture she kept on her nightstand in an old, ornate frame. But there were lots of other pictures. Over her bed, a large portrait of Jesus. It was one Jack liked because it made Jesus look like a real guy. And the wall opposite her bed was covered with photos of smiling kids. He couldn't guess how many had gone through her care over the years.

Her kids. That's what she always called us.

The first time he'd headed down this road, he'd just been thrown away like a piece of trash—abandoned by his mother, picked up by the police, tossed into the foster care system. Seven years old; his birth mother a whore. That was the word he used. There was no other way to describe her. "Prostitute" covered up her sins and sounded too kind.

Jack hadn't thought about her for a while, but as the buildings and surroundings became more familiar, questions flooded his already overloaded brain.

Why?

Why keep a kid for seven years and then give him up?

"You should have taken that right. Take a right up here." Replacement pointed with a frown.

She thinks I've forgotten the town. She thinks I forgot about them. I haven't. I'm just remembering too much.

Hennessey's, the little bait and tackle, Bob's Coffee, the old candy store... It was almost all the same, yet everything had changed.

He turned down Marshall Avenue and slowed down.

"Right here is fine." Replacement's hand was already on the door handle as he pulled over. "Here." She handed him a folded piece of paper. "Read it when you get home." She hopped out and ran up into an apartment building without a backward glance.

Jack unfolded the scrap of paper. On it was written in a delicate script: *CHECK THE STOVE. TY FOR HELPING.*

No signature.

He still didn't remember her real name.

Check the stove? What the hell does that mean?

He floored it and broke the speed limit all the way home.

7

PERPETUALLY WEIRD

Jack stood in the hallway and let the door of his apartment swing open. He was relieved not to smell gas. Still, he wasn't going to risk switching anything on. The hallway light and windows gave him enough light to see.

And it was quite a scene. Someone had ransacked the apartment—or that's what it looked like at first. Then he noticed a pattern to the destruction, particular items missing. Gina.

She'd really worked the place over. The worst of it was in the bedroom. Pillows, sheets, and the comforter—gone. All the drawers pulled out and their contents strewn across the floor.

Jack knew there would be a message in the bathroom. There always was. He was past the odd feeling of having been through this before, and had moved on to where the perpetually weird seemed normal. This was at least the third time a girl Jack knew he should've had nothing to do with had left him a massive red lipstick message scrawled across his bathroom mirror.

YOU SUCK!!!

She didn't even have the imagination to make little smiley faces out of the dots on the exclamation marks like Erin had.

Jack's gun and important papers were in the safe, so he knew they were secure. He looked into the kitchen, across the broken plates that littered the floor. What the heck had happened to him? It was like his moral compass flipped a hundred and eighty degrees after he got back from the war. Drinking, smoking, girls he would have kept his distance from before... It wasn't just about trying to kill the pain anymore, or trying to shut down the memories that wouldn't stay dead. He knew what it really was—*slow suicide.*

Suddenly he remembered Replacement's note. *The stove.* He swallowed. *What did she do?*

What remained of the shattered plates crunched under his feet as he approached the stove with almost the same trepidation he would have when clearing a room with SWAT.

All the dials on the stove were turned off. He sniffed again but didn't smell any gas. The black glass of the oven door seemed extra dark. He could see there was something inside. The light had never worked, so after a moment's hesitation, he yanked open the door.

Stuffed inside the oven was a large green trash bag. Jack pulled the bag out and set it on the counter. When he opened it, he laughed out loud; his pillow and the flowery, super-warm comforter.

Jack smiled. He'd have to thank Replacement later.

He laid out the bedding, but as much as he wanted to burrow inside and not come out for a hundred years, he had work to do. What he really wanted was a drink—or four—but instead he headed over to his computer and searched his emails. He didn't generally hold onto his emails, so the one he was looking for was easy to find.

Carlos Rodriguez. Jack had met him four months ago at the TEVOC training, and they'd gotten along. Carlos was on the police force in Sonoma, California. It was two towns over from Western Tech, but Jack knew Carlos would check to see if Michelle was there. As he finished typing the email, he thought of one detail he didn't have, and he groaned as if someone had squeezed his heart. He put his head in his hands and rubbed his face.

I don't have a current picture of her. Some brother.

He went to Facebook. His throat tightened when Michelle's picture appeared. Gone was the awkward little girl who loved her mismatched socks. The beautiful woman who sat on the hood of a blue Civic had the same bright smile and the same dark-brown eyes, but that was where the physical similarities ended.

She seemed confident and full of life.

If Jack had to choose one word to describe Michelle, it would be *happy*. When she was growing up, he had thought she was cheerful all the time because she was a little kid. He stopped thinking that after she broke her leg. They were sledding, and Michelle hit a tree. At the hospital, Aunt Haddie was beside herself, and Chandler and Jack thought they'd get a big spanking. But Michelle was lit up like it had been the best day of her life.

"Aunt Haddie, we had a great time sledding, except for my leg, but Chandler and Jack pulled me all the way downtown." She beamed. "I got to ride in an ambulance. I've never been in a hospital, and the nurses are *so* pretty. Maybe I could…"

And on and on she went. That was how Michelle truly was. Happy.

He attached the picture and sent the email, but he hesitated before closing her page. She'd matured into a beautiful woman, and he'd missed seeing her grow up. He wanted to hug her. He wanted to ask her why she was so happy then. He wished…

Want, wish… they're about equal. They come to the same thing, though: they never happen.

He left the computer on and headed to his bedroom. After a quick half-hour nap, he dressed and then headed out the door. "The glamorous life of a cop," he muttered to himself as he pulled into the station parking lot.

Part of him loved going to the new, sprawling two-story building with rows of police cars parked out front. Power surged through his muscles as he walked the halls. But there were times he couldn't stand the place because of all the people whose lives broke apart inside its walls. Their eyes told their story: the life they'd known would never return. And then there were the victims, glancing up when he walked by, silently communicating their unbearable pain. Every one of those anguished looks had seared itself into his soul.

He checked in, picked up his car, and went straight back out.

Today was patrol day. A while back, Sheriff Collins had received a call from the county commissioner's office asking how often a marked cruiser patrolled the homes at the county line. One call and now, every week, some lucky stiff had to drive in a gigantic circle around the outskirts of the whole county.

Today Jack was the lucky stiff.

Not what Jack was hoping for when he decided to become a policeman. He'd figured that after the Army, he'd be a cop for two years, then go for something more exciting, like the FBI or the CIA. He kept putting that next step off, but he didn't skimp on getting all the training he could manage.

In the Army, he'd taken specialized classes in everything from terrorism to profiling, high-speed pursuit to sniper training; he just couldn't get enough. Same thing when he joined the police force. After 9/11, money poured in for police training. In fact, training was one of the reasons he'd transferred to Darrington. Jack had no idea how Sheriff Collins did it, but the police department's training budget was a well that never dried up.

Collins was initially hesitant to let Jack take so much training, said he wanted to give everyone else a chance. But it soon became clear that the only one who wanted that chance was Jack; the other cops here were either too busy or nowhere near as ambitious. When Collins realized that those funds would go to waste otherwise, he approved almost every course Jack wanted.

The training made all the downtime bearable. Jack could learn how to wiretap, conduct electronic surveillance, survive in the wilderness, fly a drone, get TEVOC training... the list of classes went on and on. And to top it all off, he was paid to do it. Sometimes he felt like a thief.

The driver in front of him slowed to a crawl, seeing the police car behind.

This is gonna be a long shift.

8

MOMMY

Jack passed by Mrs. Stevens's door on tiptoe. He made another mental note to pick her up an appeasement present, then headed upstairs. As he turned the corner of the stairs, he stopped dead. A light shone from under his door.

His apartment door was solid wood, but there was a good half-inch gap underneath it. Gina always nagged him to get one of those door sock things because the apartment was drafty, but he was glad he hadn't, because now he could see that someone was inside.

He thought about who could have a key to his apartment. It was a long list. He knew it was beyond stupid to hand out keys to his place, but girls seemed to relax if you gave them a key, and Jack wanted to keep the girls happy. He would have thought Gina was gone for good, but he couldn't be sure.

Shaking his head at his weakness, he unsnapped his holster and opened the door. No sound came from inside the apartment, but when he looked into the kitchen, he knew something was terribly wrong.

It was clean.

The list of people who'd come into his apartment and clean was short. In fact, only one name came to mind: Mom. She must have flown up from Florida to surprise him.

"Mom?" he called as he trudged into the living room.

"Surprise!" Replacement sang the word as she walked out of his bedroom, drying her hair with a towel. Holding on to the doorframe and arching her back, she struck a comically seductive pose and batted her eyes. "Not your mommy."

"Don't do that." He wasn't up for this. "What're you doing back here?" He emptied the contents of his pockets onto the counter.

"Hey, I just cleaned that." Replacement's hands waved back and forth.

"Good thing you're not my mommy, then," Jack shot back. "So, how did you get in?"

"Key under the mat." She rolled her eyes and made a face. "Pretty surprising for a cop. It's the most obvious place to look."

Jack cursed under his breath. *Gina must have put it there.*

This was getting a little old, coming home from a shift, finding Replacement walking around, fresh from the shower—okay, that part wasn't so bad.

She walked over to his desk in the corner of the living room, and he couldn't help but notice the immaculate work surface, arranged neatly with his desktop computer, a laptop he didn't recognize, a photograph, a stack of papers, and a notebook.

"Thanks," Jack said. "This place never looked so good."

Replacement grinned.

The photo was of Michelle, smiling, her head tipped slightly to the side. She was standing on the steps of an imposing building, a book bag slung over her shoulder. He could see the pride in her eyes.

"Jack." Replacement's hand was soft on his arm. He had started to grip the photo too hard, and it was crumpling in his hands. "I thought you might need a photo to show around." There was concern in her voice and in her eyes. "It's the most recent."

"Smart to bring the picture," he muttered as he turned the photo over. It was printed on photo paper with a home printer. "Where'd you get it?"

"Michelle emailed it to the nursing home Aunt Haddie is in."

"Aunt Haddie's in a home?"

Replacement paused. "She's old, Jack. She started forgetting things. The doctors said it might be early Alzheimer's. I think she's just tired. Michelle got her into a nice place, Wells Meadow."

"Why didn't—?"

"I don't want to talk about Aunt Haddie." Replacement folded her arms across her chest.

Jack hated to admit it, but he didn't either. It hurt too much.

"Do you have an electronic copy? I want to email it to a cop I know in California."

"She didn't go out there," Replacement protested.

"Humor me, okay?"

"Well, I scanned it and put it on your computer desktop. I printed some missing person flyers and passed them out, but you didn't have a lot of paper."

Before he could even clear it with his brain, he was giving her a fist bump, the way he and Chandler used to celebrate a job well done. "Awesome," he said awkwardly. "We can print some more." Jack sat down and pulled up his emails. Maybe she wasn't a total liability.

Replacement walked into the kitchen to start the teakettle while Jack emailed this photo to Carlos, too. "We need to rule out the possibility that she went to California," Jack called to her.

Replacement appeared at the door to snap, "She didn't. See? I just ruled it out." But, sensing the annoyance barreling toward her from Jack's direction, she quickly added, "You're right, sorry."

"Can you go get us more paper for the flyers?" Jack asked.

Replacement was silent. Her mouth opened, then closed. Finally she nodded. "Sure."

Jack turned back to the computer. *Why would she be freaked out about getting paper?*

"You need money?" She didn't say anything, so he had to continue on his hunch. He took some cash out of his wallet and put it in the pocket of her jacket, which was hanging on the back of Jack's chair. The jacket looked too light for the weather. "Use this, okay?"

"Don't do that. I'm fine… I have money." She rushed over.

"Don't argue with me about money. I'm Italian. It's part of our heritage."

"Really?"

Jack gave a one-shouldered shrug. "Actually, I have no idea what I am; I'm adopted. But I sort of look Italian and it sounds cool when I say it." He made a tough-guy face. "Besides, I'm not asking, *capisce?*"

"I thought you knew your parents. Aunt Haddie said you came to her when you were seven."

"I knew my birth mother. I have no idea about my... the... guy. She never talked about him."

"Are they alive?" Replacement asked.

"They could be."

"They *could* be? You didn't try to find them?"

"What for? What would I ask them? 'Hey, how come you threw me out like trash?' I don't want to know. I don't care."

"Not even a little?"

"Well, trying to figure out why my birth mother left me on my birthday... it made me a little crazy. So I stopped doing it."

Replacement's mouth dropped open and her eyes rounded—like a mother when she tries to comfort a hurt kid. "On your *birthday*?"

"Don't be so dramatic." With each question, she was moving closer, till he could smell her shampoo.

He was never the one who initiated this conversation. Everybody seemed to think it would be *good* for him to get it out, talk about it—*yeah, right*. His skin crawled with her nearness and his discomfort, but he forced himself to go on. Maybe it would give *her* some comfort.

"It wasn't my real birthday. I don't even know when that is. We never celebrated it or anything. I figured my birth mother regretted even having me, so why throw a party? My official birthday is the date they wrote on the form when I got to Aunt Haddie's—the same day I got thrown away. My adoptive mom tries to make it nice, but to me, it's kinda like celebrating trash day."

Like everyone when they compelled him to tell this story, Replacement looked like she had dived into waters way too deep.

"What happened? I mean how did... uh... she do it?"

"Remember, we're supposed to be looking for Michelle," he said gently, in a last-ditch effort to deflect the subject. He tried to keep his eyes on the computer, but Replacement kept watching him. She wasn't backing off.

"We were in a bus depot. She said we were going to Vegas. I had no clue where that was. She left me on a bench and said she was getting tickets. When she came back..."

He looked off into the distance, trying to detach from the story.

"She just stared at me for a while and didn't hand me my ticket. She always looked at me weird anyway, like a mixture of love and hate. She'd left me alone before, and I was getting a bad feeling. And then she said something like, 'You got needs, kid. School, friends, crap like that. I'm no good at being your mom. I can't take care of you.'" *Maybe the only time she ever even acknowledged that I was her son.* "'You'll be okay.' Then she turned around and went to the bus."

"What did you do?"

"Flipped out. Ran after her, begged. She hit me. Not the first time."

"In the middle of a bus station?" Replacement's eyes were huge.

"Not exactly the middle. Sort of to the right—"

She smacked his shoulder. "You know what I mean. Keep going." She sounded urgent, like she really wanted to know.

He squinted, trying to see a detail that was just out of sight. "I didn't know really know about drugs then, but there were times when she was... out of it, totally crazy. I thought that was one of those times."

He stared down at the floor. Replacement put a hand on his shoulder. "She wore these super-big heels, and she was wobbling. She hit me again, and she said, 'You don't know jack, kid.' That was the last thing she ever said to me."

Replacement gave his shoulder a squeeze and let out a deep breath, saying only, "Wow."

A surprisingly comforting, if simple, response.

Jack jumped up from the desk, shaking her hand off, as if his work was done now and he needed to get on to the next task, but he wasn't sure what it was.

Michelle. Find Michelle.

But Replacement wasn't done with him yet.

"So she just up and left?"

Jack nodded.

"What did you do then?"

"What every seven year old would do if they got dumped in a bus depot at night." She waited.

"I got caught stealing a handbag."

"Really?"

"Yeah. I stole it so I could get money for a ticket and follow her. It was all I could think of. But I got pinched, and then... police station, youth services, counselors, court, lawyer... I never had so much attention in my life. No one talks to a whore's kid, but now everyone was asking me questions."

Jack raised his head. "Okay, enough. Really. It all ended well, you know, with Aunt Haddie and my folks... What about you?"

"I... I don't like to talk about it." Replacement wrapped her arms around her chest and crossed her legs.

"Oh, that's real fair. I have to go through my worst nightmare minute by minute and you—"

Replacement's lip quivered.

"Sorry." He held both hands up. "I shouldn't butt in." He moved to the window and watched a lone car drive down the street.

She shuffled over to the couch and sat down.

He cleared his throat. Looked like once again he would be missing his usual appointment with his old friend the whiskey bottle. He sat back down at the desk.

"Let's review some details. How often did Michelle call?"

"All the time, almost every day."

"When was the last one?"

"Here. I wrote it up." She jumped off the couch, grabbed the calendar off the desk, and flipped back two pages. "I talked to her on the eighteenth. She was supposed to come visit me on December twenty-first, Saturday. I called her Sunday, thinking that maybe she just decided to come a day later, but she never called back. By Monday morning, I freaked out and called the campus police and they said she'd transferred. I knew that was garbage, so I called the police."

"That same Monday?"

"Yep. I went to the Fairfield Sheriff's Department that afternoon, and after an hour of filling out the missing person report, the cop there said I couldn't submit the report because I'm not her *real* sister. I said that was bull—and that he sucked. And I asked if I could talk to a *real* cop."

"Hold up. Which officer were you speaking with?"

"I don't know. Officer Jerk Bag. Some creep. He said I had to be related by blood, and I told him Michelle didn't even have any blood relation living, so how was that going to work? He said he needed blood for the report, and I offered to show him some blood, and then they asked *me* to leave!" She looked genuinely surprised.

"Anyway, then I brought Aunt Haddie to the police station, and this time at least they let her submit the report. Different cop this time. But they just *kept blowing us off*, telling us to wait. We didn't know what else to do. So Aunt Haddie said to track you down."

She was hopping mad, which energized Jack again. He grabbed the notebook.

"Okay. What do we know?" He scribbled DATE and ACTIONS on one page; on the next page he wrote FACTS. He pushed the notebook and pen to Replacement.

"Can we use the computer? Hello, twenty-first century?" She made a face.

"Humor me. I like to be able to carry it around."

Replacement lifted the laptop and mimed carrying it here and there.

"Call me old-fashioned."

Replacement muttered under her breath, "Yeah, old."

The laptop case looked worn, no brand name on it. The lid was closed, but it looked powered up, and there was a cord connecting it directly to his own computer.

"Yours?" he asked.

"My baby." Replacement patted the case.

"Nice. But just use the notebook. Please. Write down all the dates from the calendar and what happened."

As Replacement grudgingly started writing, Jack went to the kitchen to get a drink. He came back with two glasses of water and set one down in front of her. When he saw what she had written, he laughed.

"What?" Replacement looked up.

"Your handwriting is perfect. I guess Aunt Haddie kept penmanship as a punishment?"

"Yeah, it sucked," Replacement said with half a laugh.

Jack remembered having to transcribe page after page from books if he misbehaved. And if his handwriting didn't meet Aunt Haddie's strict standards, she'd tear it up and he had to do it all over again.

He looked down at Replacement's intricate script—almost as nice as his own—and laughed again. "Boy, you must have been a pretty rotten kid."

"Thanks. I heard you were an angel, too." She shot him a frown. "She said if there was ever a kid who liked to do the opposite of what he was told, it was you."

"She was just trying to make you feel good. I was a choirboy."

Replacement gave him a knowing look. "Michelle backed her up."

Jack quickly changed the topic. "Okay. Let's go over the facts," he said. "One, Michelle is missing."

Replacement wrote that, and added the word *Duh*. "Two, the campus police and the roommate said she transferred. Three, Western Tech said she applied and was accepted, according to Neil Waters." He waited while she caught up. "Put that name down, Neil Waters." She rolled her eyes.

"Four, Miss Piggy said Michelle took all her stuff," Replacement growled.

Replacement turned to a new page, wrote EVIDENCE at the top, and stopped. She didn't look up. Her back was still stiff, and Jack knew she was smoldering over Michelle's missing belongings. He admired the fact that in spite of her feelings she was pressing on.

"She wouldn't leave you and Aunt Haddie," Jack continued. It wasn't "evidence" that would hold up in court, but he didn't care. He knew that fact was as real as a smoking gun. Replacement wrote, "Would not leave Aunt Haddie."

"How often did she come to visit?" Jack walked over to the window and looked out at the cars below.

"She came by about twice a month."

Jack stared into the black night. *Why walk away from a full scholarship? Why not tell Aunt Haddie?*

"Is it possible... Aunt Haddie forgot?"

"No way!" Replacement was indignant. "She forgets some small stuff, but not important things. I don't even think she really has Alzheimer's. I think she's just lonely and tired."

Great. Make me feel even more guilty.

He walked back to the desk, nudged Replacement aside, and took her place in front of the computer. "Let's back up a couple of steps." He connected to the police's computer system. "I'll run the plate."

"Okay, that's what I'm talkin' about!" Replacement gave him the plate number, which Jack typed in with two fingers. Fairfield had entered a BOLO for the car so law enforcement would be on the lookout for it, but other than that, he found nothing.

"She's never even gotten a parking ticket." Jack drummed his fingers on the desk. "Let's see if anything was going on in the area."

Replacement got right in his face. "I'll drive. You type like an old lady."

"I know the system. It'll be faster if I—"

"No. No." Replacement shook her head and pushed herself into the chair beside him.

"Hey." She left him no choice, so he stood up, looking over her shoulder.

"That's much better. Where do you want to go?"

"Start with recently reported crimes," Jack said.

With a few clicks, lines of information scrolled up the screen.

"I can limit them to the past three months," Replacement said.

"Show me what you got."

She hit a couple of keys and the data scrolled again, but the list was still long.

"You said Michelle stayed around the university. Let's limit it to the area around the campus."

A couple of clicks and a new, much smaller list appeared. Jack scanned it. One reported car theft, two break-ins, drugs, and an assault. "Check that." He pointed to the assault.

Replacement read quickly through the report, giving him the bare bones. "Right before Halloween. Eighteen-year-old woman, African American, out jogging. Male suspect grabbed her around the neck and pulled her down, but victim began screaming and the man ran away. The man in this and the other incidents was described as a white male." She turned to look at Jack. "What other incidents?"

"Check the SAR."

Quick study though she was, Replacement was puzzled and had to pause, crinkling her nose as she scanned the monitor. Jack pointed to a section of the screen. "Suspicious Activity Reports. They can link different events that may or may not be related," Jack explained. "It'll show us if there's anything it's been paired with."

Replacement nodded, her fingers flew across the keyboard, and *Suspicious Activity Reports* appeared at the top of the screen. "Bingo. Look at this. Serial assaults. Two other reports in the group. A man approached one woman while she was getting into her car. She locked the doors and the suspect tried to open them. In the other one, an African American woman was walking home when a white male approached her. The girl ran to a house and the man fled. She was nineteen. What a scumbag."

She clicked the links to get descriptions of the suspect. In all three incidents, the description was the same: a white male in his late twenties, five foot seven, about a hundred thirty pounds. They all mentioned a tattoo. Two reports described it as an eagle holding a sword, on his right forearm; the third victim reported, "Eagle, right arm."

"I just saw that database," Replacement said. She clicked and tapped, and the police tattoo database appeared. "*Eagle—right arm*. How can there be no results?" More typing, zero results; different word combinations, the outcome was always the same— nothing.

"This database blows," she said at last, pushing the mouse away.

"Chill out. We're just trying to look at all the angles now anyway."

"Well, so far this is our best angle, and we've got nothing. And I don't feel like *chilling out*."

Jack walked back over to the window. They were just beginning. He was used to the painful rhythm of information gathering—nothing, nothing, nothing… then something, and you still had to figure out what it was.

The guy shows an escalating pattern of violence. Three attacks. If Michelle ran into him…

"Did you try entering some other type of bird? Hawk? Raptor?"

"I tried everything. That system stinks. If I type in just *eagle* it has two matches. *Two*. I know more than two people with an eagle tattoo. Do you know another way to look it up?"

Jack stared out the window at the little bar across the street, lost in another memory. Shortly after he moved to Darrington, he was on a bit of a bender at that bar. Marisa sat three seats down. Late twenties, tall—about five foot ten—and beautiful. A steady stream of guys paraded by, each of them hitting on her. She ignored them all. But Jack wasn't looking at her because he couldn't take his eyes off her fingers flying over her sketchpad, and he was mesmerized as the drawing emerged, a smiling girl running in a field.

He barely remembered stumbling over to her side. He pointed to the picture and proclaimed to the entire bar, "This is art!" Then he staggered to the front door.

She chased after him and caught up to him on the sidewalk. "Why did you say that?" She grabbed him by both shoulders and gave him a quick shake to sober him up. "About my picture. Why did you say that?"

"What?" That's when he looked down and really saw her for the first time. Her eyes were deep brown and matched her long auburn hair. Her dress accentuated her hourglass figure. Jack swallowed, his mouth opened slightly, and then he looked back up at her eyes.

One of her eyebrows arched high, but the cutest smile was on her lips as she said, "You noticed my art before my body?"

"That drawing… you're a true artist! The way you hold that pencil." He pinched his fingers together to mimic her sketching. "It was…" Still deeply drunk, Jack struggled to find the words, but he didn't have to. Marisa grabbed him and kissed him. The kind of kiss a guy doesn't forget, ever.

Now he blinked, trying to drive those memories from his head. That chapter was very much closed. He wasn't so sure Marisa would even talk to him now.

"I know… I know a police tattoo expert who can help." A lie wrapped in a truth— or was it the other way around? "They should be there tomorrow."

"Who? The people at the lab? On a Saturday?"

Jack ignored the question. "It's late. Let's forget about the flyers and stuff till morning. You can stay here tonight."

Replacement grinned from ear to ear.

"But I'm going alone tomorrow."

The smile vanished.

9

INKING

The little store with the large sign reading "Vitagliano's" was nestled between an art gallery and a handmade jewelry store, and might have been mistaken for an upscale coffee shop if it weren't for the tattooed, pierced, and otherwise creatively adorned patrons sitting at the tall metal tables, draped in the comfy chairs, or milling about. They stared at Jack as he walked in, and their heads moved as one to watch him continue toward the back. They seemed to sense he was a cop, and their distrust was palpable. Vitagliano's was a sanctuary for the misfits of Darrington.

"Hey, boss!" a tall guy at the counter called out.

Jack stopped and waited in front of the thick red velvet curtain, framed on either side by statues of female gladiators, that screened off the back rooms. He'd been here before.

"What is it?" a woman called from behind the curtain, and it was pulled aside to reveal Marisa Vitagliano—owner, artist, and bouncer of Vitagliano's tattoo parlor. Leather pants and a black tank top revealed a toned canvas covered in tattoos.

Still drop-dead gorgeous. If anything, her beauty was more breathtaking because he hadn't seen her in a while.

Marisa was the type of woman every man's mother warns him about. But Jack was like a little kid with fire. Even though you told him it was dangerous, the blaze was so pretty he had to touch it.

The last time he saw her was a long summer weekend, locked away in a little bed-and-breakfast. They never came out of the room. When they were getting ready to go back to town, she'd said, "You have to decide."

"Decide? About what?"

"Me. I can't just be an accessory. I know me. *Tu sei il bello mio.*"

He didn't speak Italian, but he knew the phrase. *You're my beautiful one.* She loved him.

Jack knew he couldn't give her what she needed. He reached deep down, and he wanted to, but he couldn't.

He waited too long, and finally she decided for both of them. "I'll get a ride back to town," she continued. "We can't do this anymore." There was no malice in her voice; it was still rich and kind. "If we keep going, you'll hurt me and then..." She closed her eyes. "I'll kill you."

Her voice was so smooth that at first he smiled, but he knew right away she meant every word.

It had been almost six months since he'd last seen her—he'd forced himself to stay away. She had no idea how many times he'd driven by her apartment or started to dial the phone and then hung up. He didn't want to be here now, but he had no choice. He needed her help.

"Hey, angel," Jack said.

She didn't return his smile, but her eyes widened. "Why are you here?"

"I need a favor."

"Another one?" She lowered her chin and raised an eyebrow.

She's keeping score. This is her turf. I hurt her. Showing up here, unannounced, is wrong.

"I need your help... please?" He gave the slightest bow. He'd learned that in an interrogation class. Humble yourself and don't puff yourself up. It went against his instincts, but it usually worked. After a moment, Marisa stepped to the side and gestured for him to follow her.

Behind the curtain was a red-carpeted hallway with tattoo rooms along either side. In one, a man in his twenties was getting a large skull with torches for eyes etched onto what looked like the one remaining spot of uninked skin.

In another room, a teenage girl was getting a tat just above her bum. Tears rolled down her cheeks, but her face was set and she squeezed her boyfriend's hand as Tommy's Girl neared completion.

How long is it going to be before she's crying at a doctor's office, asking how to have the tattoo removed?

Marisa was holding open a door at the end of the hallway. Jack was used to the tight leather pants, three-inch heels, and tight tank top that seemed vacuum-sealed to her busty frame—he saw only the look on her face, the question that seemed to haunt her: *Why?* Their eyes met, and she shook her head with a knowing smile.

What can I say? Sorry? He inhaled, squared his shoulders, and marched through the door into her office.

"What's the favor now?" No small talk, not even a pretense.

"I need help with a tattoo." She'd helped him while they were together a couple of times by identifying tats: once for a mugging and once for the John Doe. Now he pulled the computer-generated sketch from an envelope. "An eagle with a sword on his right forearm."

She took it without looking at him, but he noticed her back tensed, and she didn't really look at the picture either.

"I'm looking for my foster sister. She's missing, and might have run into this guy. I don't have much to go on."

Was she going to help him or not? He couldn't tell if she was even listening.

He was close to screaming or storming out. If she wasn't going to forgive him, she could at least talk to him, or throw something at him, or something.

He looked into her eyes. "I'm sorry. I need you—"

He wasn't able to finish the sentence. She grabbed him and pulled his body against hers; the picture fell to the table. One of her hands held the back of his head and the other pulled him in closer. They crashed together like two dancers, a fierce impact filled with delicate grace.

He hesitated and then gave in. Grabbing her waist, he hoisted her onto the desk. A deep, lush moan, better described as a purr, escaped her lips. Jack's hands traveled over her taut muscles as he kissed the base of her neck.

Jack kept his eyes closed. He smelled her hair; felt her breath on his neck. He lay on top of her on the desk, one hand behind her head and the other on her waist, and breathed in her scent, and it stoked a growing fire within him. The rhythm of their movements quickly synchronized. Their mutual need was palpable, and their entwined bodies began to undulate as one.

"Jack." She whispered his name and softly kissed his ear.

He opened one eye, and she stared back. He read invitation and desire in her eyes; then they softened, and he felt her vulnerability. She reached out to pull him close again. He leaned in to kiss her, but—

I can't do this. I can't hurt her again.

He slowly pulled back and slid off the table. Her eyes traveled the length of his body, and Jack swallowed hard.

"I don't... I don't want to hurt you." Jack's jaw clenched.

The heat in Marisa's eyes cooled, along with her voice. "Really? That didn't stop you before."

Jack's chin lowered to his chest, and he sighed.

"Marisa, any guy would kill to be with you, but right now... you don't need me in your life."

Her look turned cold. She slid off the desk and went to the computer desk in the corner. "Right forearm, eagle with a sword? He got it here about a year ago."

She pressed a few keys, and a page printed out.

Jack was confused.

"I knew the tat right away. I just wanted to make you beg."

"Marisa." He touched her shoulder, and she let her head rest against his hand. She had a new tattoo on her back, a heart with a golden lock wrapped around it.

"Go." She scribbled a quick note, folded it, and placed it in an envelope with the printout. He waited for her to say something else, but she just pushed the envelope to the edge of the desk and looked back at the computer.

What was I thinking, coming here?

Jack grabbed the envelope and didn't look back. He wanted to, but it was wrong, what they did to each other. You couldn't build anything on what they had—lust and fire and jealousy and fear—all things that consume rather than nourish. What they had felt wrong because, for some reason, it could never be right.

Jack walked out front, all eyes on him. He focused on the door and kept walking, his jacket in hand. It was freezing out, but he let the cold wash over him.

Never again, he vowed as he crossed to his car.

He opened the envelope and looked down at the picture inside. A rat-faced guy was posing to show off his new tattoo. Kevin Arnold. He'd have to run his background when he got home.

On the back of the picture Marisa had written, "I'll wait." Next to it, she'd written the number 2614 and had drawn a heart around it. He remembered the new tattoo on Marisa's back: a heart with a gold combination lock. He hadn't made the connection before, but he did now. The combination was 2614.

His badge number.

A driver had to stop short and laid on the horn, even opening his window to yell at Jack as he pulled out.

Jack missed it all.

10

SHE SLIMED ME

On the way home, Jack remembered to stop by the supermarket and pick up a chocolate cake, an "I'm sorry" card, and a gigantic box of chocolates for Mrs. Stevens, but halfway to the car, he changed direction and headed to the liquor store.

I'll just have a little. Take the edge off. Nothing more.

The bell on the door rang as he entered. Cappy, the old guy behind the counter, barely looked up. Jack headed for the rum. He grabbed a half pint, took two steps, then put it back. He picked up a pint, but hesitated, returning it to the shelf with a clink of the glass against the other bottles. Settling on a fifth, he headed for the front. Cappy got off his stool when Jack set the bottle down on the counter.

"Hey, Jack, you want anything else?"

Jack stopped cold, staring at the back of the cash register.

Cappy set his hand on the counter and leaned in a little. "Hey. You want anything else?"

Jack still didn't speak. There was a flyer taped to the back of the register.

Michelle's picture. *Replacement must have put it up.*

"You want anything or not?" Cappy grumbled.

"No." Jack turned and walked out the door empty-handed. In the parking lot, shared by the Big Al supermarket, an elderly woman in a worn brown coat paused in the middle of getting into an old sedan and called his name.

Jack had met Mrs. Sawyer when she was convinced her home was being robbed after finding a broken window. Jack thought it was probably mischief by a tree branch and a bit of wind—which turned out to be the case—but he went by every day for a month to check on her, thus earning a lifelong friend and a guaranteed supply of baked goods.

He went over to accept a hug. She wrapped her arms around him and rocked him back and forth. Once he gave in, it felt really good, though he couldn't help thinking of how recently he had been crushing Marisa in an embrace with very different motivations.

After the obligatory small talk and his promise to stop by soon for cocoa and pie, the little old woman gunned her car out of the parking lot.

Jack could have gone back into the liquor store, but he didn't feel like it anymore. Instead he was very proud of himself for remembering to get Mrs. Stevens some appeasement gifts at Big Al's.

Back at his apartment building, he stood outside his landlady's door and tried to balance the cake, card, and chocolates as he knocked. He took a step back when she opened the door; it was obvious she'd been crying, and she looked scary.

Then she let out a mournful wail and threw both arms around his neck.

"Mr. Stratton, I'm so truly sorry." He could hardly understand her through the sobs and sniffling. "What a nice man you are."

Jack, though mystified by her change of heart, raced to find an excuse so he could get out from her clutches without offending her. Or dropping the cake. He extricated himself as quickly as possible and held out his peace offerings. "It's okay, Mrs. Stevens."

She patted the side of his face with her wet hand and then took the cake, card, and chocolates. "God bless you! You're an angel for what you've done for that poor girl." Another strange wail convulsed her and she ran into her apartment, slamming the door behind her.

Jack stood there and wiped the side of his face with his jacket.

Gross. She slimed me. He shook his head. *Replacement. What has she done?*

He turned and ran up the stairs three at a time.

"What did you tell the landlady?" he demanded to the empty living room and kitchen.

Maybe she went to get something to eat.

He walked into the bedroom and sat down to kick off his shoes. Replacement walked out of the bathroom wearing her long nightshirt, her head down, her hair wet from the shower.

Jack smiled mischievously. *She doesn't see me.*

"Boo!"

Replacement shrieked. Jack saw her hand shoot out, and the next second she launched the nearest heavy-looking thing—a brass candlestick from his bureau—at his head, just missing him. She ran shrieking into the bathroom and slammed the door.

Jack sat there for a second and then fell over laughing.

She ripped opened the door and yelled, "Jerk! What the hell is the matter with you?"

He only laughed harder.

She stormed over to him. He tried to stop laughing, but he just rolled over and laughed at the ceiling.

"Seriously? *Seriously?*" She slapped his legs.

"Stop. Stop. I can't breathe." Jack's sides hurt.

"Do you knock?"

"Knock? It's my apartment." He was down to giggling now.

"You're a total *jackass.*" She stomped back into the bathroom.

After a minute, Jack rose with a groan and went to the door. He shook his head and knocked softly. "Sorry." He listened and waited. "I'm sorry," he said again, louder.

She opened the door a crack. "Do you mean it?"

"Yes."

"Will you announce yourself next time?"

Announce myself? It's my apartment. Jack exhaled. "Okay. Truce?"

Replacement eyed him warily. "Truce."

"Don't you have a shower at your place?" Jack asked, trying to control his laughter. Every time he came home, she was getting out of his shower.

She deflected his question. "You have unlimited hot water. You're not one of those save-the-water-and-conserve types, are you?" She got so close to him they were inches apart. "But I did hear they have a slogan: 'Save the planet: shower with a buddy.'" Jack's mouth dropped open. "Did you want me to wait for you?" She raised her eyebrows suggestively.

"Don't go there." *Not after this morning. Too far.* Jack walked over to the computer.

"Okay, now I'm sorry." She skipped over next to him. "Forgive me?"

Jack tossed the envelope on the desk. "Got a picture of the guy with the tat."

Replacement tore it open and looked at the photo carefully. "Did you run this guy? Do you know where he lives?"

"I just got here. I was going to log in and run him."

"I thought you went to the police lab. Why didn't you run him there?" She turned the picture over, and her eyes narrowed when she saw Marisa's note. "Gee... the guys down at the lab must think you're pretty sweet." She pointed to the heart and batted her eyes.

"I said, knock it off. I'm not in the mood." He grabbed for the envelope. "Hey, what did you say to Mrs. Stevens?" he asked as the memory of the crying landlady came back.

"I bought her a pie."

I should have kept the cake.

His stomach was growling and he sensed Replacement's frustration with his typing speed, so he headed for the kitchen to scrounge for food. She immediately took his seat. In the refrigerator he found milk and a large apple pie on the top shelf.

"Wow, this looks good. Can I have some of this, please?" He sounded like a little kid begging at the refrigerator.

"I bought it for you," Replacement called over her shoulder.

"It had to be a lot more than pie to get Mrs. Stevens crying like that. What else did you say?" Jack poured a tall glass of milk to go with the huge hunk of pie he'd dished out.

"I... I just... I kept in character."

Jack shook his head, dreading what that might mean, but he didn't care; the pie was delicious.

"Kevin Arnold." Replacement pointed at the monitor. "This guy's a piece of work," she spat.

Jack rushed over to the computer. *She's logged in to the police database.* "How did you do that?"

"I just ran his name. This is the same guy. Look at the pictures." She pointed at the screen.

"But how did you log in?" Jack was trying to control his growing exasperation, but he was losing that fight.

"I used your login." She shrugged.

"How did you get it?"

"I saw you type it. *Chargers*, just with a dollar sign instead of the letter *s*. I pick up on stuff like that." Her smile seemed open and innocent.

Jack's irritation evaporated. It was his own stupidity for letting her see his password, and the look on her face showed she had no idea that she'd broken a whole string of laws.

"Okay," he mumbled around a bite of pie. "What's it have on him?" He could see how this pie might have worked on the landlady. He was already enveloped in its warm, sugary glow.

Replacement's fingers flew over the keyboard. "He's been arrested eight times: breaking and entering, drugs, and three assaults." She continued to type. "No jail time. Two restraining orders out on him. Both expired. He has one outstanding warrant." The typing stopped.

"What were the assaults?"

"One domestic. Looks like a girlfriend. That's how the restraining order came up."

"What about the other assaults?"

"First one was a girl in a bar." Replacement scanned the page. "It doesn't look like he knew her. Relationship says 'None.'"

"Second one?"

"Oh, this is different. Girl *outside* a bar. He didn't know her either."

"What's the race of the women?"

"Girlfriend is listed as white. The bar girls were"—she looked for the information—"both African American."

If this guy touched Michelle, I'm going to kill him.

"You have an address? He has no jail time, so they'd have listed it under probation records. It should be in there."

"I'll try." Her fingers flew over the keyboard again.

Jack was impressed. In spite of all his extra classes, he still knew next to nothing about their computer systems. He'd have to remedy that.

"Nothing."

Jack closed his eyes to preserve the memory of the last bite of pie, laced his fingers behind his head, and exhaled. "Check who posted his bail."

After a minute, Replacement tilted her head and shook the mouse. "That doesn't make sense. Nancy Mulligan bailed him out. That's the girlfriend he assaulted."

Jack frowned. "It happens all the time. I don't get it. Why would a girl stay with someone who treats her like that?"

"She lives at 303B Hillside Downs Road."

Jack was familiar with Hillside Downs, an apartment complex with about a hundred units that looked like something from a third-world country. Going there was about as safe. Jack made a grim list of things he'd need to take. *Gun. Taser. Vest. Mace for the dogs.* He glanced at the clock.

"'I can't go out there now. I'll need backup. I'll go in the morning. You'll stay here."

"Great. Sure." Replacement smiled and moved to the couch.

Jack frowned. *I didn't mean that you could* sleep *here.* He wanted to say it aloud, but he wasn't sure what he had meant. Instead he retreated to the bedroom for what he knew would be another restless night.

11

THE DOWNS

The next morning, Sunday, Jack drove out to Hillside Downs, followed by Kendra Darcey and Donald Pugh. They stopped before the entrance, and Jack walked back to greet them.

Donald was Kendra's partner. He'd once cajoled Jack into promising to take him to the police gun range for an afternoon, but he was still waiting for Jack to deliver. When it came to shooting practice, Jack went alone. Not because he was bad—quite the opposite. But the downside of being the fastest gun hadn't changed since the Old West: the title put a mark on your head, and everyone wanted to try to take you down. Jack didn't know whether Donald wanted tips on shooting or just wanted to take a shot at besting him.

"Thanks for coming."

"No problem." Donald gave a curt nod.

"I normally enjoy watching you get into trouble, but not here." Kendra took in their tawdry surroundings with a gesture, her eyes rounded in concern.

Jack understood her meaning and spoke in a stern, military, no-nonsense tone. "We're looking for Kevin Arnold." Jack handed them a copy of Kevin's mug shot. "He has an outstanding warrant for failure to appear from Lincoln County."

Kendra passed the paperwork to Donald.

"He has no known address, but a resident here bailed him out on the most recent assault charge: Nancy Mulligan. If we're lucky, the weasel won't be far behind."

* * *

The two patrol cars rolled through the front gates of Hillside Downs, four three-story buildings with all the warmth and charm of 1950s' Russian architecture—squat, square, and built with the cheapest materials possible. The peeled paint, rusted railings, and crumbling walls added to the desolation.

As they drove to Building Three, there were only a couple of windows with shades, even fewer with curtains. Most just had a sheet or blanket that concealed the room from the outside world.

When they parked at the side of the building, a dog tied to a railing tried to rush the car. It ran straight at them before it reached the end of its chain. The dog's whole body twisted violently, and it fell into the dirt as the three officers looked on, aghast. A moment later, the unfortunate animal scrambled to its feet and began barking nonstop.

In spite of the dog's warning, all the windows in all the buildings remained blank.

"Is this place deserted or what?" Kendra asked, clearly not needing a response, as there wasn't a soul in sight.

"It's eight in the morning. Everyone's still sleeping off the coke and booze from last night," Donald sneered.

"Kendra, you watch the back," Jack said. "This guy's assaults have all been on women, and he's jumped them. If I was putting money on it, I'd lay four to one that he takes off. See how the balconies connect the end apartments? He could try to go there. Plus, there are utility closets linking the apartments, and this guy may be skinny enough to slip through."

Kendra nodded. "I'll cover them. If he bolts, I'll nail him."

"Good."

Jack ran down his list: *Gun. Taser. Vest. Mace. Cuffs. Baton.*

Donald looked over at his partner. "No unnecessary chances, okay?"

Kendra nodded.

Jack forced himself to walk slowly, and Donald followed behind. A pair of yellowed eyes peered out from a first-floor window and hastily disappeared.

The stench of urine hit Jack's nose when he got to the exterior staircase. *Third floor. All of these apartments, same layout. Front door. Square living room. Kitchen in the back. Bathroom to the left and then the bedroom.*

The second floor had a couple of old lawn chairs next to the stairs and cigarette butts littered the cement. A chain held a mountain bike frame that was missing the tires, seat, and handlebars.

Jack climbed to the third floor and flexed his shoulders. He leaned over the railing and saw Kendra. She was watching the back, and her head was in constant motion.

Head on a swivel. Good girl.

Jack reached the unit. He motioned, and Donald stood near the window to the side of the door. Jack knocked, but he didn't pound on it like some cops did.

A dog two apartments down started to bark, and then another joined in. Both sounded like big dogs. Jack instinctively put his hand on the Mace. He knocked again. The face of a little girl appeared in the corner of the window.

Great. A little kid.

A woman in her early twenties opened the door, dressed in baggy gray sweatpants and a loose top. The baby in her arms pulled on the top so much that her left breast was almost exposed. She yanked her shirt out of the baby's hand while using her leg to try to hold back the little kid who'd been peering out the window.

Jack categorized them as a non-threat and scanned the background. The living room was dark, but there was enough light to see.

No one visible. Kitchen empty.

He listened intently for any sounds in the apartment.

"Yeah?" The woman alternated from looking at the floor to trying to get a bead on Jack. Her eyes would catch his for a brief moment and then dart away.

Red mark on cheek. Bruise on arm. Distrust. Fear.

"Good morning, ma'am. I'm Officer Jack Stratton."

"Yeah?" She pulled the baby's hand from her hair.

"Sorry to disturb you, but I have a few questions." He kept his tone light. "May I ask your name, please?"

"Nancy Mulligan."

"And this is your apartment?"

She just nodded.

"I'm looking for Kevin Arnold. Is he in?"

"He doesn't live here."

The little kid turned and looked into the apartment. *She's lying.*

"Ma'am." He gestured for her to step a little outside of the apartment. She stood frozen for a second, but Jack pinned his eyes on her. She faltered and stepped out.

His training in domestic violence kicked in. Battered women often turned on the authorities when confronted with a perceived threat to their abuser. *Better the devil you know…*

Jack leaned in a little. "I know you want to protect him. I'm not asking you to give him up, but he needs help."

"Momma?" The little girl tugged on Nancy's shirt.

Jack lowered his voice almost to a hum. "Nancy."

She looked confused for a second and then looked down at the little girl. She grabbed her daughter and pulled her closer.

"You want him to get help, right?" Jack nodded. "Everyone needs help sometimes."

A soft cry escaped Nancy's mouth, and she shook her head. She kept her gaze down and whispered, "He's in the bedroom."

That was all Jack needed to hear. He nodded to Donald and stepped into the apartment, motioning for Nancy to leave. She scooped up her children and ran down the corridor. Jack moved into the apartment, scanning constantly. The bathroom door was open. Empty. The bedroom door was closed.

Jack gestured to Donald and pointed at the closed door. He stood to the side, out of range, and slowly attempted to turn the handle, but it was locked.

He heard a door open inside the bedroom.

I knew he'd run. "Police!" Jack yelled, then popped the door with a short thrust from his shoulder. The cheap plywood shattered.

He caught a glimpse of someone running out to the mini balcony that connected to the one next door. Jack rushed after. He heard a woman scream from the other apartment. Jack jumped over the railing and onto the neighboring balcony.

"Police!" he warned as he went through the door, his gun at the ready.

The other apartment's bedroom was furnished with only a mattress in the corner. A woman sat on it, screaming and frantically pointing.

Jack raced across her kitchen to an open door and out to the back of the building, paused to listen, and sprinted after the footsteps running down the stairway.

The sound of barking dogs filled the air, followed by Kendra's angry shouts. On the second floor, Jack looked over the edge; Kendra was below, Macing an enormous dog that howled in pain but held its ground.

"Go around!" Jack called as he dashed down the stairs.

When he reached the bottom, Jack saw Arnold running for the other side of the building. A flash of metal in Arnold's hand caught Jack's eye. "Knife!" he yelled.

Arnold knocked over a chair as he scrambled away.

Jack's legs pushed into the ground; adrenaline gave him power. He rounded the corner and saw how much ground he'd gained. Arnold was now less than twenty yards away. Beyond them was an open field.

"Freeze!"

Jack grabbed his nightstick and threw it sidearm. The baton caught the creep right behind his legs, and he became entangled. Arnold's hands went wide, his back arched, and he faceplanted in the dirt. The knife bounced along the ground in front of him.

Kendra raced around the other corner of the building and tackled Arnold just as he was regaining his feet. Jack snagged his baton and took over holding the guy so she could cuff him. "Way to go, rookie," he congratulated her. "Nice job taking this guy down."

Jack didn't care who got credit for the arrest; he liked Kendra. She was short on arrests and shorter on confidence. Being a new cop was hard enough, but she was also a woman, and she was pretty, which made it a lot harder for her. The guys hit on her, and the few other women on the force were jealous.

She pulled Arnold to his feet. A string of obscenities, mixed with *don't* and *move*, poured from her mouth. She was beaming as Donald ran around the corner.

"I got him. I got him!"

"You sure did," said Donald, taking in the scene. "Nice job, Officer Darcey."

12

TRY TO OUTSHOUT ME

Jack stood with Detective Charlie Flynn behind the two-way mirror and looked into the interview room where Kevin Arnold sat chained to a table.

"How did you get the guy, Jack?"

Detective Flynn was fifty-two years old and completely bald but had thick, bushy eyebrows. His brown suit, although pressed and neat, looked to be at least ten years old.

"I got a tip that he was at his girlfriend's apartment. We picked him up this morning on an outstanding warrant. Officer Darcey made the collar."

Flynn chuckled. "Darcey. She's the one with the… um, big… *eyes*." He practically drooled.

"She's the one with the big gun," Jack said pointedly. "Anyway, she made the collar. This guy looks good for these cases." Jack patted the folder in his hands. "I put them all in here for you."

Flynn took the folder. "Thanks. This is great. Puts him on a silver platter for me. But what did you want again?"

"I just want to know his whereabouts before Christmas. See if he was anywhere near the university."

"You got it." Flynn was flipping through the folder. "Yep, he looks good for the other cases in here. He matches the description, right down to the tattoo. I think we may have found our guy." Flynn was smiling as he walked out to grill the perp.

Jack leaned back against the wall and watched. Flynn methodically picked apart the guy's alibis, and it wasn't long before Arnold started to squirm.

"So where were you before Christmas?" Flynn asked.

"I was in rehab," Arnold said.

"Rehab?"

"Court ordered."

"You know the probation office would have that in their system. There's nothing in your file here." Flynn shuffled through the folder.

"I was out of state in Sanderson County Rehabilitation for four weeks. Check it out with them."

"Don't worry, I will." Flynn looked over toward the two-way glass and nodded.

Jack stormed out of the room and over to his desk. He called the rehab and got them to pull up their records. Arnold's story checked out. And it was a county lockup, not a country club rehab, so there was no way Kevin Arnold could have snuck out of it unnoticed. Dead end.

* * *

He was surprised he could even drive—his right leg was twitching, both hands were trembling, his head was ringing.

Get a grip, Jack.

In the field, adrenaline was like a drug that pumped him up. But when it was over, he crashed—total withdrawal. Then the fear and doubt would drag him toward the pit of memories. He couldn't fill the abyss and he couldn't seal it up, either.

Jack stared straight ahead and tried to remember the young soldier's name. He closed his eyes and tried to control his breathing.

Iraq. I was on patrol with two other soldiers. Jimmy Tanaka. Tank. He was there.

Jimmy was only five foot five, but he was a powerhouse, and he never, ever backed down.

Me, Tank, and the kid.

The kid. Short red hair and freckles. So young, at most nineteen. Always chewing gum. That day they had to search a building with three doors along the front. Jack, the kid, and Tank each picked a door. They let the kid go first, and he went to the left. Tank chose the right; Jack ended up with the middle. On the count of three, they were all supposed to kick the doors open. The kid died on two. Enemy machine-gun fire blew the door apart and killed him instantly.

I can't even remember his name.

Jack pulled to the side of the road and put his head down on the steering wheel.

* * *

As soon as Jack walked through the door to his apartment, Replacement was in his face.

"You went after him without me? Without *me?*"

"When did you become my partner? Back off," Jack snapped.

Replacement froze. The problem was, she froze angry.

"Argh… I just walked in the door." Jack threw his hands up.

"You said—" she growled.

"I didn't say I'd take you." He headed into the kitchen.

"You did!" Now she was shouting.

Go ahead, try to outshout me.

"I didn't say that!" he yelled louder.

"I'm sitting around here on my ass while Michelle is out there." Her lip trembled. "You promised you'd take me. You—"

Loud hammering on the door interrupted her. They both stopped. Replacement marched over and opened the door.

Jack listened while he got a glass of water. He couldn't make out who Replacement was speaking with, but a few seconds later, Mrs. Stevens, flushing beet-red, marched into the apartment ahead of Replacement, who was twitching her head spastically.

Not again. Jack shut the water off.

"Mr. Stratton," Mrs. Stevens puffed. "While I do appreciate how stressful law enforcement can be, I cannot permit you to yell at this poor, unfortunate girl."

Jack's jaw clenched as he tried to control himself.

"Jack sorry." Replacement hopped over to him at the sink. "Jack, very sorry. Jack, you sorry?" Jack glared at her.

Replacement's arm went around his waist, and she poked him in the side. He had to force himself not to laugh.

"Yes. I'm sorry. Okay?" Jack smiled thinly. "Mrs. Stevens, my… apologies."

"Mr. Stratton, I'm trying to look out for her best interests."

"Well, thank you. You've been very kind."

"Remember, she's an angel, and when you deal with her, you need patience and love. Patience and love." Mrs. Stevens must have concluded that her work here was done, because she turned and waved as she headed out of the apartment.

"Patience and love. Patience and love," Replacement repeated as she shut the door and ran back into the kitchen.

"Well, thank you," Jack whispered fiercely. "Now my landlady thinks I'm a jerk."

"No, she doesn't. She likes you. She just thinks you make poor choices in women and drink too much."

Jack's mouth fell open. "Have you been talking to her? Stop, okay? I'm serious." He paused. "How could she know I drink too much?"

"She goes through your trash."

"She told you that?"

"She thinks I'm slow."

"You are." He headed into the bedroom. "I wanna take a shower, since it's free for once," he teased.

"Jerk, wait. You didn't tell me what happened," Replacement protested, following.

"Fine. Hold on." He shut the bedroom door to close her out. "We caught the guy," he yelled.

Replacement whipped open the door. "What? Awesome."

Jack stood there bare-chested. "Get out." He tossed his shirt at her.

Replacement didn't shut the door, but she did turn around.

"Anyway, he's a sexual predator, but he didn't have anything to do with Michelle."

"How do you know?"

"He was in a lockdown rehab for four weeks in another state. He went in three weeks before Michelle went missing and was there for a week after. He couldn't have had anything to do with it. I checked myself and confirmed it. Can you get out now?"

Replacement kicked the wall, and half her foot disappeared into the drywall. "Oh…" She knelt down and tried to pull the cracked piece back into place. "I'm so sorry." Her voice trembled.

"Forget it. I'm pretty good at patching walls. I've had a little practice."

"I'm sorry."

"I can fix it."

"Not just for that." Replacement paced around the room. "I've been a psycho. You're right. I'm a little… mental, lately."

Jack laughed.

"Thanks for agreeing." She sniffled.

He hesitated before replying, torn between whether to keep his tone light or more serious. Finally he said, gently, "Everyone's a little mental. Apology accepted. Can I take that shower now?"

She seemed relieved and calmer. Without asking, she sat down at the end of the bed beside Jack.

"So, I was working on the computer. Carlos wrote you back. He went to Western Tech and asked around, but Michelle has never been out there. He showed the picture around. Carlos said maybe she signed up electronically."

Jack had to think for a second. Carlos Rodriguez, Sonoma PD. "How do you know he emailed me?"

"You use the same password for everything. That's not smart."

Jack blinked, incredulous. "You read my emails?"

"I needed to see what he wrote. I found something else, too—an entry in the error log of the police database."

"In the error log? How could you get to the error log? Isn't that on the back end of the system?"

"Once you're in a system, it's easy to move around."

Jack glared at her as the meaning hit him. "You hacked the police database?"

"No. I just gained access to the back end."

"You hacked the database!"

"I don't call it that." She crossed her arms. "I exploited a security flaw."

"Did you use my account?"

"No. I made my own." As his eyes widened, she twisted back and forth. "Don't sweat it. They won't know. Their security sucks. I used my laptop, so they have no way to trace an IP even if they did suspect something. I mask my IP, then go through a VPN, and then double-jump high-anonymity proxies. The second proxy is offshore, so don't sweat it. No one is following my butt." She grinned.

"Okay, never mind. I can't believe this. I can't tell if you're helping me or... whatever." He shook his head to get back to the beginning. "Anything else you found out while you were casually committing felonies on your laptop connected to *my* computer?"

No question about it, she looked proud of herself, not ashamed in the least.

"Someone started to run a site inspection on Michelle's car. I don't know—"

"A site inspection? Are you sure?"

"Yeah. It was only one line; two codes in an error log. The license plate number partially matched, and the purpose field said 'Site Inspection.' I think they didn't put in enough information, and it errored out."

Jack jumped off the bed. "I have to go."

"Where? What's a site inspection?"

"That's police-speak for an abandoned vehicle in an accident. If you find an abandoned car that shows signs of being in an accident, you have to do a site inspection. You first run the plate. Someone started one. Did it have a date?"

"No. Just those two fields."

"I don't know what went wrong, but if a cop ran a site inspection, the next step is the car gets towed. There's only one impound they'd take the car to."

13

KILLER REINDEER

Jack had to keep forcing himself to slow down as they raced out to Sullivan's Auto and Salvage, a gigantic auto yard at the west end of Darrington County. Sullivan's was the main towing company the police used, and the official impound yard. If they towed a car, they'd take it there.

I should have checked there first.

He was also seriously questioning his judgment for having allowed Replacement to cajole him into taking her with him. She'd made it sound like a matter of life or death if she didn't get some fresh air. It was forty-two degrees outside, but she had her window half open and kept popping her head out like a puppy out for her first ride in a car.

He pulled down the visor mirror and glared at himself. His reflection glared right back. *Jerk.*

He flipped the mirror up.

It was starting to get dark, so once they got out of town, he punched it. The Impala's gas pedal was as sensitive as a moody teenager; the difference between twenty and one hundred twenty miles an hour was about half an inch. He decided to give Replacement the look that said, "Don't worry, I can handle driving at this speed." One glance at her and he could tell she was grateful they were getting there fast.

They towed Michelle's car. That means she hasn't had a car for a while. That isn't a good sign.

It made no sense she'd go to California, but part of him wished she had. The alternative was not good.

He barreled into a turn, and the car strained against the chassis. *Too fast.* He was going into a slip. Everything slowed way down. His adrenaline kicked in, and the world seemed to freeze. He loved this feeling. *Cut the wheel, go with the skid.* His training was taking over—kinesthetic muscle memory. Dancers, athletes, martial artists all strive for it. If you perform a motion often enough, you teach your muscles. When the time comes, the muscles repeat the motion on their own, almost independently of the brain.

Jack smiled, but when he glanced at Replacement, he saw that both of her hands were holding onto the door. He accelerated into the turn. It went against instinct to speed up as the car was going into a slip, but if you don't, you spin out.

As they straightened out, he relaxed his grip on the wheel, but Replacement didn't settle back into her seat. Her whole face was white, even her lips. He forced himself to slow down.

"I—I'm sorry about driving so fast. I just... I just want to find Michelle."

Replacement surprised him, adjusting her grip and replying, "Me too. Punch it."

Music to Jack's ears. He stomped on the gas and raced the rest of the way there.

They stopped in front of the auto yard's two large gates, which were secured by a thick chain and padlock. Jack gave three loud blasts on the car horn.

Replacement jumped out, grabbed the gates, and peered in.

Jack got out and walked along the ten-foot-tall, rusted barbed-wire fence, desperately searching for the blue Honda Civic like a mother frantically scanning faces of everyone as she looks for her lost child. And then…

Found it.

His stomach dropped.

The roof of the car was partly smashed in.

The car must have rolled over at least once.

Replacement followed his eyes to the car. Before he could stop her, she pulled the gates as far apart as the chain would allow and squeezed her slender frame through the gap.

He grabbed the fence. "No, no, no!" The warning burst out like a machine gun as he dashed back. His arm reached through the gate and he tried to grab her, but she was too fast and Jack was too bulky to fit through. "Stop!" He tried not to yell—it was more of a shouted whisper.

But it wouldn't have mattered if he'd screamed; she was fixated on Michelle's car.

Jack yelled to get her attention, but she just stood and stared at the car. Besides the roof, both the windows were down and the windshield was broken. The front end was damaged, and pieces of headlight and bumper were gone.

A sound grew closer. Bells jingling. Little bells on dog collars.

He pulled at the gates, but he couldn't break the chain; nor could he fit through.

"RUN!" Jack could always yell loudly, even as a little kid. Now sheer panic amplified his voice and he finally broke through the dark cloud that Replacement was in.

She looked up.

He couldn't even count the number of animals in the huge pack of dogs that raced toward her. Junkyard dogs—muscular, enormous beasts as mean as they come. Without a sound except the little bells around their collars, their panting breaths, and their pounding gallop.

Replacement's body tensed for the run back to the gate. The dogs must have sensed the hunt was on because now they bayed and growled.

Even if she runs now, she'll never make the gate.

Replacement froze with fear. The beasts drove forward, their mouths open.

"Get in the car!" Jack shouted. He took one look at the barbed wire at the top of the fence and knew he couldn't climb over it in time. *"Get in the car!"*

Replacement tried to open the smashed car door. It creaked, but it didn't budge. Jack could hear the dogs' claws on the frozen ground now.

"In!" he ordered.

Replacement scrambled through the open window. Jack saw her legs vanish inside the car. He could only watch as the huge, snarling dogs chomped at the window where their prey had disappeared. Their open jaws snapped, and they barked and scratched at the car. Baying and yelping, they circled it.

The biggest dog Jack had ever seen put both its front paws on the open window and rammed its giant head in. Jack heard Replacement scream and saw her feet kick at the beast's head, again and again, but it wouldn't back away.

Jack pulled the gates open as far as he could, his chest muscles straining, and tried to ram himself between the gates. But his upper body went only partly through. He struggled, but the metal refused to move.

He roared louder than the dogs in a fusion of desperation and fear. The canines stopped circling the car and, as one, looked to the sound of the challenge. They snarled, and their claws raked the ground. Then the giant alpha dog howled, and the pack ran toward their new prey.

Jack smiled. He had succeeded in luring them away from Replacement. He pushed to move himself back through the gate, but found that he couldn't budge; he was wedged fast. His legs strained, and he pressed at the gates, but his upper body stayed where it was. He tried to plant his feet, but they slipped on the frozen ground.

The dogs closed the distance. Jack's shoulders burned as his back muscles went into overdrive. His shirt ripped open, and the metal slashed his skin. He growled, heaved, and tore himself free just as the dogs smashed into the fence. When they scrambled up, they howled in frustration.

"Donner! Blitzen!" An old man dressed in dark-blue overalls rushed into view. "Comet! Heel!" The dogs turned and raced toward the man. They nuzzled up against him, eager for praise because they had protected the junkyard.

Sully. Finally. Jack winced as he got up. All the buttons were gone from the front of his shirt, and his chest was scratched and bleeding, but he was glad not to be a chew toy right now.

"That you, Jackie?" He could never figure out why older people referred to him as Jackie.

"Yeah, it's me, Sully. Let me in, please." The old man walked over and unlocked the gate, and Jack darted through and headed for the Civic.

"What the hell were you thinking, boy? Heel," the old man snapped at the growling dogs. To Jack he added, "Move slow, boy."

"Listen, Sully." Jack had to force himself to slow down and not run to get to Replacement. "I'm here about a car. My friend ran in to check it out."

"What? Is your friend stupid, crazy, or both? You never go past the gate at Sullivan's. Doesn't everybody know that?" Sully shook his head, and his wild white hair bobbed back and forth. "Go check to see he ain't bit. If he is, it's his own darn fault."

Jack jogged over to the car and found Replacement curled into a tight ball on the front seat. He grabbed the door and yanked it open. "Are you okay?" he whispered.

He touched her back, and her arms shot around his neck. She sobbed and buried her face in his shoulder. He lifted her from the car and cradled her in his arms.

"What kind of daisy is your friend, Jack? Is he bit or not? Either way, tell him to man up."

Jack felt Replacement go rigid, and he smiled. *She still has fight in her. Maybe she's okay.*

"Man up?" She wriggled her way out of Jack's grasp. "*You* man up, you killer-dog-owning psycho." She wiped her nose with the back of her sleeve. Jack noticed a small cut on her chin and another on her cheek.

"A girl? Oh—I'm so sorry, honey." Sully went as white as his hair and looked as if he was about to faint. "Jack, what the hell is wrong with you?" he grumbled, and his legs wobbled.

"Me?"

Replacement rushed to the man's side and took him by his hands, her face full of concern. How she could go from one extreme to another perplexed Jack. One second he thought she'd punch the old man in the face, and now she rushed to care for him. She shot an angry glance at Jack, but as he tried to approach, the pack growled as one.

"Easy, boys. Sit, sit!" Sully pulled one hand free from Replacement and waved at the dogs.

"Let me help you back inside," she offered, taking her new friend by the arm. "You're as pale as a ghost."

The old man grinned like a schoolboy at the attention and let her lead him to the trailer. "You got cut up," he said. "I have some bandages inside."

Jack followed the unlikely pair at a slight distance, and the dogs followed him. He might as well have been under guard. If he got too close to Sully, they growled. If he lagged too far behind, they growled.

The office was what you'd expect for a junkyard trailer office. It smelled of mildew, cigarette smoke, and motor oil. There was a small counter and a desk covered in greasy papers. An old TV was turned on full blast across from a worn-out chair. A little space heater provided a surprising amount of heat, and Jack was grateful, considering he could no longer zip his broken jacket and was basically walking around bare-chested.

Sully had Replacement sit in the old armchair while he switched off the TV. "Sorry, I'm a bit deaf," he apologized.

Probably from the TV.

"What brings you out, Jackie?" Sully was asking Jack, but he was looking at Replacement. "You want a soda?" He moved over to the small brown refrigerator in the corner.

"Sully, I'm not here officially, just yet." Jack noticed the old man's puzzlement. "I'm looking for my missing foster sister."

This latest bit of news caused him to pale even more. "Missing? I'm so sorry, Jackie. How can I help?" He handed a soda to Replacement and offered another to Jack, who mumbled a thank-you and put the soda in his coat pocket.

"The blue Honda Civic." Jack cocked his head in the direction of the car. "What can you tell me about it?"

Sully reached into a drawer and took out a box of bandages. He offered them to Replacement, but she waved them off.

"That one? Found her on Reservoir Road. Totaled. Bent frame. Some kids must have rolled her."

Jack tried not to linger on images of what had brought the Civic to its current state. "Kids? Who found it?"

"A hunter called it in. He was out on the reservoir looking for deer and said he saw a group of kids trying to start it. He thought they were stuck, but when he went to give them a hand, they all took off. Murphy said he figured we'd get the story when she showed up stolen. I haven't heard anything, so I was going to check back with him."

I knew it. Murphy, you moron.

Billy Murphy was only half a cop. And if he weren't the county commissioner's son-in-law, he wouldn't even be that. He had his own carpentry business and worked part-time as a cop for extra money. He did mostly on-call stuff, like traffic details. Sheriff Collins couldn't stand him, and neither could the other police officers. The work might be slow around here, but the other cops took it seriously at least.

Murphy working the car explained the error line in the police database. *That jackass started to run a site inspection, screwed it up, and didn't run it again.*

Jack tried to mask his frustration. "Did Murphy search the car?"

"He gave it a once-over. We picked up some pieces of it off the road, and I brought it all back here. It was just some kids, right? They okay?" Jack could see the older man was concerned. It wasn't his fault Murphy was lazy.

"Is it all right if I go take a look?"

Replacement jumped out of her chair and moved to the door.

"Sure, Jackie."

Sully went first and shooed the dogs away as the three of them walked back to the car.

Jack took a deep breath and decided to start on the inside of the car. Besides little piles of broken glass, the car was clean. The keys were still in the ignition. In the glove compartment Jack found an owner's manual, a pair of sunglasses, and some tissues.

There might be some prints left after off-and-on snow and getting towed, but no guarantees. Jack walked around to the trunk and stopped.

He closed his eyes and inhaled. He could smell the faint odor of gasoline. He looked over at Replacement, who was peering into the inside of the car.

His hand trembled.

Please, God, don't let her be in here.

Jack opened the trunk.

It was empty.

He exhaled.

Jack pulled the trunk closed. "Were you there with Murphy when he first saw the car?"

"No. I arrived a little after he got there. It wasn't real stuck. Oh—Ben Nichols!" Sully jumped as he suddenly remembered the name. "It was Ben, called the car in. He was bow hunting."

"Where can I find him?" Jack reached for his notebook, normally in his uniform pocket, and frowned when he realized it was in his car.

Sully gave him detailed directions to the house.

"Thanks, Sully. Listen, can you do me one more favor?"

"Sure thing, Jackie."

"Call Murphy and tell him the car's still here. Tell him to check that it's in the database. But don't say I was here."

Sully gave him a questioning look.

"I don't want to embarrass him, since he must have forgotten." *I don't want to embarrass him—I want to kill him. But this way Collins won't know I'm looking into this.*

Sully turned to Replacement. "Sorry about the dogs. Nice ta meet ya."

"Thank you for the soda, sir." Replacement's eyes stayed on the mangled Civic for a moment and her shoulders slumped, sort of like the smashed-in roof of Michelle's car. Then she and Jack trudged back to the Impala and he cranked up the heat as far as it would go, but they were both shivering and silent as they pulled back onto the road.

14

THAT'S ALWAYS DANGEROUS

"Where's Reservoir Road?" Replacement asked.

Jack took a hard right. "Where the car was found?"

She gave him something between a nod and a shiver.

"The hunter's place is on the way. We need to interview him and see what he knows first, then we'll check out where they found the car."

Jack lifted a knee against the steering wheel and breathed into his hands to heat them a bit, but it did nothing to warm the gaps in his torn jacket and shirt. He blew past a stop sign, and Replacement gave him a surprised look. He ignored it. They were running out of daylight.

The hunter said he saw kids run off, but why would kids have Michelle's car? Did they steal it? Were they driving it, or did they find it like that?

His knuckles on the steering wheel turned white as they sped on. He slowed down when he saw the canoes Sully had told him would be there, and pulled into Nichols's driveway. "Stay here." He left no room for argument as he got out of the car. He left it running to keep her warm, but something bothered him about leaving Replacement in his car with the keys in it.

She scooted over to the driver's seat before he shut his door.

"You're not coming with me. It would look weird," Jack tried to explain.

"You can say that again," she answered. "You look like a Chippendales dancer."

He frowned and didn't know what to say. Maybe it was a compliment; he wasn't sure. He popped the trunk and found a police sweatshirt in a gym bag. When he put it on, it was so cold he had to force himself to breathe for a few seconds.

He grabbed his notebook and pen, telegraphed to Replacement, *Do not move*, and jogged up to the house.

The door opened as he approached. A short, bald man with thick glasses stood in the doorway. "Can I help you?" the man asked. He had a blank stare on his face and his eyes looked odd.

Jack froze. He had forgotten he was a good ways out of town, and a different sort of people lived out here. Ben Nichols's left hand was visible, but his right wasn't. Jack noticed the muscles on the right side of Ben's neck stood out.

A little guy meets me at the door with that face and the way he's standing? He's a hunter. Odds are there's a shotgun in his other hand.

Jack angled his body so Ben could see the word POLICE printed across his sweater. "Mr. Nichols." Jack forced himself not to move his hands. "I'm Officer Jack Stratton.

Sully over at the auto yard said you called in the abandoned car report on Reservoir Road. I came out here to thank you."

"Thank me?" Ben's chest puffed up. "I'm just doing my duty, Officer." Jack was surprised the man didn't salute.

"I just left Sully's, and I have a couple of questions." Jack kept smiling, but stood very still.

"Yes, sir. Won't you come in?" Ben opened the door wide, and Jack's eyes went to the double-barreled shotgun in Ben's right hand. Ben shrugged and grinned. "You can't be too careful."

"Certainly. Thank you." Jack followed the man inside.

It was a pleasant home. Ben Nichols walked through a door to the left and into a large room with bookcases and a hefty, warm woodstove. Jack scuttled over to it as Ben settled onto a tan couch.

"Are you making an official report?" Ben asked. He appeared to be thrilled about the attention.

Jack coughed. "Yes. Can you please explain in your own words the events starting just before you found the car, Mr. Nichols?" Jack took out his notebook. People loved it when you wrote down what they said, and writing things down let Jack pay attention to the person. He could pore over the details later.

"I was out hunting near the Onopiquite Reservoir." Ben's voice dropped a couple of octaves, and he now sounded as if he were giving a televised report from some war zone. "I'd been out for a few hours when I first heard the kids. It was around three o'clock. There were five teens around a blue Honda Civic."

"Do you remember where on Reservoir Road this was?"

"No, not exactly. They were due west of the reservoir."

Jack continued to write.

"From a distance, I could see the teens were trying to start the car. I naturally assumed they'd just broken down, but as I approached to help, I could see the damage to the car. When they saw me, the perps fled the scene."

People loved to use police jargon. Jack tried to let it go, but the word slipped out. "Perps?"

"Perpetrators," Ben enlightened him, then continued with his narrative. "I realized afterward that the car must not have been theirs, seeing as how they ran."

"Can you tell me anything about the teens?"

"There were five guys. They were on snowmobiles. Two rode double. Umm... one had a red coat, and another guy had a Roman thing on his head."

"A Roman thing?" Jack stopped writing.

"Like a Mohawk? A gold one on his helmet." Ben's hands moved over his head. "Like a Roman soldier would wear."

"On his helmet? Like a centurion?" Jack scribbled a quick picture of a Roman soldier's helmet and turned the notebook around.

"That's it." Ben nodded.

"What about the one in the red coat? What else can you tell me about him?"

"It was a big red parka. The kid was very chunky. I think that's why he rode alone. He was stocky. Fat."

"Anything else about them? Jackets, hats..."

"Not really. They took off when I called out to them."

"Have you ever seen any of them before?" Jack continued.

"I've seen kids snowmobiling out there a lot. I think I've seen the Roman kid, too."

"You ever see the car before?"

"No."

"Was there snow on the car when you first saw it?" Jack stopped writing.

Ben thought for a minute. "Yeah, the windshield was covered. It was light. A dusting. There was some snow inside the car. I remember because I looked in the back and—"

"Did you touch the car?"

"No, sir. That could contaminate the crime scene." Ben shook his head emphatically.

"Did you notice anything else?"

Ben shook his head again.

"Thanks, Mr. Nichols. You've been very helpful." Jack closed his notebook.

"If you need anything, I'm always ready to do my part, Officer Stratton." Ben stood at attention as he held open the door.

Back at the car, Replacement stuck her head out the window. "What did you find?" The new-puppy look was now complete as she sat up on her haunches and looked up at Jack with big, dewy eyes.

"Move it," Jack said, trying to sound annoyed. Inwardly he was thinking, *I kinda like my new puppy.*

"What did he say?" she asked again. Jack watched as she scooted across the seat in a little reverse hop.

Jack climbed into the vacated driver's seat. "When he got to the car, there were five kids snowmobiling around it. One had a weird helmet with a gold Mohawk on it. It should be easy enough to find him."

"You don't think they're involved, do you?"

"No. He said there was already snow on the windshield and in the car, so I think the car had been there a while."

* * *

The Onopiquite Reservoir was the size of a large lake; in fact, many referred to it as Lake Onopiquite. No boating, swimming, or fishing were allowed—but everyone ignored the fishing ban because the fishing there was so good. The reservoir sat at the bottom of a large, natural basin, shaped like a long serving dish. Reservoir Road circled the lake on the lower side of the basin, closest to the water, and Pine Ridge ran along the eastern ridge, on the lip of the bowl. During foliage season, Pine Ridge saw a lot of traffic because the view of the lake down below with the reflection of the trees was breathtaking. However, Reservoir Road saw very little traffic and almost none during the winter.

Jack drove slowly down Reservoir Road. It was now dark, and with no streetlights, and the watery abyss next to them, it was impossible to see beyond the headlights.

"Do you know where they found the car?" Replacement asked.

"Not the exact spot. Ben Nichols just had a general description."

As they drove up and down the road, nothing stood out. Jack shook his head. "It's too dark. I'll call Sully and try to get a better description of the site the car was towed from."

"Do you think we could get out and start searching the woods on foot?"

Jack kept driving. *What am I supposed to say?* He ground his teeth and tried not to yell. "It's been two weeks, it's freezing, and you're hoping she's out there just waiting for us?" She looked so hurt, he added more gently, "We'll come back tomorrow. I promise."

He regretted his promise almost as soon as he'd made it, but it wasn't even close to the shame he felt when Replacement shot back with, "You promised to come back before."

He got back on the highway and remained silent until he passed his exit.

"Where are you going? You missed the exit."

"I'm taking you home."

"What do you mean?"

"Your apartment. You can't stay at my place anymore. I don't know what you told Mrs. Stevens, but she won't stay happy for long, so let's leave her that way… happy."

"What did I do? I won't be in the way. We can go tomorrow, like you said. But I… don't want to go home."

"I'm not doing this now." His voice was so crisp the words seemed to snap. But what she'd said was true. Fairfield was less than an hour away, yet he hadn't seen Aunt Haddie or Michelle since he came back. "I'm…"

I'm what? I'm a coward? What the hell was I supposed to say to them? "Gee, by the way, I'm really sorry I got Chandler killed"?

Jack glared at Replacement and was glad she was looking out the window. Let her come to her own conclusions about what he was.

When they got to Fairfield and where he dropped her off before, on Marshall Avenue, Replacement got out and walked away without looking back. Again, Jack didn't wait to see if she got in safely. He pulled away, tires screeching, and drove half a block before pulling over again, too upset to drive right away. He shut off the engine and pounded the steering wheel.

What does she want from me? I'm not her brother. I'm only watching out for her because of Chandler.

He grabbed the rearview mirror to see if he could get a glimpse of Replacement. She hadn't gone inside. She was walking down the street away from him.

She looked small and vulnerable, and on closer inspection, the neighborhood was pretty sketchy. Where was she going exactly? He didn't remember any residential buildings on this corner, at least when he was growing up.

He grabbed the keys from the ignition and followed her on foot. She went a couple of blocks before she turned to the left. It was a business district, but everything appeared closed. This part of the town had seen better days, but it wasn't dangerous.

A girl alone at night—that's always dangerous.

He tried to stay far back; there were very few people on the street, so he hugged the sides of the buildings and kept his head down. But all that wasn't necessary: Replacement never looked back.

She turned another corner, and Jack hurried so he wouldn't lose her if she went in somewhere. She continued for another couple of blocks and then stopped at a gate beside a small, blocky building.

It was a little hard to see what she was doing, but as he stealthily moved forward, he saw a box where a driver would normally punch in a security code, and the heavy gate was parting.

He sprang forward and slipped through. He watched her open the main entrance door with a key. He almost didn't make it in behind her before the door closed with a pneumatic *whoosh*.

It just looked like an ordinary office building; three floors, big parking lot off next to it. Maybe it had been converted to an apartment building. Then he saw a sign—STORAGE 4 U. On another sign was a bullet list of regulations.

A storage place? What's she getting this late at night?

The first floor was just an open central area flanked by two stairwells. He moved along the edge of the wall to minimize any creaks and pops, and opened the stairwell door as quietly as possible, and stopped it from clanging shut. The building seemed totally quiet. On the next level, a corridor with worn linoleum tiles ran all the way across to the other side, with four doors on either side. The last door on the right had a bit of light creeping out from underneath it.

He stood outside the door and debated whether to knock or just try to open it, or leave her to her secrets. Finally, he tapped softly. "Replacement?"

Silence.

He whispered her name again, and this time he heard movement from inside.

A couple of soft footsteps, then the door slowly opened a crack. Replacement's head appeared, but she refused to look him in the face.

Jack put his hand on the door and gradually opened it. She didn't stop him, but her lips trembled and she still wouldn't look at him.

It didn't take long to take a look at the place. Sleeping bag on the floor; a small table beside it with a little clamp-on light. Three green trash bags were stacked in one corner, a couple of boxes in the other. That was it. No place to eat, let alone cook. No table, no chair to sit on.

His anger rose. He was angry with himself. He knew—or he should have known.

She said Aunt Haddie's in a nursing home, so she can't live with her. She didn't mention any friends. She's out of the foster care system… This explains the showers every time she comes over.

"The homeless shelter… You know… it's a lot more freaky there. Aunt Haddie tries to give me money when she can, but this… It's just temporary… I mean, it's fine. I don't need much. Things will change."

She smiled at him. The smile was forced, but it contained a glint of hope, and that little bit of light cut straight through him.

"Yeah." Jack cleared his throat. "It's temporary because it's over. From now on, you're staying with me."

She looked up at him.

"Hand me a couple of things and I'll go get the car."

She started to tremble. Jack stepped forward and pulled her close.

Don't cry. Please don't cry.

Her arms started to rise as if to give him a hug, but then stopped and dropped loosely to her sides. Jack hugged her tighter. Her arms shot out and wrapped around his waist. He patted her back and held her until she stepped back, rubbing her eyes.

Jack grabbed the trash bags. "I'll get the car."

By the time he returned, she was already waiting for him downstairs with the two boxes at her feet.

"Not much of a life." The shrug that accompanied her words cut Jack to his core.

"Your new one starts today. Come on, let's go."

15

A GIANT HOBBIT

Jack looked down at the table and froze.

It's a dream, Jack. Germany. Before you shipped out to Iraq. Chandler's about to come over to the table…

"Hey, Jack." Chandler's voice was happy. "You gonna have any?" Chandler held up a plate of scrambled eggs as he tried to fit his large frame into the small booth.

Jack couldn't bring himself to close his eyes and wake up. He remembered the day. He knew he was dreaming, but he didn't want to stop replaying the memory. "In a minute."

"The best part of German food is breakfast." Chandler flashed a big grin.

"You're like a giant hobbit. What's this, your second breakfast?" Jack chuckled.

"I'm a growing boy." Chandler shrugged. "You know, if we were home right now, Aunt Haddie would be waking us with breakfast."

Jack smiled. "Yeah, how could I forget? I'd kill for one of her pancakes."

"Remember her fire drills? She'd get freaked about having so many kids in the house and have those mock evacuations. All of us standing out on the sidewalk, freezing, while she did a head count." Chandler laughed.

"She woulda made a hell of a drill instructor."

"Remember that time you and I decided to go out the window and slide out over the porch? She nearly killed us." Chandler chuckled as he tried to keep his food in his mouth.

"We had to copy that entire fire safety book."

"My hand still hurts." Chandler jokingly flexed it.

"Don't forget why she did it, big man. She always said, 'Keep your eyes on the exit whenever you go someplace new, and be prepared.' Guess she made us ready for this." Jack sighed and stopped laughing.

Chandler tried to change the subject. "Hey, I have it all figured out, what I'm going to do when I get out."

"We haven't even left Germany. Then we have to get through Iraq, and *you* have it all figured out?"

"I'm going to be a teacher. I want to teach math."

Jack burst out laughing.

"Thanks a lot, jerk." Chandler tossed down his fork. "I thought the plan was we both go in and get money for college."

Jack put his hands behind his head. "I just came to watch your back."

"Yeah, but it's been the other way around." Chandler grinned. "Seriously, do you think that's stupid?"

"No. My dad's a math teacher. Did he bite you or something? Made you some sort of math zombie?"

"He gave me the idea. It's a great job. Help kids. You get the whole summer off."

"It's not stupid." Jack held up a glass of orange juice as a toast. "I just don't know how any kid is going to have the guts to ask a question with you standing at the front of the room."

They both laughed.

"Seriously." Jack knocked back the last of the orange juice. "You'll make a great teacher."

"Do you like eggs?" Chandler asked with a big smile.

Do you like eggs? Jack heard the words again, and he struggled to stay dreaming.

"Up you go. Get up, sleepyhead," Replacement commanded, pulling the blanket off him. He grabbed it, but she still caught an eyeful. "Wow, I didn't know you slept *au naturel*. Nice butt."

"Get out—now." He was tempted to stand up and give her the full show, but from the look on her face, he didn't think she'd back down, and he'd be the one to get embarrassed. "Can't you wake me up nicely?"

"I try. I start off really gentle, but you won't wake up. So I have to escalate it. You could snore through a train wreck."

"I don't snore."

"Sure." She tilted her head at him. "I made breakfast. Get dressed now, *nudist*, or I'll eat it all." She laughed and sprinted out of the room.

Jack wrapped the blanket around himself and went to the bathroom. He pulled on some sweatpants and then smelled the eggs.

She made me a hot breakfast.

Jack had just about given up on ever having a hot breakfast again. When he had to work the night shift, he frequently woke up in the afternoon, and he didn't like to eat breakfast later in the day, so the meal was slowly being worked out of his diet.

He yanked open the bedroom door and saw the kitchen counter set with two places. Replacement stood there with a frying pan in one hand and a spatula in the other, grinning like the Cheshire Cat. She wore a big, old Fairfield High School shirt. Jack walked around the counter and saw that the shirt was *all* she was wearing.

"Knock off surprising me in my bedroom and go put on some pants." He shook his head. Jack couldn't bring himself to frown because he was so happy about breakfast, so he settled for trying to look stern.

"You like scrambled eggs?" Replacement pushed a large plate toward him. In addition to eggs, it held four pieces of buttered toast.

"I love them." Jack grabbed his fork, but stopped with his hand halfway to his face.

Replacement had the same look Aunt Haddie would give him when he didn't say grace. He sighed, folded his hands, and bowed his head as Replacement began.

"Thank you, Lord, for this food. Thank you for Jack's help. Please help him find my sister and have her be okay. Bless Aunt Haddie and say hi to my brother. In Jesus's name, thanks."

Jack kept his eyes closed and his head bowed. There were times when he felt as though he didn't have anything that was core to his being. That he was missing something about being a human. But "missing" was the wrong word. Missing implied that at one time, he'd had it, and it was now gone. But he didn't think he'd ever had what Replacement possessed. It was as if he was defective. Something inside him was incomplete.

With his eyes still closed, Jack shook his head. Replacement understood something he didn't.

He opened his eyes and dropped his fork in surprise. Replacement's face was right next to his and she was staring into his eyes as if she was searching for something.

"There you go again," Jack said. "You have to give me some space." He grabbed his fork and started to eat.

"What? I'm just looking at your face. Did you just think of something?" She eyed him.

"You can just ask me. Don't get right next to me, don't sneak up on me. Just ask."

Replacement walked over to the far counter and returned with two cups of coffee. "Are we off to the reservoir?"

"Coffee, yes… whatever you want. Wait, no," he added. "I'll call Sully first. But I was thinking, we should go see if we can find one of those kids that found the car. They may know something."

"Why are we going to look for those kids first?" Replacement didn't mask her disappointment well.

"Look, they're just kids, and we need to know if that's where they found the car or if they drove it there. And who knows, maybe they saw something. There's an Eddie's Sports on 54, and it has a small garage for ATVs, snowmobiles, and dirt bikes. It's on the way to the reservoir. It has to be local kids, so a short conversation might give us a name."

Jack looked down at the empty plate, and then glanced at his watch. Five after seven. If she was offering hot breakfast as a bribe, it worked. "How soon can you be ready?"

Replacement was already pulling out a pair of jeans.

"I need a minute." Jack grabbed his coffee and headed into the bedroom.

Twice yesterday, between Ben Nichols's shotgun and the dogs at Sullivan's, Jack had wished he'd had his gun. He opened the small safe under the medicine cabinet and took out his pistol.

16

CHICKEN HEAD

As they drove to Eddie's Sports, Replacement fidgeted in her seat. Jack turned right at the large sign that read *Ridge Hill High School*, with a drawing of a fierce mountain lion in blue and white.

"The high school? What's here?" Replacement asked.

"Kids. That kid with the helmet, and there was another one, a hefty, fat boy in a giant red parka. It's worth a drive-by."

"That's great. How are we going to pick them out of that crowd?" Replacement pointed to the sea of teens arriving at the school.

Jack scanned the crowd and began to doubt the wisdom of his decision too.

"Wait!" Replacement pointed to a heavy kid in a red parka. "Over there, too." She pointed again.

"I get it. Look for the Mohawk."

"Third red parka, but sort of thin."

Jack scanned the sea of jackets and slowed down even more.

"Fourth red parka, off the starboard bow," Replacement bellowed.

Jack laughed at her mariner's jargon, even as a large group of students turned to stare at the car. She'd rolled down her window and was now halfway out of the car as she yelled.

Jack pulled her back into her seat. "Keep it down, Captain Obvious."

Replacement sprang right back up. "There, it's him!" She almost opened the door as she frantically jabbed the air with her finger.

"What did I *just* say?" Jack was about ready to abort this mission.

"No, there he is! It's him!" Replacement yelled, gesturing wildly.

"Where?" Jack scanned the crowd milling around the buses.

"The chicken-headed kid." She grabbed Jack's chin and turned his head. Jack saw the teen parking his motorcycle, and atop his helmet, there it was, a five-inch-high gold Mohawk.

Jack double-parked right behind the bike, blocking him in. "Stay here." He jumped out of the car. The rider, who was being greeted by a group of friends, turned back toward him.

"Excuse me," Jack called. He wanted to talk to the boy without the friends. "Can you come over here for a second? I need to ask you a quick question."

The kid has to be close to eighteen. Thinks he's a tough guy, judging from his helmet and the fact he's driving a motorcycle in winter.

"You a cop?" The kid laughed, and his friends circled a little closer around him.

"I am. Just a couple of questions, please."

"Talk to my lawyer." The teen held up both middle fingers, and his friends laughed.

Replacement pulled herself up so her whole upper body was halfway out the car window. "How about you come and talk to me? I don't bite... hard." She gave a sultry wave.

The kid laughed, punched one of his friends in the arm, and sauntered forward. "Sure, I'll talk to *you*, babe." He strutted over to the car.

Jack got right up next to the boy. "You can talk to me and answer a couple of questions now, or I can have your bike towed, impounded, and checked by the MVD, and then I'll throw you in a cell."

The teen gulped and the color drained from his face. Jack nodded to the other side of the car, and the boy followed him. Jack spoke in a low voice. "I need to know about the other day, when you and your buddies were out at the reservoir and saw a blue Honda Civic."

The kid looked back at his friends, and his bravado returned. "I don't know what you're talking about." He might have some peacock DNA, with his gestures and poses.

"Okay." Jack leaned in, and his voice turned cold. "Listen up. I'm doing you a favor by treating you like a man in front of your friends. If you jerk me around again, let me tell you what I'm going to do. I noticed you swerving when you pulled into the school, and I suspect you're under the influence of a controlled substance in a school zone. Under paragraph 95 of the 1998 DEA Act, that means I can detain you until the school principal comes and the two of us will escort you down to Ms. Kazikinski's office."

Ms. K was the school nurse. She taught a couple self-defense courses at the local Y and was also the wrestling coach for both the boys' and girls' teams. She was large, burly, and, at almost six foot two, had the best frame for a linebacker Jack had ever seen on a woman. Jack was making up the DEA code, but he knew Ms. Kazikinski for a fact, and was sure the kid would be dreading whatever Jack might say next.

"As I'm sure you're aware, any student who's viewed as being under the influence of or in possession of a controlled substance can and will be subjected to a full-body *cavity* search by trained medical personnel. That would be Ms. K." Jack smiled. "So... what's it going to be?"

"Teddy, Tommy, Brian, Scott, and I were down at the reservoir."

He just threw everybody under the bus.

Jack took out his notebook. "Your full name?"

"Ricky Matthews." The kid gulped as Jack wrote it down.

"You saw the car, and then what?"

"We figured we'd just check it out."

"What did the car look like?" Jack's voice was still cold.

"I don't know. Um... blue? It had been there, you know. And—"

"Been there?"

"There was snow on it. It snowed the night before. It was busted up already. There was glass on the front seat, and the window was broken open."

Jack's hand paused with the lurch of his heart. "Did you get in the car?"

Ricky looked at his feet and shuffled them awkwardly. "Yeah, but... I just looked." The boy looked Jack straight in the eyes, then glanced away to the left.

He's lying. "Did you start the car?" Jack leaned in.

"Yeah, I was just sitting there, and the keys were still there, so I turned it over. It started right up."

Jack frowned. Ricky was holding something back. "Ricky, have you ever seen Ms. Kazikinski's hands? She can palm a watermelon." The teen was squirming, and his eyes went wide.

"You're leaving something out, and you have one chance to give it up."

"There was a smartphone. Down between the seats."

"Where is it now?" Jack's eyes narrowed.

"I took it but... I lost it." Ricky looked like a little boy who had to go to the bathroom.

Jack pulled out a pair of handcuffs.

"No, no," Ricky begged. "Wait a minute—I got it. I got it." He pulled off his backpack and desperately rifled through it. "Here," he grunted, handing Jack the phone.

"Is there anything else?" Jack's eyes bored into the kid.

"No, nothing else." Ricky waved his hands back and forth.

"Thank you for your time. I'd hurry to class if I were you. Say hello to Ms. K for me."

Ricky bolted, avoiding his friends, who called after him. Jack watched until he disappeared through the front door.

Replacement reached out and grabbed for the phone, but Jack had to stop her sternly.

"Hold on. Evidence," he warned, getting into the car. "There should be a plastic evidence bag in the glove box." It already had his prints and Ricky's on it; no use confusing things further.

Replacement found a baggie and handed it to him. After he dropped the phone in and sealed it up, he gave it back to her and started the car.

"Yeah, it's her phone." She pressed the power button and the excitement on her face melted into disappointment. "It's dead."

Jack drove around the buses and headed for the exit. "It might still work, though." He nodded back toward the school. "Think Ricky will make it to the bathroom?"

"I think he peed himself next to the car." She laughed.

"The kid's angle is what I thought really happened. Three people have confirmed the car had been there a while: Sully, Nichols, and now Ricky."

Jack's phone rang—an old-fashioned bell, like telephones used to have.

Replacement made a face. "What kind of ringtone is that?"

Jack scowled at her as he answered. "Hello, Jack Stratton... Yeah, thanks for calling back, Sully. Can you tell me where on Reservoir Road you found the car?"

Replacement tried to put her ear up to the phone to listen.

"Thanks, I appreciate it." Jack hung up.

"What did he say?"

"Near the sharp curve in the road."

"Let's go."

Jack nodded. It was nice to see Replacement getting some of her bounce back.

17

IT WAS ME

The day was very warm for January, and they both opened their windows a crack. The smell of pine trees soon filled the car.

They approached the sharp curve in Reservoir Road and scanned up and down the road and the surrounding area. Jack noticed turned-up dirt and deep tire tracks, telling him a car had gotten stuck on the side of the road. He pulled over just past the spot and got out. Replacement fell in behind him.

Bits of plastic and broken glass were still scattered about. Under the sun, the snow had melted into deep, muddy ruts beside the road. The tire tracks and the ruts told Jack where the Civic had come to rest. Deeper tracks made by the tow truck paralleled those of the small sedan, and a series of thinner ruts showed where the teens had stopped to check out the car.

Replacement walked away, following the debris trail, while Jack examined the tire tracks, not quite sure what he was looking for. Sometimes it helped just to look for a long time at the crime scene.

Possible crime scene. Jack forced himself to calm down, go over his notes. *Michelle went missing. The kids found the car here. If the car—*

Replacement was following the debris trail on the other side of the road. Jack fell into step with her, examining the scattered bits and pieces of plastic and glass, like bread crumbs, which thinned out at a certain point. The hill beside them was extremely steep for about ten feet and then rose at an easier angle. They couldn't see over the lip, but it was obvious that the car had come from that direction. Muddy tire tracks came straight down the grass, and he could see where the car's front end had scraped the asphalt as the car came back onto the road.

Could she have been driving up on Pine Ridge?

He had to pull himself over the lip of the hill, but once he stood, there were more tire marks to confirm it: the Civic veered off the road at Pine Ridge, barreled down the hill, and came to a stop beside Reservoir Road.

Jack looked over at Replacement beside him, muddied from the climb up the slope. "Walk slowly after me to make sure I don't miss anything," he told her, but that wasn't the real reason for the request. Something felt off. Other cops and soldiers had told him to put away gut instincts and go on facts, but his gut had saved his life more times than he could count.

He could tell that this section of the hill had been the scene of a terrible brushfire years back. The living trees were new and small. A few dead, charred trees refused to fall over, and some twisted ones refused to give in. The car had made an obvious trail through the brush as it careened down the slope.

They followed the path up the hill until they reached a spot where the trail veered off at almost a ninety-degree angle and large clumps of grass and dirt stuck up from a slight gully. It wasn't very low, but it dropped off more sharply after a couple of feet. Jack spotted some bits of shattered glass.

Jack pictured the crash. *This was where it rolled over.* The car flipped over and then landed back upright on its wheels. *It was going straight toward the lake. Instead, it flipped on the rocks and fell off to the road below.*

Jack studied the path again. It went almost straight up until that ninety-degree twist in the middle. He looked around the area where the car had flipped over. There was a lot of glass, a soda bottle, and some bits of trash.

They must have been tossed out when the car—

"Replacement." Jack's voice was calm, and he forced himself to adopt a neutral expression. He turned around and spoke directly to her. "I need you to go get the camera out of the trunk of my car."

"Why?"

"It's very important. I need it now."

She started to protest, but instead turned and headed back down the hill, slipping, sliding, and cursing under her breath.

Jack watched her for a long time because he didn't want to look anywhere else. He squeezed his shaking hands into fists and closed his eyes.

Please, God, help me.

His plea was always the same, whether he was in Iraq or making a drug bust.

He opened his eyes and went to the top of the rocks. He tried to picture the car. It wasn't too smashed—surprising, considering what happened to it—so it couldn't have rolled more than a couple of times. Where the car had changed direction, the tires had dug deeply into the ground in one spot. It must have landed there. He imagined the car again, and the path it took.

He walked past the spot where it had flipped, moving more toward its original path. He walked a couple of feet and stopped.

No, God, please. Please…

Jack's eyes involuntarily slammed shut, and his head fell forward. It felt as though someone was crushing his chest. A low, guttural moan exploded from him.

Michelle lay on the grass, partly hidden by some shrubs. Her face was turned away from him, toward the lake. It might be someone just sleeping with her head resting on her arm, but he knew she was dead. He could smell it, that unmistakable, foul odor of death, and her skin was ashen.

He sank to his knees and his vision blurred. He wanted to scream, then immediately thought of Replacement.

He staggered back down the hill. She was back from the car and had almost reached him.

"There was no camera in the…" She trailed off when she saw his face. She shook her head. "No, no, no, *no!*"

Jack slowly nodded.

She swayed, her feet slipped, and she fell onto her hands and knees.

Jack rushed to her and also slipped. A sob wrenched his body as guilt and pain washed over him. He'd had two real friends, Chandler and Michelle, and they were both dead now.

Images assaulted his mind: Michelle riding her bike, Aunt Haddie holding Michelle's hand, Michelle at Christmas…

Replacement was wailing and clawing her way up the hill on her hands and knees. He couldn't let her see Michelle's body. Not like that. But when he grabbed her by the waist, she turned and exploded at him in a focused rage. Her face twisted in pain, and her hand shot out to smash him across his face. He held on through her punches, the kicking, and the clawing.

"I want to see her!"

Jack just gripped her tighter.

"You were supposed to come back. You were supposed to watch out for us. Why didn't you? What did we do?"

When she pulled him down, collapsing in the mud, he still didn't let go, soothing her with empty words until he felt her body slacken and the rough sobbing taper off into hiccups.

He sat up and dug into his pocket for his phone. "Officer Jack Stratton." It was Cindy, he thought, working dispatch, but he had a hard time making out what she was saying, and his own voice sounded far off to him. "I'm on Reservoir Road. Send a car… and… the coroner." He hung up even as Cindy was frantically calling out to him.

Replacement was in shock now, breathing raggedly and shaking uncontrollably. He sat with her in the mud and snow and put his arm around her. He closed his eyes, turning to that inner abyss where he felt broken and alone.

It was me. I pushed people away. I wouldn't leave… but I made them get out of my life.

All the people he loved, and who loved him most, had been buried as he shoveled himself into his hole of self-pity. His parents, brushed aside. Aunt Haddie, his other mother, abandoned when they could have helped each other with their grief.

Michelle, whom he'd truly loved, dead on this hillside for weeks, and he hadn't even known.

"Jack." Replacement's voice was quiet and soft. "Jack, I'm sorry," she whispered. Her muddy, tear-stained face was strained with fear.

"No, you got it right." His mouth twitched, and he stared down as he shook. "I'm a rotten bastard. I can't even remember your real name." He expected to see a look of disgust, but instead her eyes filled with concern.

"Please tell Aunt Haddie I'm sorry." Jack felt the cold metal press against his temple as he put his gun to his head to silence the voices, especially Michelle's, crying out to him…

"Jack!" Replacement held out a trembling hand. "Please give me the gun."

He heard her voice from a far distance, but she was right beside him, breathing, her panting breaths making puffs of steam in the cold. Twenty-five feet away, another young woman, who would never breathe or laugh or bike or go sledding again or have children…

Jack could hear sirens now. When they came, everything would be over anyway. You can't have a breakdown as a cop. He heard voices everywhere—Aunt Haddie, Chandler, his father—all telling him to put down the gun, this wasn't the answer, this would only hurt the people he loved…

His chest hurt. His heart hurt. He was so tired of pain, of failing, of not being in the right place at the right time, of not knowing where his place or time was. He was truly lost.

A voice was calling his name. It seemed to come nearer and nearer, until he realized Replacement was right beside him. When he turned to her, barely seeing her, not quite sure who she was, she spoke calmly and firmly. "If you do it, I will too." She looked straight into his eyes.

They stared at each other, the sirens growing louder. Jack couldn't seem to think. He lowered the gun. "I'm broken," he whispered.

"Me too, Jack." Her hand came around to lie softly on his. "Don't leave me all alone."

She slid forward and placed her shaking hand over his hand that held the gun. When he realized what he'd just done—and almost done—a fresh wave of shame washed over him and dragged him back toward the abyss.

Two fire trucks, an ambulance, and three cruisers now streamed down Reservoir Road toward them. Cindy had really pulled out all the stops. Again he heard a voice from far, far away, coming closer.

"... Jack. Please. I know we can help each other... Jack..."

When he let go, she pulled the gun away and hid it in her jacket. He let her take his arm and pull him toward the Impala and make him sit beside her on the hood to wait for the final scene to unfold on Reservoir Road—the questions.

Endless questions with no answers.

The fire trucks pulled up, and Jack and Replacement watched the firefighters and policemen pour out of their vehicles and rush toward them. Replacement took Jack's hand, and he pulled her close and gently rocked her as she cried.

18

SOMETIMES... WE ALL DO

The next few hours were a blur of cops and firefighters swarming the embankment, covering Michelle's body and bringing it down to the road, pained looks... Now Jack was sitting in a hospital, a thick blanket over his shoulders, medicine clouding his brain.

How he hated hospitals. They tried to mask the smell of death with cleaners, perfumes, and disinfectants, but he could still smell it. He wondered how many people had died in the bed he now occupied.

Normally he'd never have allowed them to take him to the hospital. They should have interviewed him at the ambulance and then allowed him to go home. But this time, the EMTs checked them both out, said something about shock, and insisted they go to the emergency room. Jack had been so defeated, he just climbed into the back of the ambulance.

He shrugged the blanket off, burning with shame. He could almost feel the broken pieces swirling around inside him, unmoored. The pain had cracked through the prison within him, hidden all these years, and the long-buried lava was spilling out, burning everything it touched.

He jumped off the bed and was reaching for his jacket when he heard someone clear his throat and the curtain was pulled back.

"Hey."

Jack froze at the sound of the deep voice. Sheriff Ethan Collins. He held his hat as he looked at Jack.

"My condolences for your loss, Jack."

Collins was a good man, known for always going by the book, as well as for his fairness, and Jack knew he meant every word.

"Sheriff Collins." Jack straightened up. "I want to apologize, sir."

"We'll cover that later." Collins stiffened. "You need to take some time, okay?"

Jack relaxed, and he swayed like a deflating balloon. Collins shifted uncomfortably. The older man cleared his throat. "I talked to the girl you were with. She seemed convinced it wasn't an accident. The missing person report says Michelle was getting ready to transfer schools."

The lanky Texan waited for a moment for Jack to offer a possible conclusion to the narrative, but Jack couldn't make his throat open.

"It looks like she went for a ride, and something happened."

Jack blurted out, "I know something is wrong. I don't have any hard proof, but I know she just didn't go for a ride and... die."

"Jack, right now you need to think about you."

"Do you believe me? It wasn't an accident, Sheriff."

"Are you looking for my answer as a sheriff, or as a man?"

Collins looked at him, and Jack couldn't read him. Maybe there was nothing to read. But something about a Texan accent added weight to the question.

Does it matter what Collins says? It wasn't an accident.

"Would you like us to notify the foster mother, Haddie Williams?"

Jack's legs wobbled, and he put his hand on the bed for support. He nodded.

"Take your time coming in." Collins, who had remained standing the whole time, never even looking at the visitor's chair, squared off for departure. Not quite making eye contact, he said firmly, "You need to talk. If you don't talk to me, then talk to somebody, you hear me?"

But Jack wanted more than anything *not* to talk, or remember… in fact, he really wished he didn't have to think at all, ever again. His jaw clenched.

"I will. Thanks."

* * *

Jack and Replacement got a ride back to Jack's apartment from Cindy Grant, the police dispatcher. She'd been so upset by Jack's call that she'd gone out to the reservoir herself. She was part of a cop family; the joke was, even her dog was a police dog. She was the one who made a cake for every birthday and reminded every cop of their spouse's, parents', and kids' birthdays, anniversaries, and anything else.

The whole ride back she kept up a soft monologue of light, banal stories, and Jack was grateful for the distraction. A few inches away, Replacement watched him, trying not to let him notice. She gripped his hand; her face was very white. He wanted to tell her he was okay, but he couldn't. He wasn't.

And they didn't make it to Jack's apartment without Mrs. Stevens popping her head into the hallway, but she took just one look at Jack's and Replacement's ashen faces—and retreated without a word.

Cindy hugged them and whispered something; Jack couldn't hear what she was saying, but it was comforting. When she shut the door, the silence fell like a blow.

Replacement leaned against the counter. *Was it just this morning she was laughing?* The girl in front of him was a shell of the girl from this morning.

He clenched and relaxed his fingers, forcing blood into his hands, walked over to her, and gently led her to the bedroom. He tenderly lowered her onto the bed. She lay still as he removed her shoes and pulled the comforter over her.

She moved over and softly pulled him down to sit next to her.

He closed his eyes and sighed. "Alice," he whispered. Her name was Alice. Jack finally remembered it. When she first came to Aunt Haddie's, every time anyone said her name she'd start to cry. No one could figure out why—but Chandler solved the riddle.

He found out that she was named after her mother, but after her parents were killed, she couldn't bear to hear her mom's name. Chandler knew what she was going through because he lost his parents too. He understood her, and she got him. Chandler gave her a nickname that made her feel like she belonged. Chandler told the young girl, "I'm going in the Army, and I need someone to fill my shoes. You'll be my replacement. Do you know what that means? Everyone will treat you how they treat me. No one will pick on you, because you're my replacement. All the kisses and hugs Aunt Haddie gives me, she'll give you. And all the cool stuff my sister Michelle does with me, she'll do with you, because you're my replacement." After that, she'd only respond to her new nickname.

When Jack opened his eyes, she was still searching his face. "I'm sorry," he said. "I couldn't remember your real name." *And you saved my life.*

"I know." She looked hurt.

"It's nothing to do with you. Something's wrong with me. I can't remember names."

She looked at him, but his eyes drifted off as he struggled to remember. He inhaled and held his breath. He exhaled little by little and then stared at the ceiling.

"I was seven, but I still couldn't remember it."

"What couldn't you remember?"

"It's stupid." He put his hands behind his head. "My name," he whispered. "I didn't know my own name. How's that for a joke?"

His eyes traced the cracks in the ceiling.

"She just called me brat or moron, usually with swear words attached to the front and back."

"Your mother?"

Jack cringed and then nodded.

"After she left me in the bus station, I went into the youth system. It was like a whirlwind. Everyone was asking me questions. They kept asking me my name, but it was just beyond my reach. It's such a simple question, but I couldn't grab the answer." He shook his head. "They brought in a woman with an armful of stuffed animals and she talked to me like I was a baby. 'This is Freddy Bunny and his friend Suzy Squirrel.'" He mimed how she danced the stuffed animals around. "'And they want to say hi, but they don't know what to call you.' She pretended to speak in a cartoon boy's voice. 'What should I call you, buddy?' I wanted to die. I felt so stupid. Who doesn't remember their own name?"

"You were seven."

"What's my excuse now? I didn't know your name… and I still don't know mine."

"I don't understand. Your name's not Jack?"

Jack shook his head. "No. That's not my birth name." He hesitated. "I just wanted to get out of there and get away from that lady with the puppets, but she kept asking. All I could think of was my mother getting on that bus, and the last thing she said to me: 'You don't know jack, kid.'"

Replacement inhaled and looked at him. A tear hung off her lashes and fell onto the bed.

"I named myself. I just told her my name was Jack. To me it meant 'nothing.' You know the expression? You don't know jack. It means you don't know anything. That's what I was… nothing."

"You're not nothing."

He looked over at her. "That's how I feel… sometimes."

Replacement slid up next to him. "Sometimes, we all do."

They held each other through the night, and in the morning, when he woke up and felt Alice's hair tickling his arm and her warmth against him, he hugged her tighter and felt… alive.

19

FIRST DIBS

Replacement and Jack had spent the morning in silence—not the awkward silence of strangers, not the bitter, ungiving silence that follows a fight—but the kind that blossoms when two people have arrived at the other side of a terrible choice and realized that they need the other to feel whole. In the stillness, they consoled each other and filled each other's voids with hope. Michelle's death crushed them, then fused them together.

As they entered Wells Meadow Nursing Home, the receptionist and an orderly recognized Alice and smiled sad, knowing smiles. The well-dressed receptionist came out from behind the desk and enfolded Replacement in a comforting embrace.

"There, there, precious." She explained to Jack over Replacement's head: "Sheriff Collins came out last night. He stayed with Haddie for quite some time."

On the way to Haddie's room, it was like a solemn funeral march, as staff and nurses came out into the hallway and hugged Replacement or reached out their hands. Some hugged Jack, too, or touched his shoulder.

The door of Aunt Haddie's room was open. She sat in the corner, in a large, comfortable chair, and didn't notice Jack right away. He was glad, because he had to hide his first reaction of shock at how vulnerable she looked, how much she'd aged.

Maybe it was the contrast with how he remembered her—a tornado. She usually worked two jobs, had a spotless house full of kids, fed them all, made every nickel squeak, and taught Sunday school.

And he didn't see her initial surprise at his haggard face and how he and Alice seemed almost to be holding each other up. He hugged the frail old woman extra close and for a long time, so she couldn't see his eyes, but finally she broke the clinch. Their eyes met, and she smiled the smile he remembered and saw so often in dreams.

After Replacement had gotten equal hugging time, Jack thought he should be the first to say something; he couldn't bear seeing Haddie's face full of concern.

"Aunt Haddie… I'm so, so sorry. Michelle was such a good person; she didn't deserve this… to die so young. I just… I wish I could have brought her home."

Haddie was an expert in grief, loss, and hard times: *You hold your joy close, and your sorrows closer—they're easier to manage that way.* Now she said, in her rich voice, "Jackie, Jackie. Michelle is home. At home with Chandler. I knew it the first week. I knew God had taken her home."

Jack had nothing to offer Haddie but more grief, and here she was, giving him comfort.

"She's at peace now. She's happy. You remember how happy she always was?"

Jack nodded.

"She's happy now." She squeezed Jack's hand and tried to smile again, but her chin trembled.

Jack inhaled sharply and held her hands in his. She was still the same wonderful woman. He whispered, "I'm sorry I haven't come back."

"So am I, Jackie. You're one of my babies, too. And remember, no matter where you are, I love you, and I know you love me. Do you think I forgot that? I didn't. Neither did Michelle." She rubbed his hands.

The three of them hugged and talked, mending the gap of time as if they'd never been apart. If Haddie had cognitive impairment, it wasn't apparent to Jack, and hearing Haddie recall their shared memories was truly healing for all of them. Her strength of character—though her voice was weak and tremulous—finally pulled Jack to safe ground, and he felt centered and calm in this strange new setting, warmed by Haddie's circle of love.

After an hour, Aunt Haddie looked at Replacement and asked if she could have a moment alone with Jack. After Replacement had left to get some sodas from the vending machine, it turned out she was what Aunt Haddie needed to talk to him about.

"Alice took it very hard, Jackie. She loved Chandler like an older brother. I know she can be a handful." She squeezed his hand. "Remember, some people had it even harder than you. I appreciate you watching out for her."

What did she go through?

"She's a little spitfire, but deep down she's been wounded, too," Aunt Haddie said.

Jack just nodded as the little spitfire in question let herself back in the room and solemnly handed them their sodas.

"I understand how you're hurting," Haddie went on, including both of them now in her hard-earned wisdom. "When I lost my Alton, all I wanted to do was keep running. I know why you stayed away, I really do. But you have to get over that now.

"Michelle forgives you, and Chandler forgave you a long time ago. I'll forgive you, too, but let me be clear: I expect you to visit from now on." Her eyes were speaking their own language to him, as clear as her words.

"I need to know something. You'll tell me straight away, right?" She peered into his eyes.

"Yes, ma'am."

"What do you think happened to Michelle?"

Jack knew only one way to be with Haddie—upfront and honest—which was why he'd been avoiding her all this time.

"I think... I think someone killed her."

Her lower lip trembled. "Jackie—"

"I'll get the people who did this."

She was crying now. "I want you to stay safe. God will get the people who did this. He'll punish them. But I can't lose you, too."

God will punish them. I just want first dibs.

20

GOOD AND BAD

The following day, Jack started the Impala and pulled out. The police station was fifteen minutes away, so he had some good rehearsal time.

Sheriff Collins, I originally was not aware this had been officially—No, don't lie. Collins is so straight-arrow, he won't listen to any excuses for breaking protocol. Fall on your sword and tell it like it is.

Sheriff Collins, I didn't follow procedure... Ben Nichols? Do I tell him about that? The stupid Mohawk kid? I didn't tag the phone...

Every angle that he tried to think of to minimize damage ended the same way—with a very ticked-off Sheriff Collins. The ride went by way too fast, but when he got to the station, he marched straight in, not hesitating.

Cindy came out from behind the desk, arms open wide, and Jack walked in gladly.

"Just remember to apologize and let him do most of the talking," she whispered in his ear.

She gave him a reassuring pat on the back with a little push toward Sheriff Collins's office.

The police station was mostly two floors of open space with unassigned desks. The only people who had official offices were the sheriff and undersheriff. The layout furthered Collins's philosophy of chain of command: he was chief; everyone else was an Indian.

His door was open, and Collins sat behind an ultramodern desk with minimal furnishings. Two large computer monitors were reflected in his glasses. He swiveled in his chair and stood as Jack entered the room. His hand shot out. "Glad to see you again, Jack. My condolences."

They shook hands, and the sheriff sat, while Jack remained standing. With Jack's Army background, it was routine for him, but some of the other officers complained about Collins's habit of making you stand while he asked you questions.

"You could have taken some more time, but I'm glad you're here." Collins didn't smile, but he wasn't scowling either.

"Thank you, sir, but I need to get some things settled now. First, let me offer my apologies for not notifying you directly."

"And you also didn't notify me *indirectly*, Jack." Collins's eyebrow rose and his jaw slightly clenched. "Save the apologies and just tell me what happened."

By the book. Wish I'd thought up something about the phone.

"Last Thursday night, my friend's sister came to my apartment. She informed me that my foster sister, Michelle Carter, was missing. Her foster mother had filed a missing person report in Fairfield earlier."

Sheriff Collins nodded.

"Michelle's brother and I grew up together, served in Iraq… It sounded out of character for her to just up and go. I thought I should look into it. We took a ride over to the university and spoke with Michelle's roommate and the campus police."

Jack paused. Silence seemed to be permission to continue. "The campus police said Michelle had transferred, but we…" He cleared his throat. "I decided to look for the car Michelle had been driving, and I located it at Sullivan's."

Sheriff Collins's eyes narrowed and deep lines formed on his tanned face.

He looks a little like Clint Eastwood when he's angry.

Jack checked his notes and saw Collins's approving look, then went on and told him about speaking with Ben Nichols and with Rick Matthews, saying he had a description of the Mohawk helmet and followed him to the high school.

Sort of true. He doesn't need to know I went there to look specifically for the kid.

So far, so good; no objections from Collins. "The teen, Rick Matthews, said he started the car. He also informed me he found this phone." Jack didn't look at Collins as he placed the evidence bag on the desk.

"Immediately after, I headed out to Reservoir Road, followed the debris trail, and located… the victim's body." His eyes burned as he spoke the last few words and he paused while he waited for the sheriff's reaction.

"Jack…" Collins fiddled with a pen on his desk. "I want to apologize for Murphy. He's the one who should be apologizing anyway. You shouldn't have had to run this down."

Like Jack, the sheriff's blood boiled whenever he had to deal with Murphy's colossal ineptitude—which was daily. With noticeable effort, Collins released his tight grip on his pen, straightened his notepad, and laid the pen next to it.

Jack nodded and thanked him.

"You'll need to write it all up in a report. I'd appreciate it if you got to it directly. After that, take a few more days. When is the funeral?"

"Saturday."

Collins gave a brief nod. "We'll talk again after that."

"Sheriff?" Jack hated to wait, especially for a reprimand. "I'm sorry, but can you let me know…?"

"Let you know?" Collins had started to rise but sat back down. His face was the color of old bricks. "The same way you should have let me know but didn't?" Sheriff Collins sighed. "As of now, you're going to help the traffic detail for the next month."

Not too bad. Night shift.

"On days when there's no traffic detail, Cindy needs assistance getting caught up on reports."

Jack would have rather cleaned the bathrooms. He hated paperwork.

"We'll need to review your training schedule at a later date to see if that busy roster impacted your judgment."

This was both good and bad. Collins had said "review," so he hadn't canceled anything, but Jack was on notice. If he took another wrong step, Collins would take away the special training, and if that happened, Collins might as well just say, "You're fired," because it would have had the same effect for Jack.

"Let me make this crystal-clear, Jack, this is Joe Davenport's case now. Additionally, Michelle is your foster sister; that's a conflict of interest. I've talked to Joe about reviewing the case, and I'll personally examine it. Now, you have my utmost sympathies, but if you even think of going around me and looking into this, I'll have your hide. That is all." Collins turned back to his computer.

As Jack turned away, he let the mask fall from his face. He shut the door very carefully because he wanted to slam it—badly.

Get the report done and then get out. Now it was Jack's blood boiling. He stormed by Cindy, who held out a stack of papers to him. He grabbed them like a relay runner, never breaking stride, headed to a desk in the back, and made very sure to do everything deliberately and quietly—pulling out the chair, booting up the computer, arranging the reports—he had to watch every step now.

Murphy's a moron. If he had done the bare minimum, they...

Jack flopped into the chair and let his head fall into his hands. After a minute, he sat up and looked at the stack of papers. He couldn't help but smile a little. Cindy had filled out the sections she could. He flipped open a few of the pages.

I could be out of here in a couple of hours.

Jack had a little secret he carried around with him all the time now—actually, a pretty big secret—and he pulled it out whenever he needed a reminder: He actually wanted to live.

Everything else was the price you pay to stay alive.

21

SO MUCH FOR GREEN

Jack rolled over and looked at the clock. One thirty. He was glad, but also ticked off. On the one hand, he couldn't sleep, but on the other hand, he had to avoid getting up till the bar around the corner closed. On the one hand, he wanted a drink, but on the other hand, he really wanted nine or ten.

Drown it. Head off the rails one night and into oblivion.

He got up and headed into the kitchen for some water, and the angel on his other shoulder started up.

Don't drink. The service is tomorrow. Anyway, it's too late. The bar'll be closed by the time you get there.

He'd known even before he enlisted in the Army that he could be a blackout drinker. His drinking had never bothered him when he was younger, but there's a completely different spin on things when you wake up clueless, surrounded by high-caliber weapons.

That burn he couldn't extinguish, that lava flow of pain, seemed to be always on tap now. He tried to bury it, but it seared its way back into the open. He didn't forget his new secret—he was still glad to be alive—it just didn't hurt as much when you used some painkillers.

He turned off the water and heard the computer chair squeak.

"Nice butt," Replacement said.

Jack grabbed for the dishtowel and dashed back into the bedroom. Replacement burst out laughing.

"You should warn me," he called out as he pulled on a pair of sweatpants.

"Warn you?" She giggled. "How? Danger, Jack! You're entering the kitchen, cover your butt?"

"I didn't know you were up."

"Do you normally go around naked?" She wiggled her eyebrows.

"You know…" he stammered. "I just forgot you were here."

He was beet-red, and Replacement couldn't decide whether he was embarrassed or truly upset. "I'm sorry."

"Don't—it's my fault. This will take some getting used to." Replacement turned back to the computer. "What're you working on?"

"Michelle had a fitness app on her phone. It's called Get in Shape Girl." Her eyes stayed on the screen. She was wearing her old Fairfield High jersey and sat with her legs tucked underneath her.

"And?" Jack stood behind her.

"Part of the app monitors all your exercise. There's a walking program that shows everywhere she'd been."

"Great job." Jack grabbed the back of her chair and leaned over her shoulder so he could see the screen. "Does it give dates and times? Everywhere she's been?"

"It has everything. I just got into her phone—"

"Her phone? But I gave it to Collins."

"Umm…" Replacement hunched up her shoulders and looked at Jack with emerald eyes that hinted at a secret.

"No… You couldn't have taken it. Did you switch it? How—?" Jack squeezed the glass.

Replacement looked nervously at his tightening fingers. "I made a backup, that's all."

"You backed up her phone *before* I gave it to Collins?" His grip relaxed a bit.

"It's a smartphone; it was easy. I did it after we came home from the hospital. I didn't think it was wrong."

"Don't think. Ask. It's *my job*." Jack winced after he shouted the last two words. She looked hurt, and he felt sorry.

Don't feel bad, you idiot. If Collins knew we went into the phone, he'd have your head on his wall.

"How did you get in? Aren't they password protected?"

Replacement shrugged. "Michelle always used the same password."

Impressed in spite of himself, Jack looked back at the screen. It looked like a spreadsheet of times and dates, and his thoughts shifted to the hunt for answers. "Can you start backward? What were her last whereabouts?"

Replacement turned and began to type. "The phone was at Reservoir Road in the same place for twelve hours. December twenty-first."

"So Michelle got there on the twenty-first? What time?"

"Twelve thirty a.m."

She wouldn't just go for a drive out there after midnight.

"What happened to the phone after twelve hours?"

"The phone must have died…"

Jack put a hand on her shoulder to keep her on track. "Where was she before? How long—?"

"Hold on, I don't know the program that well." Replacement's fingers flew over the keyboard. "She was someplace for… almost four hours."

"Where?" The data on the screen didn't make sense to him.

"I have to map the coordinates." She pressed more keys, and a mapping program appeared. "Here. General Alexander Davidson Circle. It's the neuropsychology center, where she works." She zoomed in. "Why was she there from eight thirty until after midnight?"

Jack looked at the clock and raised an eyebrow. "Wanna go check it out? I can't sleep anyway." She was already getting her coat.

* * *

They tiptoed out of the apartment like little kids, careful not to wake Mrs. Stevens. The ride to the neuropsychology center would take about twenty minutes because of the winding roads. It was below freezing, so Replacement ditched the seat belt, along with any notion of personal space, and shivered next to him as the car tried to warm up during the drive.

Replacement smiled. "Thanks for everything." She curled up closer to him.

Thanks for everything? Her sister's dead. I gave her a couch instead of a closet. 'Everything' isn't much.

They pulled into a small, empty parking lot near the nature center at the top of the hill and crunched their way over frost to the front door. Apart from a faint hallway light and the exit lights, the building looked thoroughly closed.

The hours posted on a sign were weekdays, nine to seven. *Why was she out here so late?* Jack walked to the left to go around the building but stopped. The ground sloped off and revealed another level below, with the same large windows as the rest of the building. Another look to the right showed there was no easy way to walk around that way.

"Wish I could get a look around back." He turned to Replacement. Did her special research skills extend to getting into closed buildings?

Her arms were wrapped tightly around her chest, and her teeth chattered as she nodded. He saw that her jacket was more suited to fall than winter.

"Come on." Jack hurried her back to the Impala and turned the heat on. They held their hands in front of the vents.

"How accurate is that phone?" Jack asked.

"You mean for distance?" Replacement slid up against him.

"Can it tell where she was in the building?" Jack whipped his coat off, and before she could protest, wrapped it over her legs.

She looked at Jack as if he'd just done something monumental. "The app gives a rough distance, like she was around here." She made large circles with her hands.

"Did you find anything else on the phone yet?"

"I went through her emails and texts. A bunch of school stuff. She didn't have many friends. She focused on school. I'll go back and check. There are pictures, but I haven't…" Her shoulders squeezed together and she started to tremble.

Jack put his arm around her shoulders. She turned her face into his chest and cried softly.

"I'm sorry. I'm sorry I didn't come back."

"You should be." The words were gentler than Jack expected. "But you're here now. And we're going to find who did this."

The certainty in her words calmed Jack, and he put the car in gear. "We will."

As they drove away, the security camera on the outside of the building followed their car with its glowing red eye.

22

HOMECOMING

Jack shifted in his seat in the front row next to Replacement, who was next to Aunt Haddie. The lighting was subdued and the scent of flowers hung in the air. Rows of chairs in neat lines sat on thick carpet.

People filled the place. He couldn't believe how many were there. *How many really knew her?* He'd been to too many funerals of young people, where every kid that knew them turns out—their first taste of death. *Someone who shouldn't have died; it makes them think, It could have been me. But how many people here were really her friend?*

Michelle had always been quiet, and careful when she chose her friends. She wasn't arrogant at all, she just had high standards. Friends had to be loyal, honest, and truthful. Aunt Haddie used to say that if you made it out of this life with one good friend, you were blessed. Michelle was blessed.

Jack shifted. He forced a smile for Replacement, but she never looked up. He closed his eyes and let his head fall forward.

The minister had already begun the service. He was a large man with a deep voice. They sang "Amazing Grace," Michelle's favorite, with many voices cracking and some—Haddie and Replacement—unable to sing at all through their crying.

After "When the Roll Is Called Up Yonder," a girl of around sixteen went up to the podium. Her curly dark-brown hair came down to her shoulders. She was dressed in a simple gray dress, and her eyes flitted around the room. She unfolded a page from a notebook.

"My name is Selena. Michelle was my mentor and my friend," she began. "I met her through the sisters'… program where she… volunteered. She always tell… told me, that I…" It was obviously hard for her to read. She looked up, paused, and refolded the paper.

"I'm going to start again." She tried to stand tall. "Michelle believed in me. She taught me to believe in myself. I loved her very much. I was shy, like her, but she showed me an example of what I could be. My life is much better because of her."

The girl took her seat. After her, four more girls from all different backgrounds came up in turn, and each spoke about Michelle—about a Michelle that Jack didn't know. The girl who loved to learn and taught herself about computers. Not so much shy, as Selena had said, but quiet about her accomplishments and sure about her purpose. A young woman filled with hope, who passed that hope along to others, who helped her neighbors and underprivileged kids.

A tall man, over six feet, with broad shoulders and finely groomed silver hair, came forward to speak, leaning slightly on a cane.

"Michelle was one of my brightest students," he began. He had a slight European accent, maybe German, and spoke carefully. "As evidenced by the words of the people here who knew her best, Michelle was an example for us all. She worked to create change. She was always willing to help her fellow students and workers. Her enthusiasm and spirit will be missed, but it won't be forgotten. Her legacy will live on in her work and achievements."

It was Aunt Haddie's turn to speak next. The funeral director and Replacement helped her up to the podium. She could barely see over it. She looked so old. She gripped the podium for support, and gazed down for a long time.

"Michelle…" Her voice broke. Replacement squeezed Jack's hand.

"Michelle was one of my dear, dear babies. She was on loan from the Lord. Such a precious girl. God abundantly blessed me by bringing her into my life. Michelle is home with Jesus now."

Aunt Haddie paused and wiped her eyes. "Michelle always looked at the positives. She was like a little ray of sunshine all bottled up. We didn't have much, but Michelle was always looking at what we did have."

Jack could only see the people in the front row, but there were quite a few shoulders shaking from sobs and a lot of tissues being used.

"They asked me to talk about some of my favorite memories of Michelle, but how can I pick? I prayed about it. I tried to think, and then I remembered Michelle's bike."

That bike. He and Chandler found it at the dump. A boy's bike with a flat tire.

"Michelle's birthday was coming up, eight years old, and that year we had very little. I knew Michelle wanted a bike, like the big boys had. That's all she talked about."

Aunt Haddie was crying again but kept her voice strong for her story. "On the morning of her birthday, after breakfast, Chandler and Jackie told Michelle to come outside with them. Their hands, their overalls, everything was covered in pink paint, and they were smiling from ear to ear. That must be where that expression came from."

A few sniffly laughs broke out and Haddie took a deep breath.

"Well, we hiked down those old stairs, and there was Michelle's present…"

She ran out of air and had to take a big, ragged gasp.

"Jackie and Chandler had found an old boy's bike and fixed it all up. They painted it bright pink and put purple streamers on it. You'd think they both would pop the buttons off their shirts, they were so proud."

Jack looked down at his hands, almost expecting to see pink paint. He and Chandler stayed up all night, fixing the flat tire, straightening the rims, painting it, figuring out where to get the tassels—a lucky stroke, and by far the most expensive part of the transformation, when Chandler found a little girl who sold them her flashy handle grips for five bucks. Michelle teased them for two days because of the pink paint on their hands.

"Oh, you can imagine how Michelle cried and danced and cried some more. The boys taught her how to ride, and she took to it like a fish to water. She rode that bike everywhere. I can still see her smiling face riding out in the driveway. Her little wave…"

Aunt Haddie stopped, and Replacement's hand went a little limp. Aunt Haddie looked around. "I don't know what happened to the bike… she lost it… Michelle…"

She stopped again.

The thought that he might not have been here to help Haddie, to keep the tenuous circle of life connected between survivors brought shame back to Jack, but he forced himself to power through it. He exchanged a glance with Replacement and without a word went up to the podium and helped Aunt Haddie back to her seat.

The stress of the situation had clearly gotten to her. She turned to look at Jack, and he held her gaze. He could see the effects of age and unbearable grief and toil, and perhaps confusion. She looked at him, but she didn't seem to really see him.

There was a small disruption to Jack's right as a man tried to move around people to get to the podium.

"Hello." He coughed, then looked down and brushed back his dark hair with one hand. "My name is Robert, and I knew Michelle—and Chandler—since we were kids." The young man was in his twenties, wearing a nice suit. "It was hard hearing about Michelle's bike." He cleared his throat. "I know what happened to it." He looked straight at Aunt Haddie. "I stole it."

The quiet room grew completely still. Jack could hear his heart beat.

"I was a kid, and the bike was outside the library, and I took it. I brought it home and painted it blue." He paused to blow his nose. "I painted it and pulled off the tassels, but Michelle knew it was hers. She saw me riding it and she followed me home and came right to my front door."

He looked around the room, defiantly anxious to tell this story. Jack had thought at first that the guy looked a little disheveled and sketchy, but it was just rumpled hair and red eyes from crying.

"She asked me why I stole it. I said, 'What does that matter?' But she really wanted to know *why*. She said, 'You shouldn't just let evil things go.'"

He shook his head. "That freaked me out. I was like, 'I'm not evil,' but she said, 'Well, you're a thief.'"

Tears rolled down his cheeks. "She asked me why again. I told her mine broke. The frame cracked. I couldn't fix it, and it was just me and my mom. I begged her not to tell my mom or Chandler. I knew she was Chandler's sister, and he'd stomp me. I told her she could have it back.

"So she looked at me, and I'll never forget her face. She was smiling, and she said, 'You can keep it.' I couldn't believe it." He shook his head as if he still couldn't believe it. The room rustled and little murmurs and gasps rose like birdsong.

"I followed her halfway home, trying to get her to take the bike back, but she wouldn't. She told me I should have it cuz I didn't have one. She said God gave her a mom and two brothers and a bike and wanted her to share. We were just kids, but I never forgot that. We were always friends after that... I mean, I hope I was a good friend to her."

Someone handed him a tissue. He blew his nose, turned, and walked back into the crowd.

Two brothers. I love you too, Michelle.

Jack could almost see Michelle riding down the driveway, after she got good at riding, waving to him and Chandler, laughing on her way to an innocent little-girl adventure... Aunt Haddie, composed for the moment, put her hand on his thigh for a second to stop its violent shaking.

The minister rose, began to walk to the podium, then turned and came to Aunt Haddie. The large black man got down on one knee, covered her gnarled hands in his, and bowed his head.

"Lord, we thank you for the time you've given all of us to know Michelle. We thank you for her wonderful heart and the example she has been. Please, Father, be with us who are left here. Watch over us, guide us, and lead us to the rest that Your Son prepared for those whom He has called. We pray this in the name of Jesus. Amen." Aunt Haddie quickly repeated "Amen," and then some others whispered, "Amen." The ceremony was over.

Jack kept his eyes closed while people got up and made their way out or gathered to talk to friends. In the front row, the three of them just sat for a while, breathing, thinking, silently screaming.

Someone said his name and Jack reluctantly opened his eyes and turned toward the voice. It was Michelle's teacher, the dignified man with a cane and a European accent.

"Please accept my condolences for your loss."

The man had a firm handshake and a confident air.

"Thank you. You're one of Michelle's teachers at the university?"

"Dr. Alexander Hahn. Psychology. In fact, she worked directly under me. Michelle's contributions will be very much missed by the college and myself personally."

"Contributions?"

"Michelle was instrumental in bringing our computer technology into the twenty-first century. I meant that. Her legacy will live on."

"Thank you, Doctor." Jack shook the outstretched hand again.

"If you have the time, stop by the center and I will give you a tour. You would be very proud of her work."

"Thank you, I will. You can count on it."

23

THE VOID BECKONS

Jack opened one eye but then closed it again.

The knocking continued. Replacement's tuneless singing wafted from the shower.

"Hold on!" he called, rolling himself out of bed. "One sec!" He hopped into a pair of sweatpants and grabbed a clean T-shirt.

When Jack yanked open the door, he was surprised to see the potbelly and wrinkled, resigned face of Joe Davenport, the inches-away-from-retirement detective assigned to Michelle's case.

"Hey, Joe. Come on in. What brings you around?"

Joe lifted off the tan hat he always wore, a cross between an old fedora and a fishing cap. "My condolences, Jack." He shook Jack's hand but only glanced at Jack's face.

Spill it, Joe.

The detective followed Jack into the living room. "I got some good news about the phone. The tech guys were able to get into it with one of the codes you gave us."

Jack had given Joe a list of possible pins they should try. Of course, Jack knew which one would work, because Replacement had told him Michelle's pin, but he put it second on the list to make it look good.

"They got in? Great. Have they found anything?"

"They said they'll go over it with a fine-tooth comb."

Joe had a habit of nodding his head a lot. *Nervous tic.*

He handed Jack a manila envelope. "Toxicology."

Jack opened the envelope and read, "Presence of benzaldehyde, nitroethane, benzyl-methylnaphthalene." *Glass meth.*

"I'm sorry, Jack," Joe mumbled. "There's been a huge increase in the county."

Jack nodded, thinking, *No way. Not Michelle.*

Joe said, "Ninety percent pure. They've had an increase in ODs, too."

"Not meth. That's impossible. Michelle would never—"

"Not a lot, but... Even a little of that stuff can make you crazy. You can get real disoriented, and if she was driving... I've seen—"

"No way. Michelle would never do that crap."

"Jack... even good kids go off the rails sometimes. I wouldn't say anything if it wasn't my place."

Jack's head snapped up. He wanted to shout, *It's not your place!* But it was. Joe—for better or worse—was the lead detective. *He has to point these things out. But he's wrong.*

"You've seen it firsthand, Jack. I was just reading about two kids in Wisconsin who took crystal one time and ran out in the middle of a snowstorm, thinking mobs of people were trying to kill them. They froze to death."

They both looked down at the floor.

"I'm sorry, Jack. Everything points to an accident. I'll keep it open, of course."

Jack searched his face, and he knew Joe thought he was doing the right thing.

"Thanks for coming by, Joe." He held out his hand.

Joe shook it and then turned to go. But he paused at the door. "I just... I just want you to know that I did go back over everything, and I think... I think it is what it is."

Jack nodded.

The door clicked shut, and Jack walked over and leaned on the counter. A wave of doubt crashed over him and swept his anger away.

Meth?

He went to get a glass of water but stopped to listen. The shower wasn't running anymore.

He slowly opened the door to the bedroom. Replacement sat on the edge of the bed with her head in her hands, softly crying. He sat down next to her and she leaned against him.

"How much did you hear? I don't think—" he began, but she pressed her hand against his lips.

"No, Jack. Shh, I'm just gonna think for a minute. Go take your shower." She wiped her eyes and walked over to the door.

Jack sat on the bed. "We'll talk when I get out, okay?"

Replacement just nodded as she left.

Jack missed Chandler all the time, of course, but right now he really missed him. He had lots of acquaintances, plenty of colleagues—some whom he respected—but no real friends. The only people who wanted to get close were women, and he couldn't open up to them.

He stayed in the shower for a long time. He wanted to think, but his thoughts flew all over like scared sparrows. He felt old and tired. Alone and... alone.

When the hot water finally gave out, the blast of icy water revived him a little. He wasn't alone, and Replacement was a great researcher. Joe's call had really been just a courtesy call; Jack wasn't on the case and he didn't have a clue what to do next, but he had to do something.

You don't just let evil go. He didn't have to be perfect. He just had to keep from blowing his brains out.

He dressed and came out of the bedroom, still drying his hair. Replacement was standing at the front door with her bags packed.

"Jack, I have to go." She didn't look at him.

"Hold on. Why?" Jack's emotions shifted right to hurt, like the hot water suddenly turned off.

"It is what it is, Jack." Her eyes glistened.

"Don't listen to Joe. I'm not. I was about to—"

"It's over, Jack. You heard him. Michelle did meth and drove off the road and killed herself."

"That's stupid!" he yelled. "You knew her!" He wasn't sure where the anger was coming from.

"I *didn't* know her. I was just chasing after her. I didn't know her."

"That's not true." Jack took a step toward her.

Replacement's green eyes were hard. "Did *you* know her?"

"Yes," he said, desperate to contradict her.

"Really?" Her voice changed; grew colder. "What was her favorite book? Color? When did she get her first kiss? Who were her friends?"

Jack burned, not with anger but shame, because he didn't know these things; because Replacement thought of him this way.

"Look, I'm so sorry. I know—" He took another step forward, and she held up a hand.

"What do you know? You don't know crap. You think she wouldn't leave Aunt Haddie? Why? *You* did. Michelle is like you in that. She got her chance to go, and she took it. That's what I'm doing, too."

"Don't—" He wasn't sure how to finish, and she pounced on it.

"Don't what?" Her mouth was twisted. "Don't tell you the truth?" She glared; the tears had vanished, along with any trace of warmth.

Jack wanted to become as detached as she was. He could let her leave, and go back to the way things were. He could get a bottle and leap headfirst into the void. He closed his eyes. His mouth was dry, his throat was tight. They were on the edge of a cliff, and Replacement was about to jump off. Somehow she'd talked him down before; he had to pull her back now.

"Say what you want to me. You're right. I didn't know her. You did. But you need to know this. You walk out that door, and you'll bury Michelle in your head. You'll bury her in your heart. You'll lose all the times you had with her because you can't look at them, because you won't be able to look at yourself. I know that. That's… that's what I did with Chandler."

Replacement's shoulders trembled, and her hands shook as she covered her face. Jack didn't hesitate. He stepped over to her and pulled her close, wrapping his arms around her protectively. She pushed her face against his chest and sobbed.

After a few minutes, Jack led her to the bed and felt her legs wobble. She curled into a ball. He reached around her, turned off the light, and rubbed her shoulders until she cried herself to sleep.

Jack began a new list: Talk to Mark Reynolds, an undercover cop, who could help him find the meth dealers. Then go back out to the psychology center…

Pain immobilizes people; locks them in place so they spend days, years, and lifetimes held captive.

Jack knew pain. He and pain were old friends. And he knew from long experience, there's only one way to deal with pain: Hunt it down and kill it.

24

ALUMINUM FOIL AND OTHER KITCHEN STUFF

Jack was dressed and in the kitchen by 8:30. He wanted to get going, but he waited for Replacement to get up for the day.

He looked down at the two plates of food he'd laid out on the counter. Yesterday, to his surprise, he'd found that Mrs. Stevens had left four bags of food outside his door. He was no cook, but he was pretty proud of his scrambled eggs and toast—courtesy of Aunt Haddie.

He opened and closed cabinets, but he couldn't find what he was looking for. He checked beside the refrigerator and on top of it. Nothing. He pulled open the drawer under the stove and found a baking sheet. Though he couldn't remember ever using it, the cookie sheet was rusted in places, and covered with black, charred splotches. He had an idea.

He grabbed a roll of aluminum foil and covered the whole sheet. Then he found two red napkins that looked like they came from a Chinese restaurant, which they probably did, and carefully laid them over the tray, put Replacement's plate on it, and arranged the fork and knife.

He poured a glass of orange juice, added it to the tray, and stood back to survey his handiwork.

Hopefully it's the thought that counts.

He picked up the tray and walked into the bedroom. Only a small mound indicated there might be a person underneath the flowery white-and-purple comforter.

"Good morning," Jack said.

After a couple of seconds, Replacement pulled back a corner of the comforter, and one green eye peeked out. She sat bolt upright and burst out crying.

Mystified, Jack set the tray on the bureau and sat down on the bed.

Replacement grabbed him and pulled herself close, pressed her face into his neck, and sniffled and blubbered all over him as she attempted to speak. Jack could only make out every couple of words. Her nose was so stuffed up, she couldn't breathe. He jumped up, grabbed a roll of toilet paper from the bathroom, and brought it back.

"Thank you," she said, more clearly now. "I'm so sorry. I…"

Jack held out the breakfast tray, eager to get her to stop crying. "It will get cold."

Replacement took the tray and closed her eyes. After a few moments, she picked up the fork and started to eat.

Jack watched her as if she were an IED that could go off at any second. After she'd taken several bites, Jack relaxed and leaned against the bureau.

"Wait." Replacement's voice broke. "What about you?"

"What about me?"

"Aren't you going to eat?" Replacement's lip trembled, and she set her fork down.

"I made one for me too. I'll go get it." He returned a few seconds later with his own plate. Satisfied, Replacement nodded and started to eat again.

After a few mouthfuls, she lifted her head and gave a sad smile, swallowing a sob. "Thank you."

"It's nothing." *Just don't cry again!* "I was thinking you could sleep in this morning. So after you've eaten, you can just watch TV or sleep. I'm going to run a couple of errands."

"Where are you going?"

"We need some stuff. Aluminum foil, kitchen stuff."

"Okay."

They ate in silence, and Jack had to force himself to slow down so he would finish at the same time she did.

"All right." He put his plate on hers, took the tray, and set it down. "Back to bed with you."

Replacement scooted back under the covers and Jack pulled the comforter up.

"Good?" he said awkwardly.

She sat partway up and caught him before he could avoid the little kiss she planted on his cheek. "Good." Then she smiled and rolled over.

Jack hurried out of the room. He'd already put his holster in the hallway near the door. Some other time maybe he could decipher the strange bundle of contradictions known as Replacement—or Alice. Right now, he didn't want her to know where he was going or why.

* * *

Jack couldn't have asked for a better excuse to get into the psychology center, but he still had to be careful, invite or not. If he asked too many questions, someone could call the sheriff, and calls from the university always went to critical mass on Collins's radar. WRE paid the most taxes, and any issue there brought the most heat.

He turned off White Spruce Road and onto General Alexander Davidson Circle. The Impala raced up the road and hugged the turns. Speed felt good. Too good. He was always tempted to go all out. Faster. Harder. Sometimes it got him in trouble, and he didn't want to get in trouble today.

He coasted into the small parking lot, got out, stretched, and scanned the dozen or so cars in the parking lot. Nothing out of the ordinary except the silver Audi parked at a slight angle, taking up two spaces.

Jack was grateful for the brief walk to the front of the building that gave him a chance to burn off some of his nervous energy. He felt unpleasantly sweaty, and the winter blast was refreshing. When he opened the glass front door, a young, pretty girl with short black hair looked up from her seat behind a big desk and greeted him brightly. *Way too perky.*

He gave his name and asked to see Dr. Hahn, adding that he didn't have an appointment but had been personally invited for a tour by Dr. Hahn. The perky receptionist made a call, told Jack Dr. Hahn would be out in a minute, and showed him to the waiting area.

Three couches were arranged in a horseshoe pattern in front of a large lecture hall. Students sat on all three, chatting and tapping on their phones. Jack decided to stand, but when Dr. Hahn did not in fact appear within a couple of minutes, he walked over to the glass wall that looked into the lecture hall. It was smaller than Jack expected. It would hold about fifty students, and about thirty or so were now listening to... he searched for the name of the professor he met when he visited before. Dr. Franklin. Jack hadn't realized psychology could be so exciting, but the guy was pounding on the lectern, then spreading his arms theatrically, whipping his glasses on and off.

Remind me not to grow a ponytail when I'm his age. Jack moved down to stand in the open doorway so he could hear the lecture.

"Astrocytes, cluster, dopamine... the pleasure pathway." Franklin smiled at a young girl in the front row. "Your assignment will be a pro and con, not a right or wrong. Short. Four pages."

A student in the back raised his hand. "We can pick anything on the list?"

Franklin looked at the ceiling and sighed mockingly. "That's why I'm providing the list." A girl in the front giggled. "I want you to pick a subject and give a view on that subject and then select an opposing or differing view. For example, if you selected dopamine, you could write about its function in the pleasure pathway versus the view of its role with motivational or motor function. Or, if you choose nucleus accumbens, you could say..." He pointed to a young man in the front row who shifted in his seat.

"Um... right lobe?" he stuttered.

"Right lobe. And?" Franklin pressed.

The student cleared his throat and settled back in his seat. He cast a glance at the girl seated next to him, and she nodded encouragingly.

The young man's Adam's apple looked sharp enough to cut through the skin as it traveled up and down and settled back in the middle. "The connection between the nucleus accumbens and the right lobe and the theory that there's a connection between the two as far as spirituality..."

He hesitated as Franklin walked around the podium and approached him. "Some theorize, and I concur, that, according to—" He stopped speaking as Franklin came to a stop directly in front of his desk.

"You concur? Mr...?"

"Ross."

"Mr. Ross concurs." Franklin held his hands out to the class, and nervous laughter flitted around the room. "And may I assume that you're taking The Effects of Trauma on the Brain this semester?"

Ross gulped and nodded.

Franklin exhaled and walked the length of the room. "For those not privileged to be taking Dr. Hahn's class, please enlighten us with a brief synopsis."

The girl who sat next to Ross reached out and squeezed his arm.

He puffed out his chest, and addressed the class. "We've been discussing how the nucleus accumbens produces pleasure and how it works in the reward pathway. In this process, the neurotransmitter dopamine is released, and I think there may be a link between that and the right frontal lobe—"

"Eureka!" Franklin shouted so loudly that everybody jumped in their seats and turned to look at him. "Mr. Ross has done it. He has accomplished what countless before him have strived for. He has discovered"—he dramatically raised his hands above his head—"the God Spot."

Franklin clapped and walked back toward the shrinking student.

"Mr. Ross, the problem with your conclusion is—it's wrong." He leaned forward and flipped Ross's closed notebook back open. "Perhaps you should write this down."

Franklin smiled at the girl next to Ross. She shifted uncomfortably.

"For years, scientists have been looking for a certain part of the brain. The God Spot, as it's sometimes called, is supposedly the area of the brain that's responsible for spirituality. I have the highest regard for Dr. Hahn, but he's spent twenty years looking for that one spot, and he has been digging in the wrong place."

Franklin looked around the room, but most students peered down instead of meeting his eyes.

"Others, like myself and Dr. Melding, believe that it isn't one, but many spots. There have been many studies. Several have been performed in this very university." He paced and strutted back and forth, and the sleepy-eyed students pivoted their necks as if at a one-man tennis match.

"Various methods have been employed to locate it—romantic love, philanthropic love, meditation, happiness, fear. None of them worked." He sauntered back to the ill-fated student, who was trying to sink through his seat to be immolated in the earth's fiery core.

"I myself researched this exact topic you have selected for your paper. My study came to the opposite conclusion from the one with which you *concur*. In my humble opinion, it should be relatively easy to prove, through mapping dopamine release, that it isn't one spot but many spots."

Franklin spun on his heel and strutted back to the podium.

Ross glanced at the girl next to him and seemed to muster some courage. "Easy? Then why haven't you proved it?"

Kid, you should have stayed down.

"Why?" Franklin's hand crashed down on the podium. Half the class jumped in their seats. Jack was somewhat amused by the theatrics, but deep down he was appalled by the man's ego and demeaning antics. What kind of environment would this have been for Michelle?

"Knowing and proving are totally separate. If they—" The professor seized the sides of the podium and inhaled. Jack could see his knuckles turn white as his hands clutched the wood. "I digress." When Franklin continued, his voice was dripping with sarcasm. "I await reading and *grading* your paper with bated breath."

The door on the opposite side of the reception desk opened and Dr. Hahn came in, followed by his assistant. Jack remembered the kid from his earlier visit. Brendan.

Hahn leaned on the dark wooden cane in his left hand, but he had an innate grace and elegance that his colleague Franklin could never hope to achieve. He flashed a courtly smile at the receptionist and became more somber as he approached Jack with an outstretched hand.

"Officer Stratton. It's certainly a pleasure that you accepted my offer so swiftly."

"I appreciate the invitation. I really wanted to see the work Michelle has done."

"If it's all right with you, I have asked Brendan here to begin the tour while I conclude a previously scheduled appointment."

"Certainly, Doctor. I apologize for the short notice."

"No trouble at all. I won't be long. If you'll excuse me." The professor turned away, efficient but unhurried.

"Officer Stratton. Good to see you again." Brendan pumped his hand. And then the squeeze tightened just a little. "I think we should start with the computer room."

Jack followed him across the lobby. "So, Brendan, what do you do as Dr. Hahn's assistant?"

"I teach some of Dr. Hahn's introductory courses and I work here in the lab. Technically I'm still working on my doctorate in neuropsychology. Once I graduate I hope to be full-time."

"I'd have pegged you for a football player."

"I was, in high school. Quarterback—but I tore my rotator cuff. Someone thought a change from my typical classes would do me some good. I took a theory class with Dr. Hahn, changed my major, and never looked back."

"Will we see the lab?"

"Yes, but some other areas first. It's on the lower level."

"What do you do there?"

"Mostly brain scans—brain imaging."

"Imaging? Like creating a picture of what people are thinking?"

"No, that technology is still years away. We use an fMRI to perform scans and see patterns. Images of how different stimuli affect the brain."

As they headed downstairs, Jack noticed the many warning and danger signs posted throughout the building. He pointed at the *Volatile Materials—Extreme Caution* sign and quipped, "I thought the most you might have to worry about in the psychology center was falling off the shrink's couch."

Brendan laughed. "That's a good one, but you do need to be careful. This is a fully functional laboratory environment. It's world-renowned."

Jack tried to backpedal. "I'm sure it is. I just had different expectations."

Brendan continued with the tour. The whole center appeared to have been recently remodeled; that faint chemical odor of newness hung in the air. Everything seemed to have a plaque attached to it, indicating who had donated the money for it. Jack nodded his head at the appropriate times and looked for any opportunity to get in some questions.

"What was Michelle's role here?" he asked at last.

"I'll show you on the second floor. That's where the new computer lab is. Michelle oversaw the backup generators, updated the servers, and showed us how to increase our data storage capacity. More and more, we're moving to video, and that takes a lot of space."

And a lot of dedication. She must have been here all the time.

Brendan paused outside a large glass wall. On the other side, computer lights flashed and flickered in three separate rows. Jack noticed all the security cameras around the computer room and the card reader attached to the door.

"You have a lot of security here."

"A lot of it is new. That was the last part Michelle was working on. I have one of the first new cards." He pulled out a blue card with his picture on it and scanned it through the card reader beside the door at the end of the hallway.

Jack followed Brendan into a large open area. Windows along the entire wall at the far end gave a panoramic view of the woods. To one side, a solid white wall with a large double door split the floor in half.

Brendan gestured to the breathtaking view of the woods. "The university purchased the building five years ago. The makeover has been going on since then. This way."

He motioned Jack toward a staircase leading to the lowest level. At the bottom of the staircase were two closed metal doors. The door on the right had a *CAUTION—NO ENTRY* sign.

Brendan opened it but didn't step through to the cement hallway stretching out into darkness. "Utility corridors run throughout the building. I can't tell you how much cable and fiber optics Michelle ran. She'd wear this little hat with a light on it."

Jack smiled at the thought in spite of the pang in his chest. Everything seemed to point to the adult Michelle—the Michelle Jack had never gotten to know—being extremely proud of her work, vested in it, and appreciated for it. Would she leave suddenly, without giving notice, jeopardizing her whole career? Or did it creep her out and she had to run? Or…

Brendan closed the *CAUTION* door and opened the door on the left. Jack followed him down a corridor to a set of double doors. Brendan swiped his card in yet another card reader, and the doors silently swung open.

A short hallway split left and right with doors at the ends. Here everything was cold and sterile; that horrible hospital feel.

"This way to the lab." Brendan led the way down the hallway, which was lined with cabinets. He pulled a small plastic tray from one cabinet. "Do you have any ferromagnetic materials?"

"What?"

"Metal?" Brendan pointed to a sign: *No Metal Beyond This Point.*

Jack unholstered his Glock .40 caliber, dropped the magazine into his hand, and pulled the slide back to remove the round in the chamber. "Do you have a secure location for this?"

"Certainly. We get all sorts of visitors." Brendan walked over and opened a safe. "It will be secure in here."

Jack took his time placing his gun inside. He closed the door himself and tried the handle to make sure it locked. "What would happen if I went inside with it?"

"It would be bad. They made us watch safety videos where people got careless and brought wheelchairs, gurneys, and even floor polishers too close. They all got jammed deep inside the machine. And as for the gun, that actually happened one time. Some police officer had his pistol fly right out of his holster. It went off when it hit the magnet and shot a hole in the wall."

Jack raised an eyebrow. "Seriously?"

"Yeah. Google it. It was in the *New York Times.* And that was only a regular MRI. The fMRI is twenty times more powerful."

"What about the metal in this?" Jack pointed to a fire extinguisher. "Why doesn't it get sucked up?"

Brendan patted the wall. "Shielding. It was part of the biggest expense, but it's built into the walls, ceiling, and floor that surround the machine. It's like a cage and the machine is the beast." He moved over to a door. Another swipe and it opened.

Jack followed into some kind of control booth. A young man—Brendan introduced him as Pete—sat at the console and video monitors on either side of him flashed graphs and charts. A large window looked out onto a room that was bare except for a large cylindrical machine, centered over a stretcher. The space age looking equipment reflected off the gleaming black-tiled floor. On one of the monitors, Jack saw a smiling girl lying on the stretcher, inside the long tube.

Brendan beamed. "Impressive, isn't it? It's one of the most powerful fMRIs in the world, a modified experimental design, 9.4 Tesla. The University of Illinois at Chicago has been experimenting with a similar design for years with excellent results. The detailed brain scans can pinpoint reactions in nanoseconds."

"How does it work?"

"It detects the changes in blood oxygenation and flow that occur in response to neural activity. In this control booth the experimenter can control and monitor the machine and the supermagnet inside, as well as get data, both in real time and analyzed in different ways."

Jack felt as if he was in a technical infomercial. *Wait, there's more! But does it chop a tomato in just seconds?*

"It takes almost a full day to power down," Pete chimed in.

"Turn up the volume." Brendan tapped the young man's shoulder, and Pete flicked a switch.

Jack heard girlish laughter, and each time she laughed, the charts on the monitors in the control room jumped and changed. Jack looked again at the girl in the machine below and saw she was watching a monitor.

"We're almost ready to kill the TV and let her pray," Pete said as he slowly turned a dial.

Jack looked at Brendan. "Pray?"

Brendan nodded. "We're monitoring data for Dr. Hahn."

"The God Spot?"

Brendan looked surprised that Jack had done his homework. "So, you know about the theory that there is one centralized spot in the brain responsible for religious thought."

"I just heard Dr. Franklin ripping a kid apart about it," Jack said.

Brendan exchanged a sideways frown with Pete, who blurted out, "I think that's all Dr. Franklin talks about. That and which girl he's currently—"

Brendan bumped his chair and went on primly, "We can use the fMRI to see what areas of the brain are utilized for different functions."

Pete shrugged. "Whatever. Truth hurts. The guy's a—"

Brendan gave Pete a *shut-up-I'm-on-a-tour* glare.

Pete turned back to the monitors, while Jack made a note to go to Pete if he was in need of gossip about this joint.

"Excellent, you're here." Dr. Hahn eased into the small room and shook Jack's hand. "I trust that Brendan is explaining everything?"

Jack nodded. "Very impressive, Doctor."

"It represents countless hours and sacrifice by so many, including Michelle," Hahn said.

"How many students work here?"

"Several dozen. We're at full staff, and a number of students volunteer, too. Don't you wish that you had been able to get college credit for watching TV?" Hahn indicated the girl on the gurney, one gray eyebrow raised.

"I didn't realize you had so much high-tech equipment in here. And Michelle was getting it all locked down?"

"She did wonderful work. It's probably excessive for a university psychology laboratory, but still, Michelle made it possible for us to upgrade and satisfy all the security protocols," Dr. Hahn said.

"How late are people here, typically?" Jack asked.

"Typically?" Dr. Hahn paused. "Our hours are nine to seven. However, in academia, working hours are often atypical."

"And how would you describe your function here, Dr. Hahn?"

"I am just a figurehead. I like to say the center runs itself." Silvery laugh. "They bring me out for fundraisers and to teach a class or two."

Brendan stepped forward. "He's being modest. Dr. Hahn is director of the Neuropsychology Department. This whole center is really his work. He's a pioneer in fMRI research."

Dr. Hahn's hand rested on Brendan's shoulder. "My student's flattery is sure to positively affect his grades." He laughed again and patted Brendan's arm. "I'm actually co-director. Dr. Franklin runs the other side."

"I listened in on part of his lecture while I waited."

"Today?" Dr. Hahn sighed and rubbed the back of his neck. "Don't let the corduroy and glasses fool you: academia is a contact sport. Dr. Franklin was just... explaining his platform. I heard about... the incident already from my student."

"He shouldn't go off in class—" Pete started to protest, but Dr. Hahn held up a hand.

"Dr. Franklin can speak about anything he wants to in *his* class," Dr. Hahn clarified. "Conversation isn't the issue. I'll remind the both of you"—he looked back and forth between Pete and Brendan—"if you are going to defend a position, be prepared to defend it vigorously." He clenched a fist. "And if you get knocked down, get a pint and go back to the drawing board in the morning." He smiled convincingly, but Jack was wondering why he referred to it as an *incident*. Had there been others?

Brendan tapped his watch.

Dr. Hahn nodded and gave Jack a little European bow. "I do apologize for leaving you yet again, but I have a class."

"Of course." Jack shook his hand, American-style. "Thank you for the tour."

"It was the least I could do for all of Michelle's work. Brendan will see you out." He turned to go.

"Dr. Hahn, I have a rather odd request to make of you."

Dr. Hahn raised a skeptical eyebrow. "Yes?"

"After seeing all of this, I just wish... I wish I could have been a fly on the wall and seen Michelle at work. Do you know what I mean?" Jack asked.

"Actually, I do. Maybe it's the researcher in me, but wanting to be an observer is a frequent wish of mine, too."

"Do you think it would be possible for me to look at some of the video footage of Michelle working? I know it's not a typical request, but I think it would help me with closure."

Hahn shook his head. "Sadly, that wouldn't be possible..."

"I'd be happy to come back." Jack turned his hands out.

"Unfortunately, it isn't a matter of time. The security cameras were one of the last things Michelle was working on, and right now they don't record anything. They only serve as a deterrent."

"That's too bad," Jack said, not hiding his disappointment.

Hahn seemed relieved, now that his obligation to Jack had been fulfilled. "Michelle would have been very happy you came out here today. I hope you can find some closure in the fact that her work here was meaningful and will continue."

I'll get closure when I find out what happened to Michelle.

Dr. Hahn departed, and Brendan led Jack through the antiseptic maze and back to the front desk. Through the glass Jack saw it had begun to rain, and students were hurrying down the main sidewalk in large herds. He didn't change his pace or even react to the cold sting as he took long strides toward the parking lot, mulling over the glimpse he'd just had into Michelle's life—and realizing how far he was from understanding her death.

"Afternoon, Jack." Neil Waters stepped out of the crowd and held his large umbrella over Jack.

"Hi, Neil."

"I saw you were out here and wanted to offer my condolences." Neil slowed to a stop and held out a hand.

"Thank you." Jack shook his hand.

"So, what brings you out here?"

"Dr. Hahn offered to give me a tour. So I could see my sister's work firsthand."

Neil nodded brusquely. "I'm glad you got a chance to see it. If you need anything else, please give me a call and let *me* know."

His voice had lost its soft edges.

Neil gestured to the parking lot and they both started walking. He continued, "I'm sure you understand the sensitive nature of handling this matter, both for Michelle's family and the university. Because of that, it would be best if you ran any further inquiries by me first."

Jack opened the door to his Impala and got in. "Thanks."

Neil smiled down at him. "I'm glad you understand."

As Jack pulled out of the parking lot, he felt Neil watching him. He got it: a student was dead and drugs were involved; the university didn't want the bad publicity and wanted it all to go away quietly.

But there was something they didn't understand: Michelle was his sister, and nothing and nobody could stop Jack from finding out who killed her.

25

ASK A BETTER QUESTION

Jack was early for his one-o'clock appointment. He pulled over at the third lookout spot. There were many staggered along the scenic drive so people could pull off, stretch their legs, and enjoy the view. But he wasn't there for the forest scenery, and he didn't get out of the car. He was waiting for a silver Ford Taurus.

He left the car running for the heat and shook his head. *Undercover detectives.* They were a paranoid bunch, with good reason. If one wrong person saw them, months of work could go down the drain—or worse, they could end up dead. You always had to meet them somewhere strange, like the middle of a state forest, or a gas station. When he first joined the force, he had to make drops to an undercover at a golf course.

Jack was here to meet Detective Mark Reynolds. He was the man to go to for information about what was happening in Darrington County, if drugs were involved.

To Jack, it didn't make sense that Michelle, who worked hard and never did drugs, would try meth. Maybe someone slipped it to her. Were college kids using it? Who was their supplier?

As Jack worked down his list of questions, a silver Taurus backed up next to Jack, and a man in his early thirties with black, wavy hair stepped out and slid into Jack's passenger seat. He was about five foot five, and his handshake was strong—really strong, like an ironworker's.

"Jack."

"Mark. I appreciate you coming."

"I can't stay long. I'm supposed to be dropping off a package. You said you had some questions you needed help with."

"Yeah. Tell me everything I need to know about meth," Jack said, not joking.

"This related to your foster sister?"

Jack nodded.

"She died in a car accident out on Reservoir Road?"

"Yes."

"She had meth in her system."

"Yes. How did you know all that?"

"The ME's office always informs the drug task force. We keep track of any deaths involving drugs. What're you going to do with the information if I give it to you?"

"Do with it?" This wasn't going quite the way Jack had expected.

"I mean, are you thinking about kicking down the doors of all the meth dealers in the city?"

Jack needed to answer carefully. "I'll think about what you give me. If it leads me to the guy who gave her the meth, then yeah—I'll have to kick his door down. You have a problem with that?"

Mark looked at him for a minute and then shook his head. He lit a cigarette and leaned back. "Okay. What do you want to know?" His voice wasn't too deep, but it had calmness and patience, like a teacher's.

"How can you take meth?"

"Shoot it. Smoke it. Eat it. Suppository."

"Is it big at White Rocks?"

"Depends on what your definition of big is. It's available. It's always available. We shut one lab down and another pops up. Last year, there were two dealers there, but I don't know of one operating right now. It's been quiet lately."

"None?"

"Like I said, you can get it, but there isn't one dealer who's claiming the turf. Too much heat now."

Mark leaned forward and angled his head down, pretending to tune the radio. Jack looked up and saw a man on a bike. They both remained silent as the man rode past. Then the detective leaned back and took a long drag on his cigarette.

"Could someone force somebody to take it?" Jack asked.

"Yeah, I suppose." Mark eyed Jack. "Is that what you think happened?"

"Yes."

"Why?"

"She wouldn't do meth. She was a clean, hardworking kid with no previous drug use. If someone didn't do drugs, would their first choice be meth?"

"You need to ask a better question, Jack."

Jack's jaw clenched. "Enlighten me."

"First off, you don't know for a fact that she hadn't done any other drugs, right?" Jack nodded.

"Second, anyone *might*. It depends on the circumstances. I can't answer how likely it is. Who knew her best?"

"Probably her sister, her foster sister."

"Does she say that she could have done it?"

"She said no way."

"But it was in her system. What did the ME say?"

"The body wasn't discovered for some time. They couldn't tell how much."

Mark took a drag on his cigarette and blew the smoke out the crack of the window. Jack cleared his throat. "I appreciate you meeting me."

"I understand now why you asked. Family is important."

"Do you have any?" Jack asked.

Mark took another long drag and exhaled. The smoke wafted out the window. "I have a wife who defies expectations. She's like a good doctor; she has a lot of patience." Jack smiled at the joke, and Mark continued, "My daughter, on the other hand..." His voice trailed off and he looked out the window.

Jack debated for a second and then said, "She's like a pediatrician? She has little patience."

Mark looked at him, puzzled, and then burst out laughing. He started to cough and tossed his cigarette out.

"Funny."

"I just made it up."

"Thanks. I needed a laugh."

Jack persisted. "One more question. You said there are no dealers at the college now. Who was there before?"

"Carl Finn and Mike Leverone. Leverone will talk with you."

"What about Finn?"

"Dead. Suicide. Last year."

"Why will Leverone talk?"

"His lab blew up. Burned down his parents' house and got pretty fried himself. He flipped, gave us everything and everyone he had. He does Scared Straight stuff now."

"How can I get in touch with him?"

Mark scribbled down a phone number and address and handed them to Jack. "He's odd, but he's helping us, so don't go off, understand?"

"I just want to find out how she got it. I'm open to ideas."

"Talk to Mike. He knew all the players. But if it was me, I'd start with your sister's friends. Find out who she was with. Friends, start there. If not, you're chasing the wind."

"I appreciate it."

They shook hands, and Mark started to slide out of the car. Then he stopped.

"What is it?" Jack asked.

Mark held up one finger as he stared straight ahead. "There was this one kid. We followed him a few times last year. We suspected he was a runner for one of the dealers at the college, but we could never catch him red-handed."

Jack opened his notebook again.

"Lennie Jacobsen. They call him Lennie J," Mark said.

"Thanks. I'll look him up."

"No problem." Mark gave a curt nod and got back in his car.

As the Taurus pulled out, Jack had already started to dial. He wanted to see Leverone before he went home.

26

BUT FOR THE GRACE OF GOD GO I

The small yellow-and-white ranch fit right in with the rest of the quiet, tree-lined neighborhood. An old red Honda sedan was in the driveway. Jack pulled in behind it and parked. He walked up a curved brick walkway to a red door with a big pine wreath on it, rang the doorbell, and waited.

When the door was yanked open, Mike Leverone stood, smiling, in the doorway. At least Jack thought he was smiling.

Mark Reynolds hadn't provided enough information regarding Mike's accident. Whatever wasn't covered by his baseball cap was extremely difficult to look at: mangled, twisted, and scarred by fire.

Don't look away.

"Jack?"

Jack had been a soldier and had seen more than his share of horrifying accidents, but one look at Mike and he wondered how the man had survived.

"Jack Stratton." He reached forward and closed his hand around Mike's prosthetic hook.

"Mike Leverone," Mike said. "You're good. You didn't even flinch at the hook." He turned, and Jack followed him inside.

The modest living room was clean and tidy, not a spot of dust anywhere. The large book collection on the room's rear wall was meticulously arranged.

"Thank you for seeing me on such short notice," Jack said.

"Thank you for seeing *me*. I don't get many visitors." Mike held out his hand for Jack to sit in the recliner.

If a man's home is his castle, then his recliner is his throne. Jack nodded to acknowledge the gesture as he sat down.

Mike seemed pleased. "Can I get you something to drink, coffee? I'm on probation, so I stay squeaky clean and I don't have any alcohol."

"No, I'm all set, thanks."

"Give me a minute then." Mike wandered into the kitchen to a huge coffeemaker and reached up into a cupboard for a new cup. When his sweater sleeve slipped down, Jack caught a long glimpse of the scars underneath.

"Sure I can't get you one?" Mike turned.

Jack quickly pretended to be checking out the magazines that were stacked in a neat square on top of the coffee table. "No, I'm good."

Mike came back to sit on the couch. "On the phone you said you had some questions about meth up at White Rocks."

"That's right. I need some help… Can I ask you to keep this confidential?"

"Is this the face of a talker?" Mike pointed to his scarred features.

Self-deprecation. Defense mechanism. Laugh. Jack smiled. "I'm looking into a murder. The autopsy showed the victim had meth in her system. There's reason to believe the victim didn't do drugs. We think someone forced her to take it and then killed her."

"Forced her?"

Jack paused. He was trying to read Mike's face. He thought maybe Mike was raising a former eyebrow.

"Could someone have tricked her into taking it? Slipped it in a drink?"

Mike shook his head. "No. You can parachute it, but if you put it in a drink it's really bitter."

"What's parachuting?"

"Swallowing it. You can snort it, like coke. Smoke it. Slam it—you know, shoot it like heroin, or booty-bump."

Jack winced. "If someone was going to force someone else to take it, how would they do it?"

"I'd think shoot them up."

"Do they get the effects right away?"

"Not necessarily. Depends on the person. The way you take it affects the speed and strength, too. Smoking is the fastest and gets you off quickest."

"Did you know Carl Finn?"

"Yeah. Good guy. We were in some classes together."

"What happened to him?"

"He sampled. One time. He thought spiders were in his brain. So he used a nail gun to get them." Mike pantomimed the scene out as he spoke, holding his prosthetic hook up next to his temple and then jerking his head to the side.

Jack shuddered. "One time, huh?"

"All it takes."   ·

"How hard is it to make?"

"Hard?" Mike snorted. "It's not. Anyone can make it."

"Anyone?"

"If you have the Internet, you can figure it out. I learned at college."

"College? White Rocks?" Jack asked.

"Dr. Franklin's class. He taught us how."

"He's co-director of the center. He taught you?"

"Step by step. He gave me the idea. I thought he was a hero until I blew apart my life." Mike gestured wildly with his hook.

"Why was he teaching kids how to make meth?"

"Showing off? Midlife crisis? Power to the people? Who knows? It was my fault for doing it. I mean, he didn't sit there and say mix this and use that, but he gave an outline and answered any question I asked when I went back to him."

"What went wrong?"

Mike shrugged. "The whole process is super-combustible. You can see videos on the net. With me, it was the solvents, I think. I was hurrying, and I left the cover off. Making meth involves fire and explosive fumes. They mixed, and boom. Fire all over."

Jack remembered the phosphorus bombs and swallowed. *Is that what happened to Mike? If Chandler hadn't broken down that door…* Jack could still see the fire shooting out the door. Blue and white flames swirling together before turning crimson and licking at the sky.

"You've seen it, haven't you?" Mike leaned forward.

Jack nodded.

Silence descended on the room as the two men replayed their own memories of hell.

Jack closed his eyes and rubbed them with his hands. "What does Franklin teach?"

"Psychology. I was taking his class called Drugs, Youth, and the Mind. Franklin's into imaging."

"I got the tour this morning. Is that with the fMRI?" Jack asked.

"At the center? Yeah. They hook you up and give you different drugs and take images of your brain. They make you take off all your rings and stuff." He pointed at an earring that hung off what was left of his ear. "I was nervous when I first went in. I heard a story of this guy who was harpooned by a chair that flew up and crashed into the machine. Something to do with the metal."

"Because of the magnets?"

"Yeah, that must be it."

"Do they actually give you meth?" Jack asked.

"Sort of. You can get a prescription for ADHD meds and stuff like that. They do studies at the school, and I think they used it. That was a while ago. Anyway, the pill is super-low dose. A regular street hit would be like a month's worth of prescription."

"So you can legally get meth? That's messed up."

"Not really. It's way harder to get the legal stuff than the street stuff."

Jack paused. "One last question. Anyone at the college I should talk to who could have given it to the... victim?"

Mike shook his head and held up his hand and his hook. "Almost anyone. I haven't heard about anyone stepping up after Carl and me. There's still too much attention for one guy to set up shop. But you can still get it. You just have to ask."

"Did you know a Lennie Jacobsen or Lennie J? He may have been a runner."

Mike shook his head and looked down at his feet. "Meth attracts people like flies to garbage, hangers-on and wannabes." He stared down at the floor and swallowed. "For a while, I felt like a rock star with all my groupies. But they were just kids. Who knows what I turned them into? I burned myself on the outside, but they burned on the inside. I didn't even know most of their names."

He looked up at Jack and trembled where his chin used to be.

Jack tried, but he couldn't hold Mike's gaze. He stood up to leave. "Thank you for your time."

"Oh, okay." Mike looked disappointed.

"If you hear anything, please give me a call."

"Sure. If I can help at all, you can just stop by. I can't go anywhere"—he lifted up his pant leg, revealing an ankle monitor—"and I don't get many visitors."

"Thanks for your time."

"Any time." Mike followed Jack to the door, stood in the open doorway, and waved with his prosthesis as Jack drove away.

Jack looked up at his reflection in the rearview mirror.

That could have been me.

He whispered to his dead friend, "Thanks, buddy."

* * *

It was late afternoon when Jack came home. Replacement almost bowled him over as soon as he walked in the door.

"Where have you been? What happened?"

"Give me a second."

"Does your phone work? Can't you hear it ring? I've been trying to get you all day," she said, following right on his heels.

He pulled out his phone. It was turned off. He shrugged a sorry.

Replacement glared. "You didn't check your phone?" Her hands flew wide. "I was worried. I woke up and—"

"Shut up."

She slammed both hands into his shoulders, but he could tell she held back. "*You* shut up. I've been waiting."

"Okay. Get me a soda while I get ready for work and I'll tell you."

"I'm not your wife. Get your own soda."

"You're nagging at me like a wife, so get—" Jack stopped himself and closed his eyes for a second. "Fine. I went out to the center this morning. I got the full tour. I didn't get much of anything, but I'm going back for another look in a couple of days." He left off the part about looking up Dr. Franklin.

"Can I go with you?"

"Last time didn't go too well. Remember Missy?"

"Funny you brought her up." Replacement walked over to the computer.

Uh-oh. "Funny how?"

"Remember how you thought she was lying about Michelle?" She sat down at the computer. "I thought if we pushed a little more…"

"Pushed? I didn't say push. I said back off."

"It's not a big deal. I just sent an email…"

He shot her a look.

"Log in."

"Well, it kind of came from… you." Replacement's eyes grew large.

"You sent it from *my* account?"

"I thought it would look more intimidating if it came from you." She got up and let him sit at the computer.

"I don't want to be intimidating." Jack logged in to his email and checked the sent messages.

> Dear Ms. Lorton,
>
> Please be officially notified that we are continuing to look into the murder of Michelle Carter. It is our hope that you will contact me regarding all information that you have concerning this case.
>
> Sincerely,
> Officer Jack Stratton

She'd included his cell phone number!

"Have you *officially* lost your mind? My cell phone number?"

"This might shake her up. She might—"

"Yeah, she might go to the police now. About *me*."

He pulled the plug out of the back of the computer. That was the most dramatic way he could think of to demonstrate how serious he was this time.

"Stay off it."

He stormed into the bathroom and slammed the door.

27

DIRTY DANCING

Later that night, Jack was pulling traffic duty. Penance. The smell of hot tar filled the air. There always seemed to be tar ready for pouring; the stench clung to everything for days.

They'd been working on this highway since before Jack started on the force, leisurely making their way from exit to exit.

Barely two exits in the last six months. What a waste.

It was just warm enough not to freeze the light mist into snow. The highway stretched out on both sides, the droplets dancing under the enormous arc lights, little rainbows glittering on the pavement, Jack in the middle, sodden and miserable.

Officer Tom Kempy waved and smiled at Jack. He was a little older than Jack, married with three kids, one of those guys who always seems happy, just in love with life.

"Hey, Jack." Tom trotted up to him. "Billy said they're making good progress and should be done by four."

Four in the morning. That's good progress? Jack frowned.

"It'll go by fast." Tom slapped Jack on the arm and jogged toward his car.

"Say hi to Amy and the kids," Jack called after him.

Tom turned back around. "If you ever want to come over for dinner…" He trailed off.

"I'd love to. And don't worry, I won't bring a date."

Tom exhaled and smiled. "Okay. Great." He waved and ran for his car.

Jack laughed. He'd brought Gina to the last Christmas party. He didn't know it was a rather conservative event for the police and all their families. Tom had been there with Amy and all their kids. The next thing Jack knew, Gina had bribed the DJ into playing some "spicy" music—and then started to dance. The dance floor cleared as her drunken salsa began to look more and more like a striptease. When her hand slipped to the shoulder strap of her dress, he rushed in, tossed her over his shoulder, and carried her out.

The look on Amy's face as he walked by, Gina vividly describing all the erotic things she wanted to do to him…

Yeah. Definitely no date.

Five hours later, Jack felt like time had simply stopped. But the closer he came to getting home, which he assumed would happen eventually, under the normal laws of physics, the more he dreaded having to deal with Replacement.

He'd noticed that she was trying to get her schedule to match his. She'd wake up when he did and try to stay up until he returned. It drove him crazy, but he had to admit he also liked it.

On the other hand, while he was out today, she'd spent all her time reviewing the information from the phone and Michelle's emails, studying each line and each word, in case there was even a little piece of information that could hold some relevance. That girl didn't give up.

Maybe he could email Replacement and get her to look up that Lennie J kid.

But he was still ticked off about the email to Missy.

That girl will go to a lawyer. The lawyer will call Collins, Collins will go mental, and I'm screwed. I have a police delegate, but that won't matter. Collins will give me this job every shift. Or he'll assign me to paper filing and answering the phone for the rest of my career. Thanks, Replacement.

He waved a car down the lane of cones.

And what am I going to do about Replacement? She won't take the bed, and I sure don't want to sleep on the couch. I can't kick her out. I'll have to get a two-bedroom.

Suddenly Jack laughed. Not a little laugh; a big, howling sidesplitter.

A couple of guys stopped schmoozing with the Bobcat operator and looked at him. He held up his hands in a forget-about-it gesture.

He'd been thinking about Missy Lorton rolling into her kitchen, squealing. She must have died when she got that email—

He had only a second to react after he heard the car speed up behind him. He turned and headlights were bearing down on him. The engine and his adrenaline revved into fifth gear while everything else slowed way down.

He tried to jump. Too late.

Protect your head.

The bumper slammed into his thigh, and he crashed into the windshield. His back ignited in pain; a million fires burned.

For a split second, still spinning, he could see the stars, and then the arc lights, and then their reflections, twinkling and spinning. He heard swearing from the guys at the Bobcat.

Then his feet were going over his head. He was clear of the car, but he was still spinning.

Not back into the road.

Protect your head.

His feet landed first on the pavement, then his back, and then his head. He saw the car that had hit him swerve and keep going. His left hand had cushioned some of the impact, but his right arm flopped, useless.

Pain. Pain everywhere. He burned like a match held upside down.

Roll, he commanded, but his body wouldn't respond.

Jack tried to focus on the men running toward him. He could see them, but his ears didn't seem to be working. Everything dimmed. Then went black.

28

IRON MAN

The first sound as Jack came around was a slow, steady beep. It matched the thudding pulse that echoed in his head. *Hospital.*

Not dead yet, Jack.

He tried to open his eyes, but only one worked, and it wasn't working too well. He tried to blink, but everything was fuzzy. He let his head roll to the side. He tried not to breathe through his nose but then, through the stomach-churning hospital smells, there was a faint scent of flowers.

Flowers? Maybe I am dead. Body check.

He flexed his left leg, but he couldn't move the right.

Immobile from the knee down.

Hips. *Check.*

Back. Pain, but not agonizing. Lots of pain on the right side, maybe a broken rib or two.

Left arm and hand felt okay. He held up his right arm in front of the eye that was sort of working.

Splint.

"Jack?" A blurry shape called to him from beyond the flowers, then swooped in and came almost nose to nose with him.

"Replacement?" Jack's mouth was so dry it sounded more like *placemat.*

She reached her hand out to touch his head but hesitated; her hand hovered.

"Doctor!" she shouted right in his face.

His eye fluttered.

"Sorry. Doctor!" she called again. He was grateful she turned her head before she yelled this time, but his ears still rang. When she turned back to him, he could read the concern on her face.

Jack shut his eye. "You okay?"

"Me?" Replacement drew back and frowned. "I'm fine. Don't worry, you're going to be fine, too. You're good… *Doctor!"*

Darkness returned.

* * *

The next time Jack woke and tried to open his eyes, his left eyelid was like a broken garage door that went up a bit and stopped. He picked up his right hand, forgetting it was in a splint, and crashed it into his good eye.

Swearing at his own stupidity, he jerked partly upright, but came to a sudden stop as new pain flooded the broken pieces of his body.

Replacement was suddenly at his side, and placed her hands behind his back to help him. But the last thing he wanted to do now was sit up.

"Stop, stop! You're killing me."

She pulled her hands away as if she'd grabbed a hot stove, and Jack thumped back onto the bed with a loud groan.

She looked like she was preparing to roar for the doctor again, but Jack interrupted. "No, I'm fine. Give me a minute." Even the little shake of his head hurt.

"Are you sure?" She leaned in and searched his face.

She was so close, all he had to do was pucker his lips and the kiss landed right on her lips. She stood up, and her eyes were huge.

Jack giggled. The pain medicine made him a little loopy.

"Jack?" She leaned closer.

"Miss me?" His speech was slurred. He laughed again, and the room spun.

"Jack, you're in the hospital." She spoke softly and slowly. "Do you remember what happened?"

He nodded. "I got hit by a green Toyota Corolla."

"What's my name?"

I'm screwed. I forgot again. He laughed some more.

Her face grew concerned. "Jack, what's my name?"

"Replacement."

"What's my real name?" she pressed.

"I think I hit my head..."

"You can remember it was a green Toyota Corolla that hit you but you can't—"

"Alice." Jack felt like he'd hit the game-winning shot at the buzzer. He giggled, and then suddenly had to take another nap.

* * *

When his eyes half-opened a few hours later, Replacement hugged him so tightly that she choked off his groans of pain. All he could do was grimace and wait for her to relax her grip.

She stood up and wiped away tears. "Everyone was so worried."

Jack struggled not to groan. He was flat on his back, and he wanted to try to sit again. Slowly, carefully, he edged some words past his aching ribs and through his parched throat.

"Does this bed sit up without you having to lift me?"

Replacement grabbed the remote, and the bed raised him to a sitting position. The first thing he noticed when he looked around the room was all the flower arrangements.

"How long have I been out?" His mouth felt dry and slimy at the same time.

Replacement held up a cup with a straw, and he took a small sip of water. It felt so good against the back of his throat.

"You were out for a while. A couple of days. The doctors were worried about your head. Then they came back and said it looked okay."

"I've been out..." He tried to sit up further but realized that was a lousy idea as the room spun even more. "It was a green—"

"They found the car. It was stolen." Replacement stroked his arm. "We can talk about it later."

"Nothing off the car? Prints?" Jack closed one eye, and it helped bring her into focus.

"Nothing. Sheriff Collins came by. He said they had nothing on it yet." Replacement shrugged. Jack noticed how tired she looked. "Cindy came by, too. She said they'd wiped it clean."

"How long have you been here?"

She shrugged again, but the dark circles under her eyes provided the answer.

"You need to go get some rest."

She shook her head but remained silent.

He took another swig of water and tried to wiggle his toes. His right leg had been immobilized from the knee down.

"Did I break my leg?"

"Surprisingly not. The doctors thought you had at first because it was so black and blue, but all the x-rays came back negative. They call you Iron Man. You did injure your right wrist, though, and your face got pretty busted up."

Jack didn't have to touch the left side of his face to feel the swelling. It hurt even before he smiled about Iron Man, and his left eye still wouldn't open all the way.

"Officer Stratton?"

Jack looked up as a doctor and nurse walked into the room, smiling, which he took as a good sign.

"I'd like to examine you, if I may?"

Jack nodded.

Sure, give me the all-clear, and then I can go track down the guy who did this to me.

* * *

After two more days, Jack was thoroughly sick of everything about the hospital, especially the long, rectangular light fixture above his head that created a strange yellowish glow and was never turned off, day or night. He hated sitting still, hated lying down, and most of all, hated the feeling of being trapped.

"How long do they want me to stay here?"

"Maybe until this afternoon." Cindy patted his leg and sat down in the lime-green chair.

"I have to—"

"What're you going to do, Jack? The doctor doesn't want you walking on that leg, and your right hand needs time to heal." She held up her hand. "Collins said you were to take some time off, too."

"You have to be kidding me."

Cindy folded her arms and leveled her gaze at him. "The sheriff is right. You can't stand on your leg yet, and you can't shoot. You need time to get well."

Jack picked at the flowers next to his bed. "These came without cards," he said with a sweep of his good hand toward the many displays nurses had delivered to the room.

"Well, they all had cards… once…" Cindy chuckled.

"Once?" Jack didn't understand.

"Alice read a couple of them…"

"She got rid of the cards?"

"When it comes to women, you really don't know jack, Jack."

"Ha, ha." He still didn't understand but that was the least of his worries right now. "Why do I have to stay here so long?"

"One reason is to give Alice a break. Do you have any idea how long she stayed at your side? She wouldn't go home until I promised I'd stay with you today."

"You're not staying."

"I promised. That one can be scary."

"Go home, Cindy."

"I thought you'd want the company."

"I actually would prefer to sleep. Really."

"You're okay with that?" She leaned in. "My mother came for a visit, and I left her at home with my husband... They get along like gasoline and a match."

"Sounds like you're needed elsewhere. Go. Really, I'll be fine."

Cindy picked up her purse. "Don't you dare tell Alice I left." Cindy gave Jack's foot a little squeeze and headed out the door.

Jack leaned back and looked up at the jaundiced ceiling again.

Nothing is broken in my leg. Doc said I'll be on it in a week or two.

He arched his back and tried to flex his muscles. He still hurt. A lot.

A young nurse came in carrying another vase filled with flowers and set it down next to the bed.

"Someone must want you to get better," the girl gushed. She handed him a very large card.

At least I can find out who sent these.

He didn't recognize the handwriting from his name printed on the envelope. He opened the card and then closed it quickly. He could feel his face turn hot and red. The nurse took the hint and scuttled out.

No words, just a picture.

He slowly opened the card again to the exquisitely rendered pencil sketch. The problem wasn't with the quality of the drawing but with the subject—Jack, lying on a tattoo table, a sheet partially covering him—just not covering the right parts.

Marisa. Well, that explains why Replacement got rid of the others.

29

DRUNKEN GRASSHOPPER

Replacement propped another pillow behind Jack's back and stepped away, appraising her work triumphantly. Jack surveyed her accomplishment. She had transformed his bedroom into a hospital room, only much nicer, with a food tray and TV, pillows everywhere—ditto flowers without cards. Snacks, books, ice pack, heat pack, and an electric teakettle were all within easy reach; his right leg was blissfully propped up on cushions.

"Thanks. I don't know how you pulled this off. I have to figure out how you got this stuff or have you arrested."

She turned her hands up. "Donations. Cindy hooked me up at the Salvation Army. They wouldn't take a dime."

Comfortable as he was in his pillows, Jack wasn't comfortable with not being head of the household, even for a minute. "Take some money. Where'd you put my wallet? We need groceries and stuff."

"We have tons of food. Cindy brought it over." Chattering like a little house sparrow, she sat down on the bed. "She's great. I like her a lot."

"Yeah, me too," Jack said absently. "Listen, I tried calling Sheriff Collins, but he won't return my phone calls."

"Jack, I don't think that you... right now..."

He knew what she was going to say, and he just didn't have it in him to fight her. A few more hours' rest wouldn't kill him. "You do realize you didn't actually say anything just now? Not a full sentence anyway." He tried to smile.

"Just for now you need to stop. For right now, just get better." She squeezed his hand. "Please."

"Okay." He pulled the blanket up a little further. "I'll be good."

"Wait until you see this." She raced out of the room and came back with her arms full of DVDs. She stacked them on the table and gestured like Vanna White. "Pick a movie."

He grinned. *"Rocky."*

"A boxing movie?" She made a face.

"You've never seen it? You'll like it."

They spent a sweet, lazy afternoon watching movies. That night, Jack stared up at the ceiling—at least he had a different ceiling to stare at now—and waited. Replacement had gone to bed an hour ago.

She must be asleep by now.

He slipped out of bed and winced when he tried to stand, but he definitely felt a little stronger. He shuffled to the door and slowly opened it, fairly confident it wouldn't squeak after he liberally sprayed the hinges with WD-40 a few weeks ago so he wouldn't wake Gina up when he came home late.

Replacement lay curled up on the couch under the thick comforter. He was sure she was asleep.

He made it over to the desk, leaned against it, and forced himself to breathe.

Click.

There was a little chirp when he unplugged her laptop. Cradling it like a football, he limped away as quietly as he could. He was almost at the far end of the couch when he heard a soft scraping sound. He turned around, trying to pinpoint the source of the noise.

The unplugged laptop cord was slowly sliding across the desk. He watched, helpless, as it slipped off the edge and landed with a crisp *thwack.*

He held his breath and looked down at Replacement.

She didn't move.

Jack turned and scurried back to the safety of the bedroom with his prize.

The laptop's screen flashed to life, and a password prompt appeared.

Jack grinned. *You're not the only one who can look over someone's shoulder.*

He typed "XmasR0$3" and the laptop booted up.

Christmas Rose for her password? I would never have guessed it.

Jack logged in to the police database and opened the file on Lennie Jacobsen. The guy was clean, but there was a mug shot.

Why is there a mug shot, but no arrest records?

He searched further into the file and finally found an arrest record from a few years back, voided. So Lennie had been arrested when he was a teenager, and the juvenile record was sealed.

Juvie records were like vaults. To get it unsealed, he'd have to convince a judge to give him a subpoena.

As in, not gonna happen.

If Lennie was a runner for a dealer up at the university, maybe he was a student.

I have to get back on campus.

* * *

For the next couple of days, Replacement made Jack breakfast, lunch, and dinner. She lay next to him as they watched movie after movie. If he tried to talk about the college or Michelle, she cut him off and reminded him that he'd promised to wait and get better. He couldn't remember having made that promise, but he didn't say anything.

Every night, Jack sneaked Replacement's laptop and pored over pictures and files, emails and court cases.

His leg healed slowly. When he woke up, Replacement was there, and she tucked him in every night. She doted on him like a devoted wife, and though he wouldn't admit it to her or to himself, he liked it. But he was overjoyed when the day finally came for his checkup.

* * *

Jack was not as excited about *how* they were getting to the doctor's office. Because of his leg, he couldn't drive. Which left Replacement.

He watched her carefully push the front seat all the way back to accommodate his leg brace. As he settled in, he realized the problem: the front seat in the Impala was one long seat—so, if it was pushed all the way back for him, Replacement had to sit on the very edge in order to reach the steering wheel and pedals.

He laughed. "You look like a little kid."

She made a face and sat up straighter.

"Okay. Just remember that the gas pedal is—"

The car shot forward like a rocket as she pressed down too hard on the gas. She countered by jamming both feet on the brake, and Jack had to catch himself one-armed on the dashboard to keep from going through the windshield.

"Very sensitive."

Before he could say anything else, the whole process was repeated, and they headed down the street bucking and pitching.

Between the pain in his leg and the terrified yet determined look on Replacement's face, he burst out laughing again.

She muttered, "I'm doing my best."

"You have to go easy," Jack said.

"I am."

"Just press a little."

Both of them were giggling like little kids by the time they reached the clinic.

A nurse took them to a small exam room, took Jack's blood pressure, and told him to wait on the exam table; the doctor would be there in a few minutes. Yes, Replacement could stay.

Just let this guy give me the green light.

He lay down on the table and closed his eyes, worrying about work, listening to Replacement turn on the faucet and wash her hands and fidget. He was just about to tell her to knock it off when she poked his leg and he jerked open his eyes.

"The doctor can see you now." She had on rubber gloves and a surgical mask. She crossed her eyes and leaned over him, holding up a tongue depressor. "It's time for your full body checkup."

They both burst out laughing and were still laughing when the door opened and the doctor walked in. Jack swallowed, and Replacement spun around, pulled her mask down, and put her hands behind her back. The doctor's quizzical look turned into a frown.

"I'm Dr. Nieman." He shook Jack's hand. "I see you've already met my assistant." He nodded toward Replacement.

Jack exhaled, and Replacement grinned.

The first thing Nieman did was remove Jack's leg brace, which didn't feel great. After a few minutes of prodding, and Jack wincing, Nieman leaned back.

"Officer, your leg is healing up quite nicely. If my assistant here keeps up with this quality care, you can head back to work next week." He winked at Replacement.

Jack and Replacement exchanged a quick smile.

Nieman shook Jack's hand, and as he turned to walk out of the office, he whispered something in Replacement's ear. Jack watched as her eyes grew big and her face turned scarlet. She didn't say a word as Nieman chuckled and left the room.

"What was that all about?"

"Nothing."

Jack shot her a semi-glare.

"He said I can take the mask and gloves. If we want to play doctor and patient, you're healthy enough for that now." Replacement looked down at the floor as her face turned scarlet on its way to plum.

* * *

The good news put Jack in a fine mood for Replacement's driving on the ride home and his ribs were soon aching again from laughing as they lurched down the street like a drunken grasshopper. Jack was amazed she was able to park the car.

At the apartment, after Jack shimmied sideways on his crutches through the door, Replacement dropped the pile of mail on the counter and headed off to take a shower. Jack couldn't wait to take one, too. He hated the doctor's office. *Germ factory.*

He slapped together two rudimentary sandwiches for lunch and hobbled over with his to the computer. Neil Waters had replied to his email: Lennie Jacobsen had been a computer science student, but he'd dropped out in October. Neil had a home address for him in Michigan, which was a nice touch but not very useful at the moment.

Jack looked down at Replacement's notebook, which she'd made fun of when he first suggested it. He flipped it open. She'd continued to read Michelle's emails and had been making notes. She'd circled a file name in red and written *Password?* next to it. Below that, *Tried everything!!!,* with a frowny face.

Jack logged in to the file storage where Replacement had put the contents of the phone and found the file: XPC 15 Interview — Part 1. He double-clicked it, and a password prompt appeared.

He typed COOKIES and a message appeared: *Invalid Password. Type secure password and press enter.*

Jack limped into the bedroom and knocked on the bathroom door. He opened it a crack, and Replacement yelped. He jumped back and slammed the door shut.

"What's the matter?"

"I'm in the shower!"

"I have a quick question."

"Can it wait?"

"You walk in on me all the time."

"It's different! I'm a woman!"

Jack laughed and shook his head. "What makes a password secure?"

"Hold on, I can't hear you!" She shut the water off and, in a few seconds, the door opened a fraction, her body hidden. "What're you talking about?"

"That file you can't open. Did you try cookies?" Jack asked.

"A password doesn't have cookies." She looked at him as if he was stupid.

"No. For the password. Did you try the word 'cookies'?"

"No. Why?"

"Michelle always used that for her password."

"No, she didn't."

"When she was little. It was her super-secret word you had to say." Jack could see Michelle with her hands on her hips and her little chin sticking out, demanding that he say the password before she'd let him go by.

Dripping wet, Replacement yanked opened the door and raced to the computer. She jumped behind the keyboard, gave her bath towel a quick adjustment, and pulled up another program.

"I'll run it through this." She pressed a few keys and the screen flashed.

"What is it?" Jack leaned forward, but the screen was changing so fast he couldn't tell what was going on.

"It's a password cracker. It takes way too long to crack a password if you have no idea what the base password is—you'd need a supercomputer for that. But if you just forgot your password and have some rough idea of what you used, this program tries the different permutations."

"You lost me with your geek-speak."

Flattered, Replacement ignored the taunt. "A secure password uses letters, numbers, capital letters, and symbols. I can put in a base word or words and let the program do all the combinations. There are thousands, and it will try them all."

"How long does that take?"

"Hard to tell. Might take a couple of days."

When he groaned, she said, "It beats never."

Not for the first time, Jack thought he detected a silent *duh*.

"Okay." He got up and made for the bathroom. "I guess we have time." He paused outside the bedroom door. "I'm real impressed. You really are brilliant."

Replacement jumped up and spun around so fast her towel started to fall. Jack couldn't help but look. His mouth fell open, and his eyes widened. Replacement twisted and turned a deep shade of crimson as she tried to wrap herself up.

As Jack quickly tried to turn away, he slipped on some water. His full weight came down on his hurt leg, and if he caught himself it would be with his hurt wrist, so he forced his hand up and landed flat on his stomach and face. The impact knocked the wind right out of him, and he groaned loudly as he rolled over onto his back.

"Oh, no!" Replacement rushed over to him. Her small hands pushed his hair back. "Are you okay?"

He tried to swallow and look just at her eyes, and failed. He could hardly breathe, but he didn't know whether it was because he'd just taken a header or because her skin was so rosy-pearl and flawless and her emerald eyes invited him to lose himself in them. Or possibly because her mouth was only inches away.

"Jack?" Her hands grabbed the sides of his face; he lay there and inhaled her clean, soapy scent. Then his arms circled around her waist and lower back. They stared at each other. Her eyes widened and then softened as his hand glided up to her shoulder. He leaned closer and placed his cheek next to hers. Her heartbeat galloped next to his own, chest to chest.

After a minute, they relaxed into each other, and Jack pressed his face into her neck. Her breath was hot against his ear. He felt her leg slide up, and he tightened his grip to pull her in even closer. She caressed the side of his cheek, and he trembled.

Don't.

The word of caution leapt out from somewhere deep within, from some buried, dark spot, and his newfound desire for her vanished like mist at dawn.

"Fine, I'm fine," he said abruptly. He closed his eyes. "Get dressed."

Jack waited, but her hands still held his face. He softly shook his head. She slid her hands down his cheeks, and he relaxed a little. Then he felt her hands move underneath his arms.

"Let me help you up."

Jack kept his eyes closed as she struggled to lift him. With her help, he managed to stand and lean against the door. She pressed against him as she held him upright, her arms encircling his waist.

He opened his eyes and looked at the ceiling. "I'm okay." His voice sounded odd, and he realized he was holding his breath. He looked down to find Replacement's eyes waiting to search his. Her mouth was open, and her lips glistened.

Jack could feel the heat radiating off her, and he panicked. "I'm fine." He guided her away from him and looked away. "Really."

"Please let me help," Replacement protested.

"Thank you. I'm okay." As softly as he could, he slipped away from her hold and retreated into the safety of the bedroom. Just before the door closed behind him, he caught a glimpse of two very confused emerald eyes.

30

COOKI3$

Jack went to bed early, but sleep wouldn't come. Giving up, he rolled out of bed and hobbled into the living room. Replacement sat at the computer. She didn't turn around but waved him over.

"This is the file." Her voice was a low monotone, and for the first time he heard real fear in her voice. A video was playing on the monitor. Her notebook lay open. *Password = COOKI3$* was scrawled on a page.

The video showed a man's face, shot from above. A leather band encircled his forehead, strapping him down against a bed. It was hard to judge his age, but probably in his thirties. His hair was long, greasy, and unkempt. He had sores on his lips and face.

Drug addict, definitely... maybe a bum.

His eyelids were taped open, while his mouth was gagged.

"Is there audio?"

Replacement cringed but turned up the volume. Moans and muffled cries echoed from the speakers through Jack's small apartment.

Iraq.

Doing a door-to-door, chasing an insurgent, they came into a room with two dead bodies in chairs, their eyelids taped open. The torturers had wanted their victims to see what was being done to them.

Torture? Who tortures a homeless guy? Jack stood upright and forced himself to put weight on his hurt leg. *And why did Michelle have this video?*

The man made a gurgling noise. From somewhere off screen, they heard another voice, but Jack couldn't make out any words. The room darkened even more, then they heard computerized clicks, beeps, and a strange humming sound as the man began to struggle against the straps.

There was a loud crunch, and he screamed in agony.

From off camera, someone responded, but they couldn't make out any words even after Jack turned the volume all the way up.

The man started to thrash again. Though the gag distorted his groans, it was clear he was in terrible pain and trying to say something. Tears poured down his face and sweat matted his hair. He frantically shook his head. A massive sob erupted, which ended in his choking on his own saliva.

"Please." In spite of the gag, the word was clear.

"I can't watch this." Replacement ran to the bedroom.

Jack took the chair, so angry he didn't feel human. He couldn't tell what the person off camera was saying, but he heard all too clearly the next sound: laughter. Someone was laughing as the poor man on the table continued to sob.

Then the crunch of another bone being broken.

The man's muffled voice called out, "Please, God! Please…" Then the video ended.

* * *

In the safety of his own bed, Jack did another body check. His whole body hurt, but his head was exploding. He checked the clock. Eleven ten.

Probably too late to call Dad.

A few years back, Ted Stratton had developed a blood clot. The doctor thought a warmer climate would be beneficial to thin his blood, so Jack's parents moved to Florida. He hadn't been down to visit in a long while. Always another excuse, but man, he missed them right now.

With a groan, he rolled onto his side and reached for the phone, sitting up as he dialed. When he got his father, he apologized for calling so late, but Ted cheerfully shook off his sleep, reminding his son he should call anytime he needed to, no matter the hour.

Just the sound of his father's voice made Jack sit up straighter. He didn't know why. His dad was one of the kindest men he'd ever known. "What's up, Son?"

"Dad, I need some advice."

Jack laid out everything, about Replacement, Collins, and Michelle, as his father listened and asked a few questions to clarify a point here or repeat something there. He agreed completely that the Michelle he knew would never do drugs, and urged Jack to be careful.

At what seemed like an ending point, Jack asked, "What do you think?"

"What I think isn't important. What do *you* think?"

"I have no real proof… Maybe I didn't really know her…" Jack almost whispered the last part.

"Now you're just beating yourself up."

"I pushed them out of my life. I wasn't a good friend."

"Jack, hold up a minute. The truth is, I don't know everything about your mother." Ted paused. "I don't know her favorite movie, or what book she's reading right now. That means I should ask her; it doesn't mean I don't love her. You loved Michelle as a sister. That doesn't mean you could have prevented what happened. Do you love me?"

"You know I do." Jack was trying not to cry. He couldn't remember crying in front of his father. Laura, yes, but never Ted.

"What's my favorite movie?"

Jack babbled, "Sorry," then dissolved into tears. After a moment, he wiped his eyes and put his head in his hands. "Dad, what's wrong with me? I'm turning into a total baby."

"There I have to strongly disagree. You've always kept everything in, Jack, and that's not good. You have to let it out from time to time. You never let it out when you were a little boy, or after you came back from Iraq, and now… now it's coming out whether you like it or not. It's okay."

"It's not okay. I shouldn't… I got it good. I'm just…"

"Jack. I've always been one hundred percent straight with you, right?"

"Yeah."

"I'm no therapist, but the first seven years of your life were pretty horrific. Life after that wasn't always a picnic either. You've had it tougher than most. You tried to bury all that pain like it didn't happen and it doesn't bother you. But that's like trying to bury toxic waste in your backyard. It doesn't work. It will kill you."

"What do you mean? How do I let it out?"

"That stuff happened. You can't bury it. You have to face it so that you can process it."

"How?" Jack whispered, more to himself than to his dad.

"It'll come. Just let it."

"But Dad, I get... I get so angry..."

"Jack, I know you don't want to hear this, but you have to face your demons. Yeah, you got knocked down, but wipe your nose and get up."

Jack nodded, as if Ted was right beside him, looking into his eyes, giving him strength.

"Don't tell Mom, all right?"

"I won't. If I did, she'd come up there and kick your butt for being such a baby."

Jack laughed at the very thought of it. He'd never even heard her yell. Both of them laughed for a couple of minutes, and as Jack's head started hurting less, he realized he was better off calling his dad in the middle of the night than talking to a therapist any day. He blew his nose lustily.

"So, Dad, what's your favorite movie?"

"The Seven Samurai."

"The one where the samurai help out the farmers?"

"Yes. Listen, Jack, if you're going to do what I think you're going to do... please be careful." Ted sounded worried.

"I will. I'm not afraid of a fight, Dad."

"Well, I've known that for a long time. So I guess my advice would be, if you're going to fight, fight to win."

31

FOLLOWING THE BREAD CRUMBS

Early the next morning, Jack watched as Replacement checked her makeup in the hall mirror. Jack hardly recognized her. She'd come back that morning with her hair trimmed and colored much darker brown, almost black. Her business look was sealed with a blue skirt and blouse, lipstick, and eyeliner.

"Where are you going?"

"I'll be back in a few hours. I told you about a computer job I have—well, I used to have it. I do their website, and they need me again. The extra money will help out around here."

Jack was busy deflecting this flurry of news, while taking in the new, possibly improved but certainly transformed Replacement, and was unprepared for her request to use the car.

"*The* car? You mean *my* car?" Jack groaned, but tossed her the keys. "Now I'm trapped."

"I won't be late. Mrs. Stevens is right downstairs. 'Bye." She winked and headed out the door.

Jack flexed his wrist; his arm felt fine. Next, he tested his leg.

Yeah, still hurts like hell.

The bruise on his thigh was fading, but the muscles still throbbed. He forced himself to walk normally into the kitchen. After filling a large cup with coffee, he headed back to the computer. No reason not to work.

He sat down and propped his leg up on a little footstool under the desk. The computer beeped as he logged in to the police database to look for the guy from the video again. He pulled up the mug shots and limited them by gender, race, age, and arrests, but the list was still huge. He took a swig of coffee and forced himself to stop and think.

Too many results. Narrow the field.

He flipped back to the video file and stared at it. "XPC 15 Interview — Part 1. Date Created: December 19."

Michelle died on the twenty-first.

Jack switched over to the Internet and searched for information about "date created" on video files. He found an article that helpfully explained, "Date Created is the date the file was copied. When you copy a file, you create a copy of the file in the new location."

So the nineteenth is when Michelle copied the file to her phone, not when the video was recorded.

He continued to read. "Date Modified is the last time the file was changed or modified. Moving or copying does not affect the Date Modified."

The date recorded by the computer when the file was last modified—probably the date the video was recorded.

He opened the video and pulled up the file properties. The date modified was October 20—one year ago.

Bingo.

He switched back to the mug shots. To narrow results, he'd been searching for recent mug shots. Now he widened his search to include arrest records from over a year ago. Male, white, twenties, meth.

Yes.

Charlie Harding, the man from the video, was on the first page. His age was given as twenty-three.

He looked forty.

Charlie had been arrested a number of times, always for drinking, drugs, or… because it was cold. Being homeless in winter meant you had to get creative. If the shelters were full, there was a real danger of freezing to death, so you might try to get yourself arrested for a warm bed and some food. Trespassing or shoplifting was the usual MO.

Someone had reported Charlie missing in December. Jack frowned. Did it take two months for someone to figure out that he was gone? The person who reported him missing was named Hank Foster. Under "Relationship," the file said, "Sponsor."

Must be AA.

There was an address and number listed for Hank. Jack knew he should call first, but it would be just as easy to swing by, and he preferred that, for surprise value.

He got up, grabbed his jacket, and headed for the door—but then stopped.

No car. Great.

Throwing his jacket down, he went back and reread the missing person report. Hank Foster mentioned "substance abuse issues" on Charlie's report. That much was obvious already from the arrest records.

Jack leaned over, grabbed the phone, and dialed. A man answered.

"Hi, I'm looking for Hank Foster." He smiled. In an interview course, he'd learned that people could hear a smile in your voice, even on the phone.

"You got him. How can I help?"

"My name is Jack Stratton. I'm a police officer with the Darrington County Sheriff's Office and I'm calling about the missing person report that you filed."

"Oh, okay. What do you want to know about her?"

Her? Jack paused.

"Hank, I'd like to swing by and speak with you. Are you still located on Pine Hill?"

"That's right."

"Will you be around…" Jack tried to think if Replacement had said when she'd be back. "This evening?"

"It depends how late. I have an AA meeting at eight o'clock, and it can run late."

"Could I meet you there?"

"It's at the VFW out near Houton's Pond. Do you have any more information about Tiffany?"

Tiffany? Another missing person? One guy files two different missing person reports?

"I'll see you after your meeting. Hank, can you confirm Tiffany's middle name?"

"Tiffany Marie."

Jack thanked him and hung up the phone. First and middle name were enough to reference the case without arousing Hank's suspicion. Tiffany McAllister had gone missing in July, five months prior to Michelle, and Hank had filed the report a few weeks ago.

Looks like he was a little late in reporting her missing, too.

They had already found her body a few days before Hank filed the report and the medical examiner had originally listed her as a Jane Doe. Cause of death: meth overdose, injected. The cleaning crew had found her behind the Imperial Motor Lodge, a popular hangout for prostitutes.

Jack switched programs and ran Tiffany's information. Age: nineteen. Prostitution and drug arrests scrolled up the screen. He printed out the report and then pulled up her picture. She looked younger than nineteen. And ashamed. With her short brown hair and green eyes, she could have passed for Replacement's little sister.

Next, Jack ran Hank Foster. The man had done time for assault and armed robbery fifteen years ago. He had arrests for drugs and pimping at that time, too. Jack continued to type. Assault on girlfriend. Assault on a police officer. Hank had served five years and gotten five years' probation.

Habitual offender. Now he files two missing person reports?

Hoping Replacement would be back in time, Jack printed out Charlie Harding's mug shot and pushed the mouse away. His head pounded and he wanted a drink but knew that was the last thing he needed. With a groan, he grabbed Tiffany's report from the printer, walked over to the couch, and stretched out.

A few minutes later, the papers fell to the floor as Jack fell asleep.

32

GIRL JACKED

IRAQ

J ack's shirt clung to him like a damp towel. He shifted his assault rifle in his hands and continued to scan the crowd.

A lot of people moved by the checkpoint. The families going home chattered back and forth. Apart from the heat, the feeling was upbeat.

Jack turned to Chandler. "Are you hot?"

"Yeah." A cocky grin spread across his big friend's face as he nodded his head. "That's what all the ladies say."

"Shut up."

"You shut up," Chandler shot back. "It's two hundred degrees out. What a stupid question. I'm about to spontaneously combust." He laughed and finished off another bottle of Gatorade.

Jack turned to look at the approaching crowd. Something was wrong. People talked all around, but a strange pocket of silence approached them. He scanned the faces and found the source of the silence. A woman dressed in a black burqa walked with a little girl dressed in the same head-to-toe shroud. He could only see their eyes.

Of course, many women wore burqas, but there was something wrong with this pair. The mother kept the girl at arm's length as they walked.

"Chandler. One o'clock." Jack nodded toward the approaching pair.

Chandler's smile vanished as he watched them approach.

"The mother is freaked." Jack's chin tipped up. "Maybe she's being forced to wear a vest and is trying to keep the little girl out of the way."

"Can we separate them?" Chandler walked toward the edge of the crowd. "I can get the girl."

"No. You'll be too close."

Chandler shook his head and kept moving.

Jack moved forward and to the right.

The crowd shied away from the pair, and a pocket formed around mother and daughter. Judging by her height, the girl was five or six years old. Her rich brown eyes gleamed. She looked happy; she had no idea she was in danger. The mother's eyes darted all over, but she never looked directly at Jack.

Out of the corner of his eye, Jack saw Chandler make his move. He wanted to scream at him to stop, but he knew there was no stopping his friend. Chandler took two huge strides, scooped the little girl up in his arms, and headed back to the checkpoint.

"Stop!" Jack commanded the mother in both Arabic and English. "Hands up!"

The mother watched Chandler carry her daughter away before turning to look at Jack. He saw her eyes change from fear to relief—and then from relief to hate.

"Hands up!" he shouted again as the crowd scrambled for safety. With his finger on the trigger, Jack hesitated. He'd never shot a woman before.

She raised her arms up slowly.

Then Jack realized his mistake.

He saw the large hands of a man.

It wasn't a mother worried for her daughter. It was a man worried for his own safety, and scared because it was the little girl who'd been forced to wear the suicide vest.

"Chandler!" Jack yelled.

Chandler looked over, the little girl cradled in his big arms. His eyes met Jack's for a second before the white flash.

The explosion knocked Jack to his knees. He couldn't breathe. He couldn't see clearly, and his ears rang. His fingers clawed the ground in front of him. The hard, dry ground turned soft...

He opened his eyes and stared down at gray carpet with black flecks. He gazed at the pattern; he was sure he'd seen it before but couldn't place where.

The funeral home.

He was at the funeral home where they'd held Michelle's service. Chandler stood at the rear, near an open coffin. He wore his dress uniform, and tears rolled down his face. His arm was around Michelle's shoulder. She wore her long hair pulled back, and she had on a simple charcoal dress. She glanced at Jack, and she was crying, too.

Jack staggered forward. They were both gazing into a coffin. It was purple and white with pink flowers.

Aunt Haddie? No...

It felt as though he was walking through knee-deep mud as he forced himself to keep moving forward. Chandler glared back at him, and Michelle wept.

"My babies!"

The cry behind him caused him to turn around.

Aunt Haddie, tiny and frail, stood in the doorway of the funeral home.

"My babies," she cried again as she held her hands out, walking toward him. "All of my babies are gone."

Jack turned back around and raced to the coffin. Replacement's body lay inside. Her emerald-green eyes were gray and lifeless. Her mouth was frozen in a twisted scream. Her eyes had been taped open.

"Alice, no! *Alice!*"

* * *

Replacement was shaking him. She said something, but he couldn't hear clearly. His trembling hands gripped the back of his head. He gasped for air.

Replacement held his shoulders at arm's length. "Jack? It's just a dream. You were dreaming."

Jack grabbed her and pulled her close, crushing her to his chest. It was a long moment before his breathing quieted, and he straightened his arms and looked at her.

"You're okay," Jack muttered. "It was just a dream." He stood up, swaying like a drunken sailor.

Replacement looked up at him. "I walked in and you were… yelling my name."

He shuffled into the kitchen and looked at the clock. Eight fifteen. "I need my car." He rubbed his eyes.

"What? Why? I was going to borrow it tomorrow, too."

"That's okay. I'm meeting a guy tonight. Hey, how's the website job going?" He tried to smile.

"Good. They need some updates." Replacement followed him into the kitchen. "Nothing big. Who are you meeting with?"

"Guy's name is Hank Foster. The guy on the video was Charlie Harding, and Hank reported him missing."

"Good work. Are you sure you're okay?"

"I'm fine. The problem is that Hank Foster also reported a girl named Tiffany McAllister missing five months ago."

"He reported both of them missing? And you're sure you have the guy from the video?"

"Yeah, it's him. But I need to ask Hank about Tiffany first. She showed up dead. Then I'll ask about Charlie. Keys?"

She handed him the keys, and he grabbed his jacket.

"What about your crutches?"

"I need to strengthen the leg," he called back.

Replacement followed him out the door and hurried to catch up to him.

"You're not coming," Jack said. "Go get something to eat."

"What? No. I'll drive."

"No." Jack stopped and turned to her. "You can't come. Don't even try."

"I can help." She raised herself up on her toes.

"No. Listen. It's not happening." Jack shut his eyes, and the images from his dream flashed into view. "Seriously, no." Jack tried to soften his voice, but it still came out cold and angry.

She didn't say anything, just turned and went back into the apartment.

* * *

Jack pulled up in front of the small VFW hall, where twenty to thirty cars were in the parking lot. He headed for the main door and scanned the faces of the people outside and on the porch, smoking cigarettes. Foster's last mug shot was ten years old, and it was dark out, but Foster didn't appear to be among the smokers, who all gave him covert glances as he passed.

Jack opened the door to a medium-size room with folding chairs set up in neat rows. Less than a quarter of them were occupied. *Your typical AA meeting.* He picked a half-empty row and sat down.

A man at the front was speaking about how he stayed sober. Jack didn't pay too much attention to him at first. He'd spotted a man seated three rows from the front, next to a column, and he was pretty sure he was looking at Hank Foster.

"How many people right now want a drink?" the man at the front said. Hands shot up all over the room, and the man speaking raised his own hand. "I do, too. The problem is, I won't stop. I'll just keep going. I drink because I'm a drunk."

The man had everyone's attention now, including Jack's. "There's only one way I've stayed sober. How? Myself? Get real. That self-righteous crap doesn't keep you sober. I know what power is, and it ain't me; it's God, pure and simple. He keeps me on track one day at a time, moment by moment. But *He* expects you to step up—twelve steps exactly. Don't drink, work the program, and ask for help. That's how I've stayed sober for fifteen years."

Jack shifted in his seat. If he'd been honest, he would have raised his hand when the guy asked who wanted a drink.

After the man finished speaking, there was a small round of applause, and an older man rose and moved to the podium. "Ten-minute break. Smoke 'em if you got 'em."

While people filed out, Jack's eyes followed Foster, who rose and shook a woman's hand. After a few minutes, Foster headed for the back door, and Jack followed him onto the big porch where the smokers congregated.

"Hank?"

Foster turned. He was in his forties, and there'd been some rough miles in there. His long hair, pulled back into a ponytail, was predominantly gray, but black streaks still ran through it. A full beard and mustache partly covered his pockmarked face. The well-worn leather jacket seemed too large for his slim frame.

He narrowed his eyes. "You the cop who called?"

Jack got the feeling Hank wanted to talk alone, and saying "cop" loudly cleared the porch, leaving the two of them alone.

"Jack Stratton." They shook hands.

"What did you find out about Tiffany?"

"You're aware that she's dead?"

"Yeah. Who do you think paid for the funeral? You got anything new?" Hank took a step forward.

"I'm sorry to say, no. I was calling about Charlie Harding when you brought up Tiffany. Interesting you filed two missing person reports. One of them is dead and I'm concerned for the safety of the other."

"Me too."

They stared at each other for a moment, then Hank relaxed.

"So you still have nothing," Hank said. "Jeez."

"How did you know Tiffany?" Jack asked.

"Man. I try to do the right thing and *I* get looked at?" Hank flicked his cigarette off the porch.

"If you want to do the right thing, just answer a couple of questions."

"Fine."

"How did you know Tiffany?" Jack asked again.

"I was her sponsor."

"I thought AA didn't allow opposite-sex sponsors."

Hank peered at Jack. "Are you in the program?"

"Was. You sponsored Tiffany?"

"Not officially, but she was the same age as my daughter. I thought I could help."

"What happened?" Jack relaxed his guard a little but resisted the urge to lean against the railing.

"She missed a meeting. I called her—nothing. She missed more. I freaked. I kept going to the police, but they don't care about whores, even if they're kids. I filed the report, and they called a couple of days later and said she was already dead."

"She OD'd injecting meth."

Hank jumped up so fast that Jack's hand instinctively went out in front of him. "That's a lie."

"Easy."

"You don't give a—"

"Hey, I'm the cop who's here right now looking into this, so how about you just answer my questions?" *Okay, not officially, but…* "First, why do you think it's a lie?"

Hank paused. "She didn't do meth."

"She did drugs?"

"Not meth."

"Could it have been the first time?"

"Not meth."

Jack was getting frustrated. "She did drugs and was a prostitute. Why would she not do meth?"

"She said she saw someone go nuts and start ripping at their skin. It freaked her out. I know it sounds weird, but she was different. And she never shot up. She never would. She hated needles."

"Enough to never do meth?" Jack shook his head. "Even if she was desperate?"

"Even if she was in total withdrawal. I went through that with her. It was bad. Real bad. She didn't do needles. I know people who are so freaked they don't fly. They won't get on a plane for any reason. She was like that with needles."

"So what do you think happened?"

"I don't know. I've gone over it in my head. She was trying real hard. She was clean. No drugs and no booze."

He's not telling me everything. "Hank, look, I'm trying to find out what happened. I'm trying to help. Don't hold out on me." Jack took a step forward.

Hank looked up at the night sky. "She was having money issues. I offered her what I could, but it wasn't much. She couldn't ask her parents. It might have been she ran down for a quick trick."

Down to the Imperial. The smokers were pounding up the stairs now to get back into the warm meeting room, again giving Jack and Hank a once-over. They waited until the stampede passed.

"Okay. What can you tell me about Charlie Harding?"

"Not much."

"Were you his sponsor?" Jack asked.

"Yeah. Not for long. He'd had it hard but he was a good kid. Him, there wasn't a drug he wouldn't take."

"What happened?"

"Just disappeared. He was living at the shelter, so the stinking pigs—sorry, the police—just assumed he moved on. I haven't heard from him since. Is he dead?" Hank asked.

The question took Jack by surprise. Best to be honest, but he didn't have to tell Hank how close to death Charlie had looked in that video. "I don't know. Your report is the last official document in the file. When were you last in touch with him?"

"Maybe a few weeks before Halloween. He was happy. He'd just gotten a job, a crappy gig washing dishes, but it was work."

"What do you think happened?"

Hank shrugged. "No idea, but I sure hope he's not dead."

It doesn't look good, Hank.

Jack held out the mug shot. "This him?"

Hank held the picture and didn't say anything but he nodded morosely.

"Do you know if he'd ever been to White Rocks Eastern University?"

"Yeah, I took him there."

"For what purpose?"

"I do this Scared Straight thing every year. You know, scare the crap out of rich kids. Tell them how drugs screwed up my life."

"Charlie went with you? When did you go?"

"When school first started. September? The professor uses us to kick off the class. I know it's a dog and pony show, but it's a chance to warn them." Hank shrugged.

"You know the professor's name?"

"Dr. Franklin."

Yeah, I thought so. "Did Tiffany ever talk to the class?"

"No."

"So she never went with you?"

"No."

"Did either Charlie or Tiffany ever say anything about going there again?"

Foster shook his head as he lit another cigarette. He looked as tired and drained as Jack felt. It was time to end the interview, even if he didn't have all the answers he needed.

"Okay then, Hank. Thank you for your time."

Jack nodded. Hank did the same but didn't extend a hand, so neither did Jack.

As Jack walked away, Hank called to him. "Hey, I know Tiffany didn't do meth, no way. I'm telling you, that girl got jacked."

33

SPEED KILLS

Jack groaned and rubbed the back of his neck. Six o'clock, and Replacement still wasn't back. He'd spent three days going back and forth over all his notes and the police reports. He started a new notebook and copied everything over to organize it; created a timeline, starting with Charlie Harding in September at the college. His only deduction so far was that sitting at a desk all day and night doesn't exactly count as physical rehab. His leg was still killing him, though he wouldn't admit that to the doctor.

He pulled his sweatshirt on and headed out for a walk. He needed to think and build up his strength. He looked down the stairs with dread. The deep muscles in his thigh still throbbed. The hardest part of going down the steps was trying to put all his weight on one leg. When he finally made it out the front door, it wasn't that cold. He'd walk down to Finnegan's and then up toward the library and back. His usual two-mile lap.

He picked up the pace as his thoughts turned to Replacement. She was "borrowing" the car every day to get to her job. Not having his car was turning out to be a major logistical problem. He was considering picking up a used car for her.

Great, now we need another car and *a new place.*

A car horn sounded behind him, and Mrs. Sawyer pulled up alongside him. The boat of a car she drove made her appear even smaller than she already was.

Over the half-open window, her old eyes twinkled. She greeted Jack and asked him if he liked the flowers she sent when he was in the hospital.

"I loved them. Thank you so much."

As he got close to the car, she pulled him halfway in the window and gave him a big hug.

"You'll have to stop by. I made cherries jubilee that will put you into sugar shock." She patted his cheek and winked.

I have to visit Aunt Haddie tomorrow.

"I will. Has everything been nice and quiet?"

"Not a peep around the house," she proclaimed and squeezed his hand. "All thanks to you."

Nice to know he could always count on Mrs. Sawyer to make him feel he was useful as a cop. He cringed as she drove in the wrong lane for fifty feet before crossing back into her lane.

As he headed back into town, he realized it was Tuesday. He yearned for a real work schedule. His frustration caused his body to tense, and he stumbled on a crack in the sidewalk. He uncurled his clenched fists and shook his hands.

He needed some way to ask questions at the college. Franklin's name was coming up too often. Maybe he could call Hahn and say he was organizing something for Haddie, a remembrance book from Michelle's friends… *Yeah, that should work. And while I'm out there, I'll look up Franklin.*

As Jack looked left to cross the street, he noticed—for the second time—a guy in an oversize blue parka. The first time was two miles back, when he first came out of the apartment.

Don't rush. Left. Right. Left, right. Swing your arms normally. Look around a little.

He kept walking straight for a while, straining to hear anything behind him, then took a left down a little side street. A couple of people walked down the sidewalk; a few cars were parked along the curb. He jumped into the shadow of a doorway and pressed his back against the wall.

Wait. Listen.

He tried to drown out the sounds of cars, people talking, shop doors opening and closing.

Footsteps. Running.

The guy in the parka ran past him. His face was gaunt and marked with sores. *Another addict.*

He was about an inch taller than Jack, and judging by his thin face, Jack figured he weighed under 180.

Jack stepped out from the doorway. "Looking for me?"

As the man spun around, Jack could see a pair of glazed eyes that gave away a world of information.

Wired. Scared. Mad. Crazy. Great time to leave your gun at home.

His pupils were gone, and there was a creepy grin on his face. He took three steps toward Jack and lunged.

Jack sprang forward; his hand came down to block, and he saw a knife headed for his gut. He scooped it to the side, but as he went to grab the guy's wrist, he realized something was wrong. The thumb is the weakest part of the grip, but as Jack twisted the addict's hand, it wouldn't open.

The knife is duct-taped to his hand.

Jack pushed forward and stepped to the left, taking himself out of the knife's path, but the motion placed too much weight on his injured leg. Pain shot up his thigh, and his scream of agony turned into a guttural growl. His leg shook and went limp.

Jack fell backward and pulled the junkie with him as he fell. He held on to the guy's knife hand while they crashed into a parked car and landed on the sidewalk.

He twisted the guy's wrist fast and hard. Something snapped.

The man screamed, but so did Jack as the man's knee landed right on his injured thigh. Jack's hand reflexively opened, and the guy pulled his injured arm away. With his other hand, the junkie punched Jack in the face. A quick punch, but it caught Jack across the chin with plenty of power behind it. While Jack tried to clear his vision and spit the blood out of his mouth, the junkie stumbled backward.

Jack rolled onto his side and pushed himself up, but his thigh muscles contracted, and he fell right back down.

The junkie turned and ran.

Jack howled in frustration. He'd never be able to catch the guy. As he fumbled for his phone, a small crowd rushed toward him, asking if he was okay and if he needed help.

Jack punched in a number he could dial in his sleep.

"Darrington Police," the dispatcher answered.

"Bev, this is Jack. A guy tried to knife me. Need pursuit."

"Where?"

"He's running south down Oak. Male suspect about six feet, one eighty, dark-blue parka, blue jeans and boots. He has a knife taped to his broken wrist."

"Broken wrist? So he has a cast on his arm?" she asked as she repeated his information over the radio.

"No, but his wrist is broken."

"How do you know?"

"I broke it."

Jack stretched his leg to try to get the circulation flowing. He winced and his eyes narrowed.

Finally, a live suspect.

34

LOOSE ENDS

"I'll see you later. I won't be home until late," Replacement called on her way out of the apartment. Jack heard her pick up the car keys from the hall table and then open and close the front door.

"'Bye." Jack stared at the door. A whiff of her perfume wafted toward him. Another thing to add to the list of mysteries recently, and at the top of the list was her work, which she kept saying was no big deal but seemed to require her presence every day for many hours, always wearing makeup and perfume…

Something's up.

He shook himself out of his thoughts and moved back to the computer. He certainly didn't mind having the apartment to himself again, and he'd almost gotten used to being without a car. After a swig of coffee, he got back to work. His attacker had vanished. They had an APB out in all the surrounding towns, but Bennie was a ghost.

Jack had picked the man's mug shot out in under thirty minutes: Bennie Mayer, from Rockland. He had a long list of priors: B&E, assault, marijuana, cocaine, and meth. Bennie also did time off and on.

Jack stared out the window, aggravated. He wanted to be out looking for Bennie the Goon right now, but on top of everything else, his injuries were screaming again after their wrestling match.

The guy was watching my apartment. Waiting for me. It wasn't random.

Jack saw the man's face, saw his eyes.

I don't think he started out trying to kill me. He just wanted to follow me. When I surprised him, he panicked. He was scared.

Jack had seen it before. He'd never met anyone who killed and just tossed it off, all in a day's work. Most people were freaked out at taking another person's life; very few were just plain evil. Most were scared, and their fear turned into anger or need or hatred, and that's when they killed.

This guy had looked like that, like he could have run, but he chose to kill instead. It might have been the drugs, but Jack saw him make the decision.

Jack pulled up a list of hospitals in the surrounding area and groaned. It was going to be a long day.

* * *

He had spent hours calling every nearby hospital. When that turned up nothing, he called every regional clinic. Finally, he ran through the alphabet and called doctors' offices. No one had walked in with a broken wrist. Nothing.

Switch gears. I'm spinning my tires. He was reporting back to work the next day and he wanted to show he hadn't just been wasting his time off.

Jack flipped to Tiffany's autopsy report. No sexual assault. Meth OD. As expected, a ton of medical jargon. Jack kept hitting the page-down key.

The autopsy photos were all high-resolution and took forever to load. They had photographed the entire body, but Jack wanted to see a close-up of her face. The pages continued to load until that face filled the monitor. Jack shut his eyes for a second. He'd seen death many times, but it still made him feel surreal. And angry.

Maybe all I can do for her is find the monster that did this.

He scanned around her eyes, looking for something. There was slight bruising around the right eye. And there it was. He clicked and zoomed in. It was faint, very faint, but clear. A small rectangular patch on her cheek.

Her eyes had been taped open.

The medical examiner can find out a lot more, but it's there. Just like Charlie Harding.

Jack leaned back in his chair and made a new list.

1. *The computer lab has Michelle's phone with the video of a guy getting tortured. I have proof it's related to Tiffany's death. They can get a warrant with that.*
2. *Tomorrow, lay it all out to Joe face-to-face.*
3. *Once they get the video, I can fill in the details of who and what and lead them to Tiffany.*
4. *They'll have to reexamine Michelle's autopsy photos for tape around her eyes.*

He got up and stretched. His leg hurt from sitting for so long. *I should tell Joe right now.*

He dialed Joe Davenport's cell phone and voice mail picked up. It was dinnertime; he could try again later. He looked over his notes again and saw only loose ends. But one of those ends hadn't even been tried yet—Western Technical University. Still afternoon out in California.

After Jack explained who he was to three separate people, and was put on hold each time, an hour had passed and he hadn't even asked a question yet.

"Mr. Wellington's office, how can we help?" The woman had an irritating singsong voice.

"How can you help? Miss, I have been on hold for over an hour. I'm calling concerning my sister Michelle Carter. She supposedly transferred to your college but then... she was killed." Jack heard the woman gasp. Maybe he had her attention now. "Can you please answer a few questions about her transfer?"

"I'll certainly do whatever I can to help, sir."

"Michelle Carter..."

"I'm looking at her transfer now, sir."

"Did she register for classes?"

"Yes. She signed up for a full course load."

"Did she sign up for housing?"

"No."

"Meal tickets?"

"No."

"Library access?"

"No."

"Anything besides the classes?"

"Not that I can see."

"How long does it take to get approved for classes?"

"Instantly."

Jack held the phone away from his head. "Really? You can get accepted to a college instantly?"

"Well, we're a sister college and she was just transferring credits. She can take any classes here that she wants."

"So you're saying she just signed up for classes? She didn't really transfer in?"

"We're a sister college, so, technically, yes."

Technically, I might have to strangle you.

"When did she apply?"

"December twentieth."

"And where does it say that?"

There was a pause. "It's the date that's written on the form."

"Lady…" Jack's frustration was getting the better of him. "Is there a way you can tell when they electronically submitted the form?"

"Hold, please."

"No, don't—"

Jack waited on hold for another fifteen minutes.

What's it… four forty-two on the West Coast? I need this information today.

By the time the hold music stopped, he didn't know whether he'd be able to speak without swearing.

"Hey. You still there?" It was now a young man on the other end of the line.

"I'm on hold for…" *Oh, great… I don't have her name.*

"Are you the guy looking for the date on the form?"

"Yes."

"I'm from the computer help desk. How can I help?"

"Can you get a date… can you please tell me the date that Michelle Carter signed up for those classes? Electronically. Not the date written on the form."

"Sure, dude. Hold on."

Jack heard typing in the background.

"The time stamp on the doc is December twentieth at ten-oh-three p.m."

"Are you sure?"

"Yeah. The computer records it. I'm looking right at the electronic time stamp."

She could have signed up herself while she was still at the school. Dead end…

Wait.

"You're talking Pacific Standard Time. Eastern would make it December twenty-first, one-oh-three a.m. here?"

"Yeah."

"I'll need a copy of that report."

35

THE PIT

Early the following morning, Jack walked through the doors of the police station with a large folder in his hands. Even though his first shift back wasn't until later that afternoon, he had Replacement drop him off early. He had stayed up half the night getting everything prepared to give to Collins. As he forced his leg to take him steadily down the corridor, other police officers came over and patted him on the back or shook his hand. He hated the attention.

He was just about to break free of the latest welcoming committee when he heard a woman call his name, and turned just in time to brace himself as Kendra crashed into him, wrapped her arms around his waist, and pressed her cheek against his.

After a couple of seconds, he joked, "This is getting awkward."

She stepped back, still beaming. "Everyone was worried about you. Did you get my flowers?"

"I did." *I think.* "Thank you." He nodded down the hallway. "I have to go check in."

"Welcome back." Kendra started to open her arms and move in again, but caught herself. She gave him a quick shot in the arm instead.

On to Sheriff Collins's office. A new police secretary looked up at him and shook her head. "Sheriff Collins is away at a conference."

He hadn't seen this coming. *It never goes the way you plan.* "I had no idea he'd be gone," he groused.

She smiled sarcastically. "I wasn't aware you were on the list of people to be informed of his scheduling."

Jack exhaled and pressed his lips together. "Is Judy around?"

"I'm covering for her while she and Sheriff Collins are away at the National Sheriffs' Association Conference in Charlotte." She swiveled back to her keyboard.

"When will he be back?"

"It's a four-day conference; he'll be back on Monday. He can be reached if it's an emergency." Her look was a dare: *Go ahead, make my day.*

"Do you know when Joe Davenport will be in?"

She went back to typing. "Nine a.m. When he gets back from vacation."

"What?" Jack snapped.

"Detective Davenport is on a fishing trip in Canada." She continued to type, striking the keys with more force now. "If you want a copy of the schedule, it's posted near the water cooler."

"When will he be back?"

The secretary stopped typing and swiveled back to glare at him. "It's posted on the schedule"—she leaned forward and read his badge—"Officer Stratton. Detective Davenport will return on Saturday. If you—" She stopped and her eyes went wide. "Jack Stratton?"

Jack nodded.

"You should have said something. I'm so sorry. How are you?"

Said something? Like, hey, I'm the guy who got hit by the car. Can you be nice and answer a simple question for me?

"Much better, thank you. I just need to speak to Collins or to Joe as soon as possible."

The woman's hands went up and out as she now spewed forth useless information. "Sheriff Collins checks his messages between meetings, or you can text 911 if it's an emergency. Undersheriff Morrison is available, and Detective Flynn is covering for Detective Davenport. Can they help?"

Jack tapped the folder against the edge of the desk. *Collins doesn't like Morrison so much. I can't give it to Flynn after what happened, and Joe won't be back for two days. I'm screwed.*

He shook his head, thanked her, and walked away. He tried Davenport and didn't have to wait; the voice mail picked right up.

Jack hung up and tried Sheriff Collins. His voice mail clicked on right away, too. "Sheriff Ethan Collins. I'll be in and out of conferences all day. If this is an emergency, text me and I'll call you back immediately. If not, Undersheriff Morrison is covering and can be reached…"

Jack debated for a second and then hung up.

He called Davenport again and left him a message that he wanted to talk about his sister's case.

He'd be better off at home with his leg in a sling.

* * *

Later that afternoon, Jack stood in the police parking lot again. He was still on the night shift, four to midnight.

At least getting hit by the car got me off traffic duty.

Jack's anger and frustration vanished for a moment when he saw that the Charger was all his. He slid behind the wheel, and the engine purred as if it was glad to see him again.

Since he had the freedom to patrol where he wanted, within boundaries, he let those boundaries bring him out of town and close to White Rocks.

He drummed the steering wheel as he waited to reach the back roads and open the Charger up. He needed to clear his head. He needed speed.

"Ten-ten in progress at WRE," the dispatcher's voice said over the radio.

Perfect. Jack heard the location and jumped for the radio.

"This is car sixty-eight. I'm north on Piedmont crossing Bridge Street."

"Ten-four, car sixty-eight. The location is Two Jefferson Avenue."

Sweet. Right in the pocket. The address was for The Pit, a bar in the basement of an old converted administration building at White Rocks. Jack hit the lights and sirens and punched it.

He settled back in his seat as adrenaline flowed along with the gas. He kept his foot down, and the Charger roared its approval.

Two campus police cars were parked outside The Pit, and a large crowd was forming outside, where a sort of temporary triage had been set up at a picnic table. A couple of guys held bloody towels to their heads, and about twenty kids were gathered around them, shouting and talking.

He recognized the two campus cops on the scene. Chad Tucker was busy trying to hold back Milton Anderson, off to the side. Milt's nose was bloody, and he also held a towel to his face.

"Chad, Milt, what's going on?"

"Inside." Chad motioned with his head. "We got two guys with cuts and another one who may never have kids, if you know what I mean." He adjusted himself.

Chad led the way into the building.

"What happened to you, Milt?" The tall, thin man was trying to hold his head back to stop the bleeding from his nose.

"That psycho down there hit me in the face when I went to break up the fight." The towel muffled his voice.

Jack could only assume things would become clearer once he was at the scene. He motioned to them to follow him down the stairs, but Milt declined to join them.

"Careful, Jack. She doesn't look tough, but she's dangerous," Chad said quietly.

"She?"

"You'll see."

The door was ajar, and Jack pushed it open cautiously. The Pit was never much on looks, but you could tell a good fight had taken place. Tables were overturned, and in one corner, glass littered the floor.

"A girl did this?"

"Shh." Chad's eyes went wide, and he pointed as he moved behind Jack.

I'm so glad they don't give these guys guns.

Jack now saw a girl sitting at the end of the bar, facing away from them. Around five feet tall, a hundred pounds soaking wet, she looked about as dangerous as a puppy.

"Excuse me, miss?" Jack held his hands out, palms up.

The girl swung around on the stool. Jack gasped and stepped back on Chad's foot.

"Yes, sir?" Replacement said.

Jack just stood there with his mouth open.

Jack could tell that Replacement was trying to convey something to him with her expression, but his brain was struggling to respond. His courses at the academy had never covered anything remotely like this situation.

"Ah… Chad, I've got this. Go check on Milton," Jack ordered without turning around.

"You sure?"

Jack turned to glare at Chad, who was already almost out the door.

"Don't say anything," Replacement whispered. "I'm undercover."

"What are you talking about?" Jack stammered, just as Chad came back with Milton.

"How come she's not in cuffs?" Milton demanded. Poor guy's voice sounded like his nose was completely blocked up.

"Once I ascertain… what happened to this poor girl—"

"Poor girl?" Milton said. "I think she broke my nose."

Replacement let out a wail and covered her face, sobbing. "I'm sorry. I thought you were one of them… one of the men who attacked me," she bawled.

"Attacked you?" Replacement was hamming it up, but *something* had happened to her.

"Ken put something in my drink. Him and his friends." There was genuine anger and disgust on her face.

She'd never make that up about someone to get out of a bad situation.

"Bring them in, and keep them quiet," Jack ordered Milton and Chad. "I'm speaking with the girl first." He took Replacement by the arm and led her across the large dance floor into a back room.

"What the hell are you doing?" he whispered.

"I told you, I'm undercover."

"Well, your cover is blown. What happened?"

"It's not blown." She crossed her arms and huffed. "They don't know who I am."

Yeah, join the club. "Talk. You got a lot of explaining to do."

"Okay, I went to go talk to this guy, Ken, and he put something in my drink. It freaked me out."

"How do you know? Did you drink it?"

"I saw him do it, *and* he told me." She stamped her foot.

"What do you mean he told you?"

"We were over in that corner. I came back from the bathroom, and I saw Ken put something in my drink, and when I confronted him, he had the nerve to say, 'I *just* put in a little something to help you relax.' Then he put his hand on my thigh. *High* up on my thigh." Her hands turned into fists. "So I punched him in the face. Then his friends came up and tried to grab me, and I had the glass in my hand, so I whacked one guy with it."

Replacement acted it out. "The guy behind me had both my arms, and he pushed me into the table, and there was a beer bottle on it, so I got one hand free and I grabbed it and hit him, like this." She mimed smashing a guy in the head with the bottle. Relishing it all over again. "It didn't break, but he sure did scream."

Jack cringed. "What happened to Milton?"

"Who?"

"The campus police officer whose nose you probably broke."

"It's his fault! He snuck up behind me, grabbed me. He didn't say he was a cop." She shrugged.

"Replacement—"

"Alexis," she corrected him with a deadly serious look.

"*What?*"

"That's me. My undercover name. Alexis Holmes."

"Will you forget about that for now? You're not undercover!"

Jack pulled her by the arm back into the bar area and sat her at a table as far away as possible from the trio of miscreants Chad and Milton had assembled for him to question.

"Please. *Alexis.* Stay here. Do not move. Do not talk to these people or engage with them in any way, or you will jeopardize my ability to help you. Do you understand, *Alexis?*"

Alexis smiled demurely and batted her eyes. *Remind me never to get a puppy.*

He motioned for one of the guys. A tall man with a bloody towel pressed to his head, stepped forward. Jack led him into the back room. His face was hard as he shoved the man into a chair.

"ID?" Jack waited for the man to hand it to him.

Dillon Cole, 21.

"Were you the guy who grabbed her from behind or the guy who came at her from the front?" Jack took out his notepad.

"What? She punched Ken in the face."

"So what did you do?"

"It was more like a slap. I didn't mean to hit her."

"You hit her?" Jack fought to stay professional.

"No, I… She punched Ken and I tried to grab her… It was an accident."

"Listen, Dillon. What we have here is an underage girl who says you were part of a group of guys who tried to drug her."

Dillon's eyes went wide and his mouth flopped open. "I didn't know she was underage, and I had no idea Ken was going to do something like that. Honest."

"Will you empty your pockets for me, please?"

He stood up and turned out his pockets. "I don't got nothing."

"Did you see any of the other guys with drugs?"

Dillon nodded. "Ken said he got some Ecstasy or something to impress Alexis. She asked me if I had some drugs, but I don't do drugs. I don't even know where to get—"

Jack turned and called, "Chad?"

A disheveled head appeared.

"Stick this guy in the corner and send the next one in."

Another student walked in and slumped forward in the chair. Paul Denning, 22. Jack could see the bump on his head even through the towel.

It might have been better for him if the bottle had broken and he didn't get clubbed.

Paul's story matched the other loser's. He had run over and tried to grab Replacement, and she'd decked him with a bottle. Jack shook his head, pointed to the door, and waited for the final kid.

After a couple of minutes, Chad and Milton appeared, supporting and helping a guy in obvious pain.

"Sit him down," Jack ordered. "Everyone else, clear out."

Jack looked at the license.

Ken Fenton, 21.

"What's your version of the events, Ken?" he asked smoothly, keeping himself in check.

"I met that crazy bi—" Ken stopped as soon as he saw the look on Jack's face. "I was having a drink with Alexis, and she, um, sort of freaked out."

"Was this before or after you put drugs in her drink?" Jack's voice was as cold as his darkening eyes.

"What? I— I don't know—"

Jack put his face inches away from Ken's and didn't move, didn't say a word, just smoldered.

"It was Ecstasy," Ken said quietly. "I asked her. I mean, I told her." He leaned away from Jack.

"You asked her?"

"I swear. I did. I told her it was in there. She wanted it."

"*What* did you say? You're saying she *wanted* you to drug her?" Jack grabbed the arms of the chair and shook it hard. Ken's face contorted in pain.

"Crystal," he whined. "She kept asking for meth. I didn't know where to get any, but she was real insistent. I asked around, and this guy had some Ecstasy. I wanted to impress her. Before she went to the bathroom, she asked me if I could find some drugs. I just wanted to surprise her, so I put it in her drink. She must have seen me do it and misunderstood. I just wanted her to have fun and relax." Ken was on the verge of breaking down now.

Jack just glowered. "Who sold you the Ecstasy?"

"I don't really know him. I've seen him around campus. I think his name is Lennie."

"Lennie Jacobsen?"

Ken shrugged.

"When did you see him before?"

"Just around the school. He was in one of my computer classes. He's a little weird."

"What do you mean weird?"

"He's real goth and has long black hair."

"Can you point him out to me?" Jack gestured toward the door.

"Yeah, but I'm pretty sure he's gone. When I was outside and heard everyone start moaning that the cops were here, I saw him hop in a car and take off."

"What did the car look like?"

"Um, silver."

"Do you know what kind of car it was?"

"No, no clue."

"What was he wearing?"

"Black. A hooded sweatshirt, I think, and black jeans." Ken shifted in the chair.

"When did you get hit in the groin?" Jack tried to think of how to control this.

"After she hit Paul with the bottle."

"Did you grab her?"

He shook his head but didn't look at Jack.

"Did you grab her?" Jack repeated.

"Yeah, but…"

"Go sit back there in the corner," Jack ordered.

Jack followed him out, waved Replacement over, and nodded toward the back room. He set her down in the same chair that Dumb, Dumber, and Dumbest had occupied.

"Listen to me, okay?" Jack hoped his tone conveyed the gravity of the situation. "Ken in there said you asked him to score meth for you. True or not true?"

She gave him a *duh* look. "I'm trying to find out how Michelle got meth in her system. I figure someone must have slipped it to her. If I can find out who—"

"So that's true."

"Yes, but—"

Jack held up a hand. "Listen. If I take him in, it will come out that you asked him and the other boys for drugs, and it's going to turn into a he said, she said. And your whole"—*what to call it?*—"impersonation thing is going to come out."

And I'll have to waste time on this when I have a solid lead to hunt down.

"But—"

"Do you really want me to arrest him?"

She scrunched up her face. "I guess not, if it blows my cover. And I doubt he'll ever do it again." She grinned.

"Your cover? Get that smile off your face. You beat the snot out of three guys and broke a security guard's nose. I'm still trying to figure out how not to arrest *you*."

As Jack walked her back to where the three students and two campus policemen were waiting, he whispered, "Don't say anything. But if you can, cry." She immediately started to wail. "A little. Cry a little."

Jack sat Replacement at a table in the middle of the room, then motioned for Milt and Chad to bring the boys over.

"Milt, Chad, I'm going to try to contain this for your sakes."

"Ours?" They both looked at each other.

"Right now I have an underage girl in *your* college bar accusing one of your students of providing her with illegal drugs, and she's alleging that you manhandled her and didn't disclose you were law enforcement." He raised an eyebrow at Milt, who looked away, muttering.

"But if it was all just a misunderstanding and no illegal drugs are visible"—he glanced around the room—"then I'd be fine considering this just a mix-up. Unless, of course, you want me to file a report that she"—he pointed to Replacement, who was still working on her Oscar for best crying scene—"gave you a bloody nose." He glanced at the boys. "And beat up the three of you. In that case, I'd have to close the bar down indefinitely, and then we would have to go through every drink here"—he eyed Ken meaningfully—"to determine if there were any drugs on the premises. And I have to warn you, that would lead to other charges."

He watched as the boys' flushed crimson and then turned ashen during his speech.

"So I believe this situation was due to 'misinterpretation' and may best be handled as a White Rocks matter." Jack exhaled as everyone relaxed at his words. "That's if no one requires medical attention?"

All the students shook their heads.

Chad took a step forward. "We'll take it from here, Officer. Everyone is fine. It was a misunderstanding that will be addressed." Chad saluted but Milt yanked his hand down and snarled, "Yeah, we got it."

Everyone moved toward the door.

"I'll deal with you later," Jack growled to Replacement. "I assume you have a ride?"

Nodding her head, she looked like she had a thousand and one defenses, excuses, or apologies bursting to be set free, but he stepped around her.

"Stay out of trouble, if possible."

"Undercover?" he muttered to himself as he walked to the car, his anger rising with each step.

What was she thinking? How was he supposed to protect her if she threw herself in harm's way?

Even being behind the wheel of the Charger failed to register. Just before he started the car, the image of her in the coffin flashed in his head.

Jack spent the next couple of hours of his shift driving around, looking in vain for a silver car and a goth drug dealer on the run.

36

STUPID BUT BRILLIANT

Jack paced the floor and glanced at the clock. Twelve forty.

"Why isn't she home?" he muttered.

For the third or fourth time, he stormed over to the window, yanked the curtain back, and glared into the darkness. This time he went so far as to grab his jacket and head for the door. But when he reached into his jacket pocket, he stopped.

She had the car. With a snarl, he ripped his jacket off and beat it on the floor.

Keys jingled in the lock, and he froze. The door slowly opened, and Replacement peered in.

"Get in. *Now*," Jack's voice rumbled.

"You're mad." She closed the door but didn't come in any farther, leaning against the door for support.

He stalked forward. "No. I'm way beyond mad. They need to come up with a new word for just how angry I am."

"I had to." Her head snapped up, and she glared at him.

He slammed his hand into the doorframe. Wood cracked.

"Three people are dead. Three. You're hunting a monster, and you don't have a clue. Do you have any idea what Chandler would say to you?"

She burst into tears and shook her head. "No," she whispered.

"He'd tell you that you're out of your mind! Any other cop would have arrested you. You assaulted a security officer. You solicited drugs. Chandler would say just what I'm saying."

"No." She shook her head. "Chandler never yelled at me."

Jack turned and took four steps away. "Don't. Don't turn this around on me. I'm not Chandler. He would... I don't know what he would have done. He'd handle it!"

He stormed over to the bedroom. "Don't leave the apartment or borrow my car *ever again*," he yelled, slamming the door.

* * *

After tossing and turning for two hours, Jack opened the bedroom door. Replacement was asleep on the couch, curled up in a ball. The comforter had fallen to the floor. He picked it up, then fanned the comforter out and gently laid it over her.

Her eyes fluttered open, and she sat up. He cleared his throat so she wouldn't be alarmed to see him.

"Jack, I'm so sorry." She gathered the comforter tightly around her.

He went over and sat on the arm of the couch. "No, I was… upset. I—I shouldn't have yelled. You're right, Chandler wouldn't have yelled."

She nodded.

"But we need to get one thing straight."

She bowed her head. "I can't leave the apartment and I can't use the car."

"No. That was a stupid thing to say. But this whole undercover thing is done."

Replacement took a deep breath.

Jack held up his hand. "I'm not arguing."

She started to speak again. He gave her a look.

"Let's do this the right way." He walked over and picked up his notebook and pen. "Start at the very beginning. How did you get into the college?"

She tossed the comforter off and jumped up. "Oh, that was pretty easy. I already had an alias. I've had it for like two years."

"Ah, yes, the mysterious Alexis Holmes. How?" Jack sat down at the desk.

"A lady from youth services came by Aunt Haddie's a couple of years ago. I watched her connect to the state database and she used a really simple password. I logged in and figured I'd just make someone up to see if I could. I was just messing around. Then I decided to keep it in case I ever needed it." As if that explained everything.

"How did you get onto campus and into buildings?"

"When we went to the campus security office, and you went into that guy's office—"

"Neil Waters?"

"—I saw the secretary's login. She had her password written down under her keyboard. That gave me full access to the college computer system."

"You didn't tell me?" Jack was more surprised than angry.

"I didn't know if I could get into either of the systems until after… after you were in the hospital." She started to move forward and stopped. "I made a push after that. I got into the college's system, and just made myself a student. I don't think I could take it to graduation or anything, but I got into classes and a key card, all that stuff."

Jack looked up. "Why did you leave me out?"

"Because you'd lose your job. You told me about what your boss said." She went over to the couch, putting distance between them, but Jack jumped up and grabbed her by the shoulders. "Did you think about what could happen to you? I have training. I have a gun. What do you have?"

"Nothing to lose?"

They stared at each other, until Replacement blinked.

"If you ever pull something like that on me again…" He struggled for words.

"I won't," she whispered. "I promise."

He hugged her. *She could have gotten herself killed. Stupid! No, not stupid… fearless.*

He held her for a moment and let himself relax while her hand moved in little circles at the small of his back. He closed his eyes and electricity tingled up and down his spine.

She made a faint, soft moan, barely a sound, really, but Jack held her at arm's length. He scooted back to his seat and picked up his notebook. "Did you find out anything?"

"Not too much." She scrunched up her face.

"Getting into the college was brilliant. Stupid but brilliant."

Her smile vanished. "Oh, really. How can I be stupid *and* brilliant?"

"Not you… what you did. It was dangerous. Three people are dead. This isn't a game."

She nodded.

"Have you seen any drug use around campus?"

"Not besides that spineless—"

"Besides him."

"Not really. I haven't been out much. I had a couple of study dates…"

Jack cocked an eyebrow. "Do you know a Lennie Jacobsen?"

"No, never heard of him."

"He was at the bar tonight. Dresses goth. He has long hair and was wearing a black hoody sweatshirt and black jeans."

"No, I never… Wait a minute. Goth? I've seen a guy with long dyed-black hair hanging around the school."

Jack pulled out Lennie's mug shot.

"Yeah, that's him. I saw him in the computer lab."

Jack's heart rate quickened. "Where Michelle worked?"

"No, not at the psych center, the one at the student union."

"Was he with anybody?"

"No… I'm not sure. I don't remember." Her face brightened mischievously. "Maybe if you tell me more about what you're looking for next time, I can help you look."

Yeah, good try. But she might have a point. Jack stared down hopelessly at the picture. "Is there anything else you can remember about him?"

Replacement paused for a moment, then shook her head. "Do you think he was involved?"

"I don't know. After what just happened at The Pit, I wouldn't be surprised if Lennie went into hiding."

After a meaningful pause, Jack continued with his semi-interrogation. "Have you had any classes with Dr. Hahn?"

"Yeah, he's boring. He was great in class, but get him in the lab? He's cold, like Mr. Spock or a robot. Super-focused. Everyone has to be quiet. No sound. Nothing." She rolled her eyes, and Jack suppressed a smile.

"Have you talked to him one-on-one?"

"Nope."

"What about Dr. Franklin?" Pages of his notebook flew back and forth as he took new notes and tried to reference the old ones.

"I don't have him for class, but rumor is he hits on the girls pretty hard. Everybody knows he's married, but he takes his wedding ring off before class. Nice."

"Anything else?"

"I heard a guy say he can be charming one minute and then flip out the next. A girl in my psych class said he's a few fries short of a Happy Meal."

"Are you out at the center a lot?"

"All the time. If we're not in a class there, we're in the lab. Huge pain."

"Are you ever there late?"

"No. We have to leave by seven, but we start early. There's mountains of homework. One of the grad students has been helping me."

"Who?"

"His name's Brendan."

"Phillips?" Jack's eyes narrowed.

"Yeah. How did you know?"

"I met him when I went to go on the tour. He showed me around. Dr. Hahn's assistant. How did he seem? What read did you get?"

Replacement shrugged. "He seems nice. He teaches one of my classes."

"He had a blue security card. Does that get him into the computer room?"

"Probably. I knew he was Hahn's assistant; that's why I picked him. He has access to the other parts of the building. He likes to show off, like he's a bigwig. I'm working on getting closer to him."

Jack's eyes narrowed. "You mean you *were* working on it. Not anymore."

Replacement's grip tightened on the comforter. "I found something about Missy Lorton."

"Michelle's roommate?"

"The thief," Replacement spat. "She definitely took some of Michelle's stuff. A box of it."

"How do you know?" Jack stopped writing.

Replacement rolled her eyes. "Come on. I'm undercover. I peeked."

"Peeked. Did you break into her apartment?"

"It isn't breaking in if I'm undercover."

Jack could feel the blood rush to his face.

"I didn't take anything so I wouldn't contaminate the crime scene." Her look and shrug said, *So that explains it all. Glad I could help.*

"You *made* it a crime scene! It's called breaking and entering."

"Don't yell. She made it first. It's called big-jerk-stealing."

"Just stop. Okay?" Jack rubbed the sides of his head before he continued. "You didn't take Michelle's box, then?"

"No."

"Did you see what was in it?"

"It's just a big box of Michelle's stuff. I don't know, I figure she must have wanted it. Can I get it back now?" Her lip trembled, and she looked down at her hands. "It's all... it's all I have left of Michelle."

Jack melted. "I'll get it. I promise." He put his hand on her shoulder.

She leaned her head onto his hand and closed her eyes. "Thank you," she whispered, and then her eyes snapped open. "Nothing I'm doing is going to get you in trouble, right?" Her eyes rounded in concern.

"Trouble?" Jack stuck his lower lip out and shook his head. "Nah, you've pretty much blown up my life. What more trouble could you cause?"

"Are you serious?" She grabbed his arms. "Don't say that. You're good, right?"

"I'm good. It's not your fault. Look. I've gone at this the wrong way. From the beginning, I should have gone to Collins, but I didn't." Replacement started to speak, and Jack held up both hands. "Joe Davenport is... damn it. I forgot to try him again. I wonder why he didn't—" He looked down at his phone; two missed calls. "My phone rang, and I didn't hear it? Smartphone my eye."

"Let me see." Replacement took the phone from him, scrolled through some menu, and a dog barked out. "It's working."

"What the hell was that?"

"Your new ringtone. I thought it fit you better than that old grandpa one."

"You messed with my phone?"

"No. I updated it for the *twenty-first century*." She waved the phone over her head. "If you can't even change your ringtone, how am I going to get you to use a computer instead of a notebook?"

"Ain't gonna happen. So don't change my phone and *don't* try to change me."

"Fine."

Jack paused and rubbed his eyes with his thumb and index finger. "I'm going to Joe and giving him everything."

"But you'll lose your job." Replacement's shoulders slumped.

"I might and I might not." *Or I might wish I had.* "Either way, we know someone who has access to the center has killed at least three people: Charlie, Tiffany, and…" He couldn't bring himself to add Michelle's name to the list. "And we know that Michelle didn't apply for a transfer because the transfer went through on December twenty-first at one a.m."

"What?"

"I didn't have a chance to tell you, what with all the, um, extra drama." After pausing for effect, Jack explained how he found out someone had just filled in December twentieth on Michelle's form, but the time stamp on the application was December 21 at 1:03 a.m.

That got Replacement's attention all right. "Michelle was already dead by then! She was at the reservoir at twelve thirty. Someone else submitted it. But—" She looked away.

"But what?"

She looked at the ceiling, thinking. "If it was electronic, then they'll be able to tell the IP, too. It will say what computer it came from. Move."

Replacement shoved Jack out of the chair and handed him back his phone. As she logged in, Jack moved over to the window.

"All night, I kept thinking I was hearing dogs barking," he muttered to himself.

Replacement either didn't hear or pretended not to.

"If you can just sign up for classes at Western Tech as a transfer," she said, "then their system and White Rocks' are linked. I didn't even think of that. I'm a moron."

Jack watched in amazement as Replacement's slender fingers sped across the keyboard. Every couple of seconds she'd huff or shake the mouse, waiting for a screen to catch up with her commands.

"Got it!" She hopped up and down in the chair.

"Will that tell you the computer they used?"

Her fist smacked the desk. "No. It's the forward-facing IP of the psych center."

"Can you translate that geek-speak back into English?"

"Every computer has an IP address, but if you connect in a building, all those addresses can get funneled together for security and then go out as one IP. That's what they do at the psychology center. This IP address covers the whole building."

"And you're sure it came from there?"

"A hundred percent." They each considered the ramifications of this certain fact in silence for a moment. Then Replacement asked quietly, "So what's our next move?"

Jack was ready for her. "*I'm* going back out there tomorrow to talk to Dr. Meth—I mean, Franklin. There's also Hahn."

"You think Michelle's boss might be involved somehow?" She seemed horrified.

"The person in charge either knows everything or nothing." Jack sighed and ran his hand through his hair. "Hell, it could also be a student or a janitor. And I need to find this Lennie kid. But right now, Franklin is the best fit. He also does research with meth, so he knows how to cook it."

Replacement looked like she was following a swarm of ideas down the corridors of her mind. "I bet Michelle found the video of that poor guy in the psych center."

Jack paced back and forth. "She was overhauling the computer systems. She'd have access to everything."

"Hey, remember that guy at the funeral who talked about Michelle tracking him down when he stole her bike? She was like that—she never gave up. If Michelle found that video, she'd keep digging. And there's no way to log in to the center from the outside so she had to do it there."

Jack stopped pacing. "That's why she was there so late."

Replacement crossed her arms. "I'm trying to get into the computers there right now."

"Trying? Don't you have access already?"

"No. The lab computers are completely separate from the college system. I have a student's account that has limited access, so I wrote a Trojan."

"A what?"

"You know, like a virus. I named a file SuperHotPornBabes. The antivirus program flags it and moves it to a holding folder. Most computer administrators are horny computer geeks, and when they see a title like that, believe it or not, nine times out of ten, the blood rushes from their brains and they open it to see what it is. Once they run it, it runs under their permission. Get it? It will run on and on, mining their system for data, with administrator rights, *and* it will create another admin account for me." She held up her hand for a high five, but he disappointed her.

"I got about half of that. You wrote a program that will give us access?"

"Yeah."

"Did it work?"

"Not yet. I only put it on today. I was hoping to get a hit by tomorrow, and I have to go there to log in."

"No way. Can you talk me through it?"

Replacement shook her head. "As discussed, I can't even get you to use your phone. No. Let me. I can be in and—"

"No. That's off the table. I have the next two days off. I'm going to the campus in the morning by myself. I'll need the car."

Replacement turned back to the computer while Jack headed with his verbal victory back to his room.

"Good work," he muttered as he shut the door. He knew he was facing yet another night of tossing and turning and trying not to think about the beautiful, stupid, fearless woman outside the door—who made everything so absurdly complicated.

37

PENDULUM

Bark, bark, bark. Bark, bark, bark.

"Hello? Stratton," Jack answered the phone sleepily.

"Jack? Undersheriff Morrison. Can you meet me down at the morgue?"

Jack straightened up. "Yes, sir. How soon?"

"How soon can you get here? It's eight now—eight thirty?"

"Yes, sir."

No time for a shower. He shaved and brushed his teeth and dressed quickly in some semi-preppy clothes for going out to White Rocks later. He rushed into the living room to get his coat and Replacement was looking out the window.

He yelled excitedly, "I just got a call to go and meet the undersheriff at the morgue."

"What… the undertaker?"

"No. Undersheriff. The guy who's next in line to Collins." He grabbed his coat from the door.

"Okay, cool, um… I was going to run a couple of errands." She bit her lip. "But I'll just walk."

"Are you sure? I can drive you when I get back."

"It's not far."

"Okay, I'll see ya later."

As he pulled out, once more master of the Impala, he looked up at the third floor. Replacement was still standing at the window.

* * *

In the black-tiled crypt, Jack stood next to Undersheriff Morrison beside a stretcher with a corpse laid out on it. Robert Morrison, a tall African American man in his late fifties, wore the tan uniform of the Sheriff's Department, without the hat. His curly black hair was short and graying at the temples. The coroner's assistant, a petite woman in a white hospital coat, stood at the head of the stretcher.

"That's him," Jack said.

"You sure?" Morrison asked.

Jack nodded. He looked down at Bennie the Goon. His face was heavily bruised, but he was sure it was Bennie.

Morrison nodded, and the woman pulled the sheet back over the corpse.

"Did he have anything on him, Mei?" Morrison asked.

"Just these." She adjusted her rectangular blue-and-pink glasses and pulled a metal cart closer.

Jack couldn't tell much from the items: a crushed package of cigarettes, a fast-food receipt, three quarters, a scrap of paper smeared with black ink.

"Might have had to bum a light?" Morrison pointed. "No lighter."

Jack leaned down so he could read what was on the scrap of paper.

"It looks like an address," Mei offered, smiling sweetly at Jack.

"It is." Jack smiled back tightly. "Mine."

Morrison's eyes narrowed. "You never saw him before that night?"

"No. I noticed him when I came out of my apartment and he started following me."

Morrison thanked Mei and left her to her work: covering Benny, straightening his toe tag, lowering the stretcher, and sliding him back into his drawer.

The two men walked out into a slightly warmer hallway. Morrison took out a pack of gum and handed Jack a piece.

"You'd just been clipped by the drunk driver, right?" Morrison pondered out loud. Jack nodded.

"And you hurt your leg. You still have a little limp; how's it feeling?"

The observation took Jack aback. "Much better, sir."

"You can save the sir stuff for Collins. Call me Bob." Jack gave him a short nod of respect before Bob continued, "Anyway, is it *possible* that maybe the guy thought you were an easy mark?"

Jack bristled at the comment and straightened up.

Bob looked at him and chuckled. "Then again, maybe not."

"No cause of death yet?" Jack looked back into the room.

"Preliminarily, it's an OD."

"Where was he found?" Jack asked, a hunch forming.

Bob stuck two more pieces of gum in his mouth. "Imperial Motor Lodge."

Bingo. Now we have two bodies found there.

Morrison's phone rang. "Morrison." He listened for a second. "I'll be over as soon as I can." He hung up. "Fatal car accident on the highway. Two semi tractors."

Jack nodded.

"Jack?" Morrison's voice got even deeper. "I've been doing this too long to think that two close calls in short order don't warrant closer attention. Do you think they're related?"

Jack scratched his neck and looked down the hallway before he admitted, "Yes, sir, I do." He just couldn't bring himself to call the man Bob.

"If you have any ideas, now's the time to speak up." Morrison eyed Jack for a moment. "I don't know you that well, Stratton, but all I can say is… trust your gut. If you think I'm the type of guy who's going to jam you up or throw you under the bus, shut your mouth. If you think you can trust me, tell me what you've got, and we'll take it from there."

Jack respected the man's forthrightness, and made his decision quickly. He laid out everything. Morrison cracked his gum occasionally but remained silent. It took a while, but when he was done, Jack was more sure than ever that he needed to tell somebody this, and now was the time.

"Okay, you have this video?" Morrison said when Jack finished.

"Yes. The guys in the IT lab have it. They also have the password. I don't know if they've looked at it yet." Jack clenched and relaxed his hands.

"If the guys at the lab haven't seen the video yet, *then neither have you*," Morrison stressed. "Chain of custody is already gone with the phone, but it's explainable given the circumstances. Davenport gets back tomorrow. I'll call the lab and the forensic people, and we'll all sit down first thing in the morning."

"Thank you," Jack replied, truly grateful.

"Do you have any idea who at the university it could be?" Morrison asked.

"Nothing definite."

"Okay, we'll go over it all again tomorrow."

Jack shook his hand, and Morrison's phone rang again. "Morrison... I'm on my way." He nodded back to Jack and then headed out the door.

Jack turned to go.

"Officer Stratton?" Mei ran around the corner after him.

"Yes?"

"Oh, I'm glad I caught you." She smiled up at him and adjusted her glasses. "We also found a baggie with some money hidden in his left shoe and a small piece of paper."

Jack looked down at the evidence bag. The piece of off-white paper was card stock, about two inches by one inch, jagged where it had been ripped. Only three printed letters remained: *lin*.

Not much to go on.

"Thanks." Jack nodded. "Can you make sure these get over to Undersheriff Morrison's office right away?"

"Of course." Mei grinned.

* * *

Jack eased back on the gas as the Impala swung into the turn. He had a stranglehold on the steering wheel. Bennie the Goon had been his best lead. *Best living lead.* He could have led Jack to whoever hired him to watch his apartment.

No money to follow. They'd have paid him in cash. And what would he have gotten? For fifty bucks, he'd have watched my place all day and night.

Jack was still bothered. It felt as if something was about to break. He'd felt that way before.

Weird.

He was apprehensive, as though time was slipping away.

Think, Jack, think. A crushed package of cigarettes; typical. Fast-food receipt; could be nothing, but maybe he met someone there. The money. nNothing unusual about that. The scrap of paper; stock paper... card stock. Why would a junkie have—

"Business card!" he shouted.

Jack watched the Impala's speedometer rise as he headed toward the college. The three letters, *lin*, clicked into place.

His hand pushed a Johnny Cash CD into the player. "God's Gonna Cut You Down" blared over the speakers as he flew out to the psychology center. The ride took fifteen minutes. He went through "I Walk the Line," "It Ain't Me Babe," and "Busted." "Ring of Fire" was just finishing as he pulled into the parking lot.

Jack combed his fingers through his hair as he walked into the center and smiled at the blonde behind the counter.

She leaned forward and looked Jack up and down. "How can I help you?"

Jack grinned. "I'm here to see Dr. Franklin."

"Is he expecting you? He's in class right now."

"I just have a quick question. Is he in the new classroom upstairs?" Jack was guessing. "Can you show me?" He leaned in close and smiled.

"I can't leave the desk." The girl shrugged and leaned closer.

"That's fine." Jack smiled. "I didn't catch your name."

"Stacy."

"Do you have a long shift ahead of you, Stacy?"

"Yeah." She pouted. "I have to work until noon."

Three hours? Killer shift. Wait until you graduate, kid.

"That's rough." Jack tried to look sympathetic. "Do you ever have to work a late shift?"

"No. We close at seven every day." She put her chin on the back of her hand as she looked up at him.

"Does the whole center close or just the reception area?"

"People with card access can stay after hours, I guess. Why?"

"I'm just curious. I hate those cards. Your picture always looks funny."

She sat up straight. "Mine doesn't look funny."

Jack gave her an exaggerated wink. "Sure."

"It doesn't. Look." She handed Jack her card.

Computer chip inside. Card reader. No key punch access. All doors monitored and recorded. The cards are color-coded. Hers is yellow.

"It's a beautiful picture, but it doesn't do you justice." Jack made sure that he brushed her hand as he handed the card back to her.

"Thank you." She sighed.

"You said Dr. Franklin was in Room…"

"Two ten," she said.

"I'll only be a second. Be right back."

"You have to sign in… and you can't go unescorted," she called out.

"It's our secret." He winked and hurried up the stairs, but the girl still reached for a phone.

Jack took the stairs two at a time without looking back. When he reached the top, he quickly scanned the posted room assignments and headed to Psychology Classroom 210. He opened the door and slipped inside as quietly as he could.

It was a small classroom and a dozen students were there now. Franklin stood behind a desk at the front of the room. Apparently the class was just coming to a close.

Perfect.

"The assignment is due next class," Dr. Franklin was saying. "As always, thank you." Franklin's attention immediately turned to a young girl who had hopped up and rushed to his desk.

As the rest of the students got up to leave, Jack weaved his way to the front. The girl now stood at the edge of Franklin's desk. She kept leaning in toward the professor, who was quite obviously appreciating the view her low-cut blouse gave him.

Jack waited. Dr. Franklin looked up and frowned. So did the girl. She picked up her books, gave Jack a dirty look, and stomped past him.

"Dr. Franklin? Jack Stratton." Jack smiled. The doctor didn't.

"Yes?" He looked past Jack, eyeing the girl as she walked out of the classroom.

"I have a couple of quick questions for you."

"I'm sorry, I have another class." Franklin turned back to his desk.

"I spoke with Mike Leverone—"

Franklin's hand slammed down on his desk with such force that everyone left in the room turned and stared.

Damn. I should have said Hank Foster.

The doctor's voice was clipped and rapid fire. "Mike Leverone making his own meth lab and blowing his face off had nothing to do with me. Who are you? Get out."

That was a mistake. Take it down. "I didn't say you had anything to do with it. I just need to ask you—"

"You need to get out of my classroom. Are you a lawyer? I'll call security." He stepped around the desk toward Jack.

Jack shook his head and held up his hands. "You have it wrong. I'm here for your professional opinion. I'm a police officer and I'm looking at a missing person case. I've spoken with a few different people who recommended I speak with you, including Hank Foster."

Franklin glared at Jack for a moment, and then it was as if someone flipped a switch. He smiled. "My apologies, Jack. The situation with Mr. Leverone was… traumatic for me as an educator. You said you're a police officer? You're working a missing person case? I don't see how I could be of any assistance with that."

"I'm looking for a girl who did meth. One time."

Franklin frowned and looked at Jack with a mixture of scorn and pity. "People don't do meth one time."

"They do if they die."

"That's a trick question then." The doctor's lips pressed together.

"The question I had is, how does meth influence someone the first time they take it—psychologically?" Jack added the word *psychologically* at the last second to try to hook the doctor back into the conversation.

"Another trick question. There are too many variables and too many inconsistencies. What's the person like physically? Tall? Short? Fat? Thin? What's their emotional state? The drug? What's the mixture? How much? How taken? I could go on and on. A trick question again." Once more his hand came down on his desk.

Whoa, off the rails. "Doctor, thank you for explaining the complexity of how meth affects people. Since there are so many variables, how do you figure them out?"

"There have been a number of studies on the effects of meth and the mind, including my own," Franklin said. "Although my personal study has been placed in a status of indefinite hold, thanks to the aforementioned Mr. Leverone."

"That's unfortunate—"

"You've no idea of the hours wasted. Not just mine, but my students'. The whole study was frozen, just like that. Now the data is useless. You can't just pause a study. Gone. All of that research is gone."

"Doctor, for the test subjects, did you accept volunteers?"

"Of course. We don't pay more than a small stipend, if anything, but—" His eyes widened and his nostrils flared. "This supposed missing person case… who? Who's missing?" Dr. Franklin pointed a finger at Jack.

"I can't divulge—"

"Get out. Now. I have a class." He took two steps toward Jack.

Is this wacko on meth? "Doctor, I'm sorry I imposed. I just have one more question. Do you know a Lennie Jacobsen?"

"Yes… no… maybe. I have so many students," he spouted, his head shaking. "Get out!" He waved his hands at Jack.

Jack forced a smile. "Thank you for your time. You've been very insightful."

Franklin looked confused for a second and then smiled. "I'm glad I could be of assistance. You can make an appointment, and we can discuss this further. I have another class. Good day." He turned his back on Jack and arranged his desk.

Jack headed for the door, slipping past students coming in for the next class and weaving through crowds of kids on his way down the hall. One look at his snarl and smoldering eyes and everyone moved aside for him. Outside, he jumped into his Impala and gunned it out of the lot.

But the Impala didn't hug the curves like the Charger, and Jack kept having to slow down, which gave him too much time to think, and to regret opening with Leverone. Tomorrow he would talk to Morrison and have him look at Franklin.

That guy's a lunatic. I think he's taking meth himself. He's his own research subject—

Jack yanked the wheel to the right and pulled over to the side of the road.

Charlie Harding. He looked like a torture victim on the video…

… or maybe some sicko's research subject.

38

BOX FULL OF MEMORIES

At six o'clock, Jack was once again pacing the living room, waiting for Replacement. He checked his phone. *Nothing.* He tossed it down on the counter next to Replacement's note.

She said she was running errands. She had no car, so she must have taken the bus downtown.

Get a grip, Jack.

As he headed for the window again, the phone rang. He reached the counter and hit Answer before the first ring stopped, without even looking at the screen.

"Hey. Where are you?"

Pause. Jack checked the number. He didn't recognize it. Not Replacement, though. "Hello?"

"I'm looking for Jack Stratton." It was a girl's voice.

"That's me."

"This is Missy Lorton. Can we talk?"

You betcha. "Certainly. Where are you?"

"My apartment." She hesitated. "I—I kept some of Michelle's things. I want to give them back. I'm not in trouble, am I?"

"You're off to a good start at getting out of any trouble by calling me. I can be there right away," Jack said.

"Okay. I'll be here." Click.

Jack gathered up his jacket, keys, and gun as fast as his leg would allow, and two minutes later the Impala was racing back to the college. He didn't try Replacement again; she knew how to reach him. Probably just out doing errands.

* * *

Jack parked right outside Missy's apartment. She immediately buzzed him in, and he hurried up to the third floor. When she opened the door, her face was splotchy, and her eyes were red.

"Thank you for calling, Ms. Lorton."

"I don't want to be in trouble." She was hard to understand, holding back tears.

"I do have some additional questions."

Missy nodded and moved into the apartment. "Sure." She motioned Jack into a small living room.

It looked as if Missy still didn't have a new roommate; the furnishings were sparse. The coffee table, pushed against a long couch, was where Missy had tossed her purse, keys, and a blue student ID card with the chain snaking around the pocketbook and partly hanging off the table. A cardboard moving box was conspicuously placed on the seat of a chair near the couch.

Missy stepped toward the box. "So, here's Michelle's stuff." *Replacement was right.* "I didn't mean to keep it."

Jack remained silent. He wanted her to talk.

"I just… I thought she was throwing it out."

Jack eyed the blue ID card, and something clicked into place. He posed his next words carefully. "Ms. Lorton, how did Michelle seem to you when she told you she was transferring?"

"Happy. She was really excited about it." Missy turned her back to Jack and reached into the box.

Jack drew his gun. "Freeze." He growled the command. "Michelle never transferred and never intended to. She never talked to you about it."

Missy didn't move.

"Slowly raise your hands over your head and turn around," Jack ordered.

When Missy replied, her voice had transformed. Gone was the weepy roommate; in its place was a voice that was calm and collected. "You should hear this first."

"Show me your hands!"

"You need to look at my phone." Missy kept her back to Jack and her right hand in the box. She slowly raised her left hand and held the phone up where Jack could see it.

Jack could make it out from where he stood. His worst fear—Replacement, strapped to a gurney—fell like an anvil in his chest and his heart pounded in long, hard beats that rang in his ears.

Missy turned around. In her right hand was a Taser. In her left she held up the phone so Jack could watch Replacement thrashing and hear her scream, "Wait until you see what I do to you! I'm going to rip your face off!"

"Throw your gun on the couch," Missy said. "Or I disconnect the call and she's dead."

Jack's finger eased back from the trigger.

"Do it now, or she starts losing pieces," Missy hissed.

The Taser was a knockoff civilian model with a ten-second burst. Jack had been shot with a police tactical Taser in training before; he knew he could ride the wave of pain.

Jack tossed his gun onto the couch. "Where is she?"

Missy answered by pulling the trigger. The Taser's barbs embedded in Jack's chest and the electricity froze his muscles, but he didn't drop. Missy had made the mistake of being too close to Jack when she fired. The prongs need to have distance between them to affect the most muscle groups; shot from close range, they remain closer together. Jack gritted his teeth and waited. His muscles twitched and burned, but it was nothing compared to the rage surging through him. Five more seconds, and then it would be *his* turn.

But when a second Taser hit him from behind, his muscles seized and he pitched forward. As he lay writhing on the floor, a wet cloth was pressed over his face and a chemical smell filled his nose.

He fought, but he knew it was a losing battle. His vision blurred, the blackness rushed up to envelop him, and he toppled into the abyss.

39

UNDER THE ROCKS

Jack woke and opened his eyes a fraction to check out his situation. What he saw didn't look good. Thick leather straps bound his arms and legs to a hospital stretcher. *Just like Charlie Harding.* His head wasn't strapped down—yet. Small mercies.

A large circular vault arched above his head—which told him exactly where he was, even before he saw the control booth.

The psych center. The fMRI.

Through the large viewing window in the middle of one wall, he saw Missy, talking animatedly to someone out of his view in the control booth.

He tried to remember the layout of the lab. When he slowly, painfully turned his head to the right, he saw the edge of the heavy door. He remembered a corridor running along that wall and tried to envision where the exit was; it would be on the north side, he thought.

Jack tested his restraints. These straps were leather; there would be no breaking them. His wrists were fastened, and thick straps held his thighs and ankles. Bile and anger choked his throat.

Stay calm. Try to get them talking.

The door to his right swung open, and he heard footsteps. Someone scraped a chair across the floor and sat down next to the stretcher.

"Hello, Jack."

Jack buried his fury. His voice was low and steady. "Brendan."

"So calm. Did they teach you that in the Army? You're a soldier, right? You served with Michelle and Alice's brother in Iraq." Brendan smiled.

Jack's rage seethed back to the surface. *Bluff.* "So you figured out that you're under investigation? The police have been looking—"

"Very good." Brendan chuckled. "You're clever. You should have been an actor, Jack. But you've got it all wrong. You see, *you* were the one under investigation. I've known all about you and Michelle and Alice for a while."

Jack pushed with every muscle against the straps, but it was useless.

Brendan watched him flailing and thrashing for a minute and smiled. "Good. Good." He lifted a syringe and held it to Jack's arm. "I need you to help me today, Jack. Your anger issues are going to play a part in that." Jack gritted his teeth as Brendan inserted the needle and pushed the plunger. "Ever done meth? This is the good stuff. I added a little extra kicker for you."

Jack felt the needle burning in his arm and then the drug racing through his system. The door opened, and Missy, scowling self-importantly, pulled in a gurney. Missy turned her head, and the scowl on her face twisted into a sneer. Replacement was strapped to the gurney. One whole side of Replacement's face was red; blood trickled from her nose and the corner of her mouth onto the stretcher.

"I'm going to kill you!" Jack yelled.

"I don't think so, Jack." Brendan shook his head.

"You loser!" Replacement raised her bloodied head and spat at Brendan. "If you hadn't Tasered me, I would have kicked your teeth down your throat." Her voice was very hoarse, and got louder and then softer, as if she couldn't quite control it.

"Screw you, you scrawny wench," Missy hissed before turning to Brendan. "What happened to your arm?" She pointed at the bloodstain on his shirt.

"She bit me in the chem lab," whined the former quarterback.

"What was she doing up there?" Missy demanded.

"She ran in there when I went to grab her. We have to clean it up after we're done tonight. She trashed it." Brendan glared at Replacement.

"Are you out of your mind?" Missy looked furious. "Everything in there is combustible. You'll blow this whole place up."

"Calm down. I got two batches." Brendan held up two syringes. "I gave him one already."

Missy huffed. "Hold off on hers. It may be a long night." She turned and exited, reappearing a moment later behind the glass in the control room.

Brendan leaned down till his face was inches from Jack's. "Well, now that everyone is here, let's get this party started."

"Wait," Jack said. "Everyone knows I'm watching you. Do you seriously think you can get away with this?"

"Yeah, I do. Tonight, you and Alice are going to die."

"I'm a cop." Jack spoke calmly over his racing heart and tried to rein in his cloudy thoughts. "They'll come straight here. They know about Charlie Harding, Tiffany McAllister, and Michelle. The trail of bodies will lead them right to you. You can still stop this."

Brendan shrugged. "I know they'll come, but it won't matter." He placed his hand on the side of the large machine, like he was the owner of a very big, steel dog. "As for you and Alice... I could cut you up and toss your bodies deep in the woods. But I think a fire at your apartment building would be better. They'll find you and Alice in bed, with some empty rum bottles and some drugs. The police will want to cover that up, and that's that."

Jack's head was spinning. "But we have proof. We know what you did."

"Proof? You met Dr. Franklin? He's my backup plan. With all the rumors about him using meth, a suicide note and his corpse will end any investigation. How do you think Bennie had Franklin's business card tucked into his shoe? That's why you came by today, right?"

Dammit.

"I know all about your research," Jack said. "That's what this is about, research? You're looking for the God Spot."

Brendan looked down at Jack and studied his face. "Impressive. You've done your homework. Well, so have I, and I'm almost there. Do you know how long Dr. Hahn searched for it? How close he was?"

"Dr. Hahn's involved?" Jack asked.

"No. Dr. Hahn's fault is that he's too kind. He knew what he'd have to do to prove it, but he wouldn't go there. So instead he became the butt of everyone's joke."

"Hahn's right," Jack said. "This is a line you shouldn't cross."

Brendan shook his head. "Quite the opposite. It's a line that *must* be crossed. Do you have any idea of the significance of finding the God Spot? Once I locate it, I'll shut everyone up."

"The God Spot doesn't exist." Replacement picked her head up as she spat. "You should take Dr. Melding's neuropsychology class, you moron."

The veins on Brendan's forehead bulged. "Melding's a fool. She always attacks Hahn, but she's the imbecile. Did she say that? Did she say that in class?"

"Yeah. She said Dr. Hahn is a loser who wasted twenty years of his pathetic life. Any undergrad could poke a million holes in his theories."

Brendan jumped off his seat and cut off her tirade with a brisk slap that made the gurney tremble.

"I'm going to rip your heart out," Jack growled.

"*She's* the fool, Alice," Brendan said menacingly, then turned back to Jack. "As I was saying, Jack, Dr. Hahn couldn't do what needed to be done. He relied on emotions like hope and love to try to locate the God Spot, and they didn't work. But I found the key: pain."

Replacement laughed. "If you think pain is the way to find God, then all you had to do is take your class. It was so *painfully* boring, I prayed a piano would fall on my head. Or better yet, yours."

Brendan slapped her again. Replacement laughed, but Jack could see she was hurt.

"That'll cost you, Shrimpie. That's what all the girls in class call you. Did you know that? Did you *date* one?"

Brendan punched her in the face and her head lolled to the side, saliva dripping off her chin.

"Stop." Missy's voice crackled over the speaker as she glared out the control room window.

"Stop!" Jack's body lifted off the stretcher as he strained against the straps.

Replacement lifted her head and looked at Missy in the control room. One eye had already started to swell shut. "Your boss hits like a girl."

"He's not my boss," Missy snapped, and then smiled suggestively at Brendan.

"Ewww." Replacement's reaction wasn't taunting but honest disgust. "Brendan, you're banging Miss Piggy? That's gross."

A stream of profanities poured through the speakers.

"Shut up!" Brendan yelled. He grabbed a plastic bit from a metal cart and forced it between Replacement's teeth, finally silencing her.

40

YOU ARE SICK

Brendan sat back down. "Dr. Hahn tried love, meditation, happiness, and then fear to find the God Spot. None worked. *I* thought of pain." Brendan was enjoying spinning it out. He moved unhurriedly to the rolling cart. Jack tried pulling up the rail attached to his wrist, but it held firm. "Human subjects were necessary, but there are so many rules now about the methods you can use in experiments. I had to find subjects who wouldn't be missed: drug addicts, prostitutes, and such."

"They're not subjects, they're human beings." Jack had told himself over and over again not to react, let the guy talk, watch everything he did, conserve his energy, but he couldn't help himself. "You're like that sick Nazi doctor. Mengele."

"Mengele was a pioneer, too," Brendan said, efficiently filling syringes as he talked. "People like that are invisible. No one cared enough about them to even look. They're not people, they're a means to an end."

Replacement moaned and struggled against her restraints. Brendan looked at her and smiled a little. "At least their lives were useful at the end. Unfortunately, their lifestyles had deteriorated their minds—which made them inferior test subjects. Even though I gathered a great deal of data, much of it was useless."

He paused to enjoy the process of tapping syringes—Jack counted six—for air bubbles. Then Brendan pushed the cart next to Replacement, right where she could see it.

"I found that meth enhanced the brain scans. I learned how to make it in Dr. Franklin's class. Some of his work is brilliant, really. Anyway, I had to tweak the meth a little so it will cause pain. That's what I injected you with, Jack, a derivative of methamphetamine. It opens all the pain sensors in your system and makes them even more receptive to pain impulses. That's the warm glow you're feeling right now. Soon you'll feel as if you're being roasted alive."

Jack's whole body felt as though it was smoldering.

Michelle...

"Dr. Hahn saw my true potential. Now I'm his protégé, and that got me the keys to the kingdom." Brendan patted his security badge. "All I needed was subjects."

"How many?" Jack recoiled at the thought.

"Nearly a dozen. Because of the people we select, no one even came looking for them—until you. It's sad, really. If one disoriented dolphin swims into New York harbor, it's national news; everyone rushes to save it. Yet all these people disappeared, and all you hear is silence."

"But why Michelle? She didn't fit your pattern!"

"No. Michelle was… unfortunate. I had no intention of using her for my study, but she was too gifted with computers. She found a hidden file on our research."

Missy's voice crackled over the speaker. "Her mistake was being too trusting. She confided in me about the file. This save the world complex must run in your family." Missy's words dripped with sarcasm.

"We had to get rid of her and since we didn't think she had any living relatives, we decided to include her in the experiment." Brendan shrugged.

Jack screamed and thrashed against his bonds.

"There was a bonus, though. Her brain images were spectacular. *C'est la vie.*"

Brendan nodded to Missy, who began adjusting her monitors.

"I couldn't believe it when you showed up claiming to be her foster brother," Brendan said. "I still thought our story about Michelle transferring across the country would hold up."

"It would have if you had just put the car in the lake," Missy chided.

Brendan shot her a look and then turned back to Jack. "I was a little nervous when you came snooping around, but after you sent the email to Missy, we needed to act."

Replacement gasped.

"How's the leg?" Brendan's fist slammed into Jack's thigh, eliciting a scream. "I should have stolen a bus to run you down with."

Jack groaned.

"It's taking effect, I see." Brendan leaned in to examine Jack's eyes. "In some ways I'm glad you weren't killed instantly. Now I get to use you."

Replacement growled through the bit in her mouth.

"And when Alice came to our school, it was perfect; we welcomed her with open arms." Brendan leaned over his cart with renewed focus.

"Leave her out of this!" Jack pleaded. Every movement caused pain now, even blinking.

Missy taunted, "You screwed up, Jack, bringing her along."

Replacement looked over the metal cart of horrors and stared at Jack. He tried to read the expression in her battered face, expecting to see fear, hatred, but instead…

Hope. For some reason, she thinks I can still do something. She thinks I'm going to get her out of this. I can't! I got Chandler killed. I got her into this. Brendan knew we were coming. I'm no hero…

Jack's shame added to the burning in his body, and he groaned.

Now I've gotten her killed, too.

41

THE BEAST

"Let's get started."

Jack was helpless to resist as Brendan taped his eyes open, strapped his head in place, and slipped a bit into his mouth. Brendan wheeled the gurney to the fMRI scanner and slid the stretcher into the tube. Inside, behind glass, Jack had his own personal video camera and monitor. Brendan used a remote control to angle the screen directly over Jack's face.

"You should be feeling quite a bit of discomfort now." Brendan reached in and squeezed Jack's upper arm; it felt like a chainsaw ripping into him. "Good. You see, physical pain is quite effective. But for you, I think emotional pain will be even more efficient. Pain that hurts you at the core of your being." He turned toward Missy in the control room. "Put the imager up to full power."

In a few seconds, Missy's voice crackled, "All set, Dr. Phillips."

Brendan strolled past Replacement toward the door and gave them a little wave. "I really hope you have some shrapnel embedded in you."

In spite of the pain, Jack struggled against his restraints. The sound of a low buzz vibrated around him, then gradually increased. Jack tried to calm his breathing, but his heart pounded louder than the roar of the machine.

Brendan's voice echoed over the speakers. "I had planned a video of the battlefield to show you. I thought maybe reliving some of the horrors you saw in Iraq might help elicit that mental state. But then you gave me the perfect idea."

The monitor crackled, and a nightmare began. Michelle was strapped to the stretcher, her eyes taped open and black-and-blue, nose swollen and bloody. Her features, so familiar to him, were disfigured by pain and terror. By torture.

"You wanted to be a fly on the wall," the torturer said. "Do you remember when you asked Dr. Hahn to see video footage of Michelle? Well, here's your chance."

Jack attempted to break free from his head restraint, turn his head away, close his eyes, anything—but all he could do was watch.

"Missy, please turn up the audio," Brendan murmured.

Right before Jack's eyes, Michelle cried and begged, over and over, "Help me. Please!"

He lay there, powerless now to help himself and knowing that her cries for help would never be answered. "Please stop." She wept. "Please." Her mouth twitched and trembled. A memory of her as a little girl, crying after she broke her leg sledding, ripped through Jack as she continued to plead for her life in front of him.

Bile rose up in Jack's throat.

He broke.

He stopped struggling; he stopped fighting. He hadn't surrendered; he had been defeated. All his demons rose up inside him and tossed him into the void. He felt himself tumble down into the nothingness. No feeling. No pain. Nothing. He lay there, his eyes forced open, but saw only the abyss. His mind had lowered an invisible curtain.

How long he stayed shrouded in the empty, shifting mist, he didn't know. Senseless, he hovered in gray nothingness.

From far away, he heard a sound. He wanted to continue his free fall into the vacuum and embrace death, but from somewhere outside the ether, a voice called to him.

"Jack!"

The mist began to clear, and the monitor emerged.

Michelle's voice. She looked directly at the camera, straight at him, and called out his name.

"Jack..."

"Jack..." Replacement's voice echoed in the tube.

"Please," Michelle and Replacement called out at the same time—one voice in the here and now, and the other from the video, blended together.

Then another voice emerged clearly. "The scrawny bitch is loose!" Missy shrieked. "Brendan, you idiot! I told you to check the restraints!"

The fog swirled. Jack was being pulled out of the tube. Replacement was tugging at the strap on his wrist.

Brendan rushed up behind her, grabbed her around the waist, and hoisted her into the air. She twisted and flailed in his arms, raking her fingernails across his face.

Brendan shrieked and dropped her, and she fell back against Jack's stretcher.

"Punch her in the head!" Missy screeched.

Replacement went back to work fumbling at Jack's wrist strap and managed to pull the first part out of the buckle. She flashed only a brief smile before Brendan's fist slammed into the side of her face so hard her head snapped around. Her body went limp, and she crumpled over Jack's legs. Her eyes were open, but black. She was knocked out cold. Or dead.

Brendan pushed her limp body onto the floor.

"Is she dead?" Missy hissed.

Brendan looked toward the control booth. "We can't use her now anyway." He walked over to the cart and took up one of the syringes.

Jack lay on his back, counting the ceiling tiles and his options. He knew he was a violent man, deep down inside. There had always been a beast inside, rattling the bars of its cage. He feared it. He knew it for what it was: hate, pure and simple. He'd locked it away, but the monster didn't die, it grew.

Finding Michelle that day had awoken it. Ever since then, it raged inside, only semi-restrained in its broken cage, while Jack tried to control it.

But now Jack embraced the hate.

If you have to fight, fight to win. His father's words.

He released the beast.

When he yanked up, his chest muscles tightened, and he felt as though his ribs splintered apart. He screamed, frothing at the mouth and biting the gag. Spit flew upward into a red mist. Jack felt something on the gurney crack as he contorted his body.

Brendan turned to Jack, interested but unconcerned. "Go ahead and fight. You'll never break those straps." He leaned down again over Replacement, and pushed the plunger of the syringe, watching the reddish liquid arc into the air.

The pain didn't feel like pain anymore. All Jack felt was hate coursing through his battered body—fueling his rage. He pulled his arms down against the restraints, and his eyes rolled back in his head. He forced his legs to go stiff as boards and shot them up and out. Screaming, he planted his heels and pushed with everything he had, until his legs ripped free and pieces of molded resin flew through the air. A buckle landed on the floor.

The beast was free.

Brendan turned, startled, and Jack kicked him square in the face. The meth speeded up time so it felt like he'd had weeks to plan it. Brendan reeled into the glass wall and fell to the floor, letting go of the syringe.

Jack struggled to release his arms. Brendan was retrieving the syringe from the floor. Jack roared in frustration and pulled up against the wrist straps.

"Get him, Jack!" Replacement's unsteady voice came from below.

Suddenly, Jack's arms were free.

Replacement slid out from underneath his stretcher, holding up two cotter pins in her trembling hand. Tears mixed with the blood on her face, but she still smiled up at him. "Get him, Jack."

"Kill him!" Missy's order thundered over the speakers.

Jack staggered, and his vision blurred, but he ripped the bit from his mouth and the tape off his eyes and leapt to his feet. Brendan stepped back, unprepared for the sudden turn of events, then regained his wits and charged.

Jack's left foot flashed out and smashed into Brendan's hand. The syringe flew out, but Brendan's momentum kept him coming forward. Jack stepped to the right and crashed his elbow into the side of Brendan's head. He grabbed Brendan by his collar and belt. Pulling him against his leg, he twisted his body and pivoted his hip, crying out in agony. But his rage was still stronger.

Brendan's feet shot straight up, and when he reached the apex of the flip, Jack slammed him down. Brendan hit the floor with a sickening thump and his body went limp.

"Jack!" Replacement pointed to the control room.

In the control room, Missy held a gun—*his* gun—and was pointing it straight at him. Her lips curled back in a triumphant snarl. Everything slowed. Jack stumbled sideways. Then Missy turned and aimed the gun at Replacement's chest.

Pain tore along his thigh as he pushed off his rear foot and ran forward. He was too late. He saw the muzzle flash, then the small flames flicking out of the barrel, as the glass in front of Missy spiderwebbed.

"*Alice!*" he cried, lunging forward. They crashed together onto the floor and slid across the black tiles.

He jumped up and knelt over Replacement. His hands frantically searched her body, looking for the entry wound. She gazed up at him in bewilderment and shook her head. They stared in disbelief at the window.

In the control booth, Missy was screaming and holding her bloody hand.

The bullet had lodged in the thick glass; it hadn't passed through.

Jack knew what had happened. Another rookie mistake. She had wrapped her fingers around his gun too high, and the slide action had probably at least broken her thumb, if it hadn't removed it altogether.

Jack and Replacement got up and stumbled for the door, but it was locked from the outside.

Replacement's eyes flashed alarm. "Jack!" He tried to move, but he wasn't fast enough. Brendan smashed into him and slammed Jack up against the wall.

Brendan's fist caught him in the jaw, and Jack's head snapped to the side. He saw stars, and his feet slipped. His left arm grabbed for the wall as Brendan's weight drove him to the ground. The back of Jack's head smashed into the floor, and his whole body shook.

Brendan knelt down on top of him and raised his fists. He punched with his right and then his left. Jack's head whipped to the side with each blow. Jack knew what to do, but his body wasn't cooperating. Pain burned through every cell as the punches rained down on him. A blow from the right split his lip open.

Then a loud twang rang out, and Brendan's eyes rolled back in his head. He pitched forward like a marionette cut from its strings.

Replacement stood victoriously behind him, a stool clutched in her hands.

Jack shoved the body off him and forced himself to sit up. He struggled to stand; each movement sent a wave of agony crashing over him. His hands violently trembled as he tore through Brendan's pockets. "Where's his pass?"

Suddenly the whole room shook, and a muffled roar thundered from above. The lights flickered, and dust fell from the ceiling.

Jack looked to Replacement. "That was an explosion."

He turned toward the control booth, but Missy also looked perplexed.

The second explosion was so loud and powerful it knocked Jack off his feet. Ceiling tiles fell to the floor; the lights flickered and then went out. Sprinklers hissed, but no water came out.

"Replacement?" Jack stumbled over to her.

"Jack?" He heard the panic in her voice.

Emergency lights flicked on. The small lights cast a strange amber glow around the room.

"What the hell happened?" Jack helped Replacement to her feet.

"I may have done that…" she said sheepishly.

Behind them, the large machine was emitting a high-pitched whine that was rapidly increasing in intensity. The electrical wires and hanging lights bent toward it, as the uncontrolled magnet continued its insatiable pull, even without power.

"We have to go!" Replacement cried out.

Jack slipped his arm around her waist and moved for the door. He tried the handle, but it still wouldn't budge.

"It's a keypad." Replacement ran to the wall and frantically punched in codes. "Four digits. I saw the first three." Replacement typed in numbers, pulling the handle after each attempt. "Bingo."

The door swung open. There was smoke in the hallway.

"Wait!" Missy's muffled scream came from behind the glass. "Wait!" She pounded on the window. "I can't get out! Something fell in front of the door. I'm trapped!" Missy yelled.

Through the glass, Jack could see that the explosion had bent the control room door out of its frame.

"You wanted to find the God Spot? It looks like God has come looking for *you*."

"Please," Missy begged. "You have to help me. You're a policeman!"

Smoke was seeping into the room.

Jack glared at his torturer. He grabbed the stool, rushed toward the window, and slammed the stool against it, but the glass didn't break, it only spiderwebbed. He groaned and swung the stool again with everything he had.

The fMRI whirled louder and louder. A metal pipe ripped through the wall behind Missy.

"The shielding's broken. Please!"

Metal objects from the hallway flew through the air and slammed into the fMRI. The metal pipes of the sprinkler system above the ceiling were pulling—shrieking, twisting—toward the colossal supermagnet, now that the explosion had cracked the shielding.

The ceiling of the control room cracked as the metal bent toward the machine. The broken window was finally pulled out of its frame in a shower of glass. Then, with a deafening roar, the whole control room collapsed in on itself—and Missy's screams were silenced.

Jack grabbed Replacement and hurried her through the door into the hallway. It was their only choice. Holding each other up, they limped down the corridor. The smoke was already thick, especially along the ceiling, and they had to walk hunched over. Beneath their feet, the floor was moving.

They could just make out the emergency exit sign and were stumbling toward it when there was a loud crash, and they were flung several feet nearer to their goal. Ceiling tiles and lighting strips rained down on them as the hallway behind them disappeared into rubble.

There's no way I can get Brendan out now.

"Jack! Come on!"

Replacement's voice, and the need within it, gave Jack just enough strength to shrug off the debris that littered his shoulders. He staggered back onto his feet. Keeping low, he grabbed Replacement's hand and made a final dash for the exit sign.

They reached a stairwell that led up.

"Here." Jack took off his shirt and ripped it in half. He handed half to her and put the other half over his face.

Replacement looked up at the staircase filled with thick black smoke. "We can't go up!"

"Over here." Jack had seen a utility door at the bottom of the stairs, and it opened. The door opened onto a narrow service corridor with no emergency lighting.

"Follow me and don't let go." He took her hand and with his other hand, felt his way along the corridor. Even here, farther from the center of destruction, the whole building continued to shudder, and debris rained down on them.

He felt the cold touch of metal. *A door.* He waved his hand around until he felt a handle.

They burst through the door and out into the night. Coughing, they staggered forward. A light snow was falling, mixed with glowing embers. Broken glass, bricks, pipes, and unidentifiable shards lay everywhere, while flames from the burning structure behind cast strange shadows and made everything dance and sway before their eyes.

Stumbling, they climbed the small hill and found themselves at the corner of the parking lot.

Replacement reached out and took Jack's hand. Sirens sounded in the distance, approaching. They could feel the heat where they stood, but Jack wasn't cold; his body still burned from the drug.

Half of the psychology center had blown up, and the entire building was engulfed in flames.

Replacement closed her eyes and whispered, "Thank you, God."

Jack pulled her close. They held on to each other as the flames flickered in each other's eyes and the snow sparkled around them.

Jack watched the snow create a veil of white on Replacement's hair and shoulders. He smiled; he knew a miracle when he saw one. Her right eye was swollen shut, and her whole face was smeared with soot, blood, and tears, but she smiled back.

"How did you do that?" He nodded toward the fire.

"Brendan chased me into the chem lab. I started trashing the place and mixing everything together, hoping it would set off the fire alarm, but I never thought..." With a look of surprise, she gestured to the destroyed building.

Jack laughed so hard that tears ran down his face in spite of the pain, and he pulled her in closer, as if he would never let her go.

42

I GOT THIS ONE

The Impala cruised down the highway toward Fairfield. Replacement stretched her legs out onto the dashboard, and Jack winced. Her ankles were bruised from the restraints. Her jaw was swollen, and her eyes were black-and-blue. He caught a glimpse of himself in the rearview mirror. *I won't be winning any beauty contests, either.*

"What's your favorite color?"

"What?" She wiggled around in her seat.

"What's your favorite color?" he repeated.

"Green."

"Like your eyes?"

"Yep." She perked right up. "What's yours?"

"Black, like my heart." He laughed.

"Seriously, what's your favorite color?"

"Pink."

"Hey. You started this." She crossed her arms.

"Fine. Red. Like your lips." Jack grinned.

A tide of crimson rose from somewhere he couldn't see, up her neck, and over her cheeks. "Okay," she said, pretending nothing had happened but clearly enjoying the game, "I start next. Favorite movie?"

Jack smiled. *"Rocky."*

"That boxing movie you made me watch?" She rolled her eyes.

"It's a great movie. It won an Oscar! Whatever. What's yours?"

She wrinkled her nose as she thought. *"The Wizard of Oz."* She sighed. "It's like my life."

"Your life?" Jack raised an eyebrow. "And who are you, Dorothy?"

"Yes. You're in it too."

Jack sat up. "Me? Who? The Tin Man?"

"Nope." She shook her head and impishly grinned.

"If you say the Cowardly Lion…" Jack scowled.

"Nope." She giggled.

"The Scarecrow?"

"No brain? A possibility but… nope." She hugged her legs to her chest.

"Who's left? The Wicked Witch of the West? Glinda?"

"Toto."

"The dog?" Jack looked at her in disbelief.

"Yeah. You're always running around, barking at me, yapping at my heels. You follow me everywhere but... you're loyal too."

"Seriously?"

"See. There you go, getting yappy, but if I give you a pat on the head you're all lovable again."

Jack frowned.

"Why do you think I gave you that ringtone?" Her hands shot up.

"The stupid barking dog? That's for Toto?"

She burst out laughing. Jack shook his head, but he still smiled.

"Favorite sport, Toto?"

Jack winced and shifted his leg.

"Do you want me to drive?" she offered, concerned.

"No. I'm fine. Baseball."

"Football," she shot back. "Superhero?"

"Iron Man."

She closed her eyes for a second, and when she opened them, they were glistening. "Batman."

He remembered—Chandler was Superman, and he was Batman.

"Thank you for coming back," she said softly. They smiled at each other. "TV show?"

"The Rifleman."

She laughed. "Never heard of it."

They kept playing the game until they reached Fairfield. As they drove into the town, they both drifted off into their own private thoughts. The silence that followed ended the game, but it was a companionable silence.

Jack parked the car and looked at Replacement. Her eyebrows rose, and he understood the unspoken question. Jack started to get out of the car.

Replacement reached out and grabbed Jack's hand. "Do you want me to do it?"

"No, I got this one."

Walking slowly, he stuffed his hands into his pockets and hunched his shoulders, focused on what he had to do. He wasn't looking forward to this, but he knew he had to do it himself. A few moments later, he stopped and stared down at the ground.

"I'm sorry I'm late," he muttered. "I put off... coming to speak with you." He inhaled deeply. "I didn't want to... you know... but I need to tell you what happened. They caught the people responsible for Michelle's murder. It was this guy who worked at the psychology center with Michelle. Him and Michelle's roommate. They're both dead. The Sheriff's Department is opening cases to look into the other people they murdered. They'd been killing people for years, and the victims' families should know what happened." Jack cleared his throat. "Alice should get the credit. If it weren't for her..."

He stopped talking. He wrung his hands together and waited. He was nervous when he heard nothing but silence.

Jack tried to keep going. "She's going to stay with me now. I'm going to get a two-bedroom apartment. My landlady already offered me the apartment below mine. She said the people moved out because the guy above them was too loud." Jack shrugged and smiled faintly. "That's me. Anyway..."

He closed his eyes and exhaled.

"I miss you. Both of you. I'll take care of Alice and Aunt Haddie. I promised her I'd stop by a lot."

He walked forward and placed a flag on the left side of the tombstone and flowers on the right. Then he looked up and sighed.

"I've been thinking about it. If it weren't for Replacement, no one would have known what happened to Michelle. More time would have gone by, and we might never have known. You can tell she's your sister. She has your courage, Chandler. You should have seen her at The Pit." He laughed. "Michelle, she said you taught her computers. She's pretty amazing. Anyway, I see both of you in her."

Jack started to turn to go, but stopped.

"Thank you, for everything," he whispered.

He closed his eyes. He could almost see them. Michelle was riding her bike, and Chandler ran alongside her. They both waved and smiled. Jack laughed and waved back.

He returned to the Impala.

Replacement looked up at him, hopeful.

"How did it go?"

Jack gripped the steering wheel. "Good." His fingers tightened until the leather creaked, and then he relaxed his hands. "Ready?"

Replacement grinned and cracked open her window. "Ready." She smiled, and they headed down the road… together.

EPILOGUE

Alice's hand covered the phone, trying to muffle the beep. She held her breath as she peered back at the couch. Jack was still sleeping.

She bit her lip and her eyebrows knit together. He hadn't slept the whole night through since their ordeal at the lab.

He moaned and rolled over again. She waited a minute until she was sure he hadn't woken up, then she picked up Jack's phone to check the email that had set it off. She tapped the display and the message appeared.

Hi Jack,

Just checking in. Hope you're feeling better. I just read about your exploits in the paper. Like to get together sometime?

Marisa

P.S. If you need any nursing, I give great sponge baths. ☺

"He doesn't need your nursing," Replacement muttered, and stabbed the close button.

She turned back to the computer and continued her hunt. Every night for the last few days, Jack had woken up screaming and covered in sweat. He wouldn't tell her what the nightmares were about, but she heard him muttering in his sleep.

He was looking for his mom.

As the case had grown and the police had found additional victims, Jack had grown more and more restless. She wondered whether the victims who were prostitutes had something to do with his struggle.

Alice had wanted to help, but she knew he'd say no, so she hadn't told him she'd started a search of her own. Every chance she had, she scoured through online records and hunted databases for clues.

The first thing she found out was that Jack's adoptive father, Ted Stratton, had hired a private detective to track down Jack's birth mother for the adoption. Reading through the court documents was frustrating, because Jack's birth mother's name had been blacked out on every page.

But now, pay dirt. She discovered one page where the photocopy of the old records had bled through.

Jack's birth mother's name was Patricia Cole.

She followed the woman's trail through the police database. The mug shots told the tale; prostitution and drugs had worn down the beautiful woman into a shell of who she once was. Alice compiled the photos into a sort of facial smash. They showed Patricia's descent into drugs and despair, like one of those Scared Straight campaigns.

The arrest records stopped a few years ago; it was as if she had fallen off the planet, and Alice thought Patricia Cole might have died. But then she came across an address scribbled in the margins of the paperwork.

She looked back at Jack and bit her lower lip.

How do I tell him?

He groaned and turned over.

Alice got up and walked to the window. Her resolve started to fade as she stared into the darkness. How could she tell him?

Jack, your mom is alive but... she's institutionalized.

She exhaled.

And I think there's more...

THE DETECTIVE JACK STRATTON
MYSTERY-THRILLER SERIES

The Detective Jack Stratton Mystery-Thriller Series, authored by *Wall Street Journal* bestselling writer Christopher Greyson, has over 5,000 five-star reviews and over one million readers and counting. If you'd love to read another page-turning thriller with mystery, humor, and a dash of romance, pick up the next book in the highly acclaimed series today.

AND THEN SHE WAS GONE

A hometown hero with a heart of gold, Jack Stratton was raised in a whorehouse by his prostitute mother. Jack seemed destined to become another statistic, but now his life has taken a turn for the better. Determined to escape his past, he's headed for a career in law enforcement. When his foster mother asks him to look into a girl's disappearance, Jack quickly gets drawn into a baffling mystery. As Jack digs deeper, everyone becomes a suspect—including himself. Caught between the criminals and the cops, can Jack discover the truth in time to save the girl? Or will he become the next victim?

GIRL JACKED

Guilt has driven a wedge between Jack and the family he loves. When Jack, now a police officer, hears the news that his foster sister Michelle is missing, it cuts straight to his core. The police think she just took off, but Jack knows Michelle would never leave her loved ones behind—like he did. Forced to confront the demons from his past, Jack must take action, find Michelle, and bring her home... or die trying.

JACK KNIFED

Constant nightmares have forced Jack to seek answers about his rough childhood and the dark secrets hidden there. The mystery surrounding Jack's birth father leads Jack to investigate the twenty-seven-year-old murder case in Hope Falls.

JACKS ARE WILD

When Jack's sexy old flame disappears, no one thinks it's suspicious except Jack and one unbalanced witness. Jack feels in his gut that something is wrong. He knows that Marisa has a past, and if it ever caught up with her—it would be deadly. The trail leads him into all sorts of trouble—landing him smack in the middle of an all-out mob war between the Italian Mafia and the Japanese Yakuza.

JACK AND THE GIANT KILLER

Rogue hero Jack Stratton is back in another action-packed, thrilling adventure. While recovering from a gunshot wound, Jack gets a seemingly harmless private investigation job—locate the owner of a lost dog—Jack begrudgingly assists. Little does he know it will place him directly in the crosshairs of a merciless serial killer.

DATA JACK

In this digital age of hackers, spyware, and cyber terrorism—data is more valuable than gold. Thieves plan to steal the keys to the digital kingdom and with this much money at stake, they'll kill for it. Can Jack and Alice (aka Replacement) stop the pack of ruthless criminals before they can *Data Jack?*

JACK OF HEARTS

When his mother and the members of her neighborhood book club ask him to catch the "Orange Blossom Cove Bandit," a small-time thief who's stealing garden gnomes and peace of mind from their quiet retirement community, how can Jack refuse? The peculiar mystery proves to be more than it appears, and things take a deadly turn. Now, Jack finds it's up to him to stop a crazed killer, save his parents, and win the hand of the girl he loves—but if he survives, will it be Jack who ends up with a broken heart?

JACK FROST

Jack has a new assignment: to investigate the suspicious death of a soundman on the hit TV show *Planet Survival*. Jack goes undercover as a security agent where the show is filming on nearby Mount Minuit. Soon trapped on the treacherous peak by a blizzard, a mysterious killer continues to stalk the cast and crew of *Planet Survival*. What started out as a game is now a deadly competition for survival. As the temperature drops and the body count rises, what will get them first? The mountain or the killer?

Hear your favorite characters come to life
in audio versions of the
Detective Jack Stratton Mystery-Thriller Series!
Audio Books now available on Audible!

Novels featuring Jack Stratton in order:
AND THEN SHE WAS GONE
GIRL JACKED
JACK KNIFED
JACKS ARE WILD
JACK AND THE GIANT KILLER
DATA JACK
JACK OF HEARTS
JACK FROST

Psychological Thriller
THE GIRL WHO LIVED
Ten years ago, four people were brutally murdered. One girl lived. As the anniversary of the murders approaches, Faith Winters is released from the psychiatric hospital and yanked back to the last spot on earth she wants to be—her hometown where the slayings took place. Wracked by the lingering echoes of survivor's guilt, Faith spirals into a black hole of alcoholism and wanton self-destruction. Finding no solace at the bottom of a bottle, Faith decides to track down her sister's killer—and then discovers that she's the one being hunted.

Epic Fantasy
PURE OF HEART
Orphaned and alone, rogue-teen Dean Walker has learned how to take care of himself on the rough city streets. Unjustly wanted by the police, he takes refuge within the shadows of the city. When Dean stumbles upon an old man being mugged, he tries to help—only to discover that the victim is anything but helpless and far more than he appears. Together with three friends, he sets out on an epic quest where only the pure of heart will prevail.

INTRODUCING
THE ADVENTURES OF FINN AND ANNIE

A SPECIAL COLLECTION OF MYSTERIES EXCLUSIVELY FOR CHRISTOPHER GREYSON'S LOYAL READERS

Finnian Church chased his boyhood dream of following in his father's law-enforcing footsteps by way of the United States Armed Forces. As soon as he finished his tour of duty, Finn planned to report to the police academy. But the winds of war have a way of changing a man's plans. Finn returned home a decorated war hero, but without a leg. Disillusioned but undaunted, it wasn't long before he discovered a way to keep his ambitions alive and earn a living as an insurance investigator.

Finn finds himself in need of a videographer to document the accident scenes. Into his orderly business and simple life walks Annie Summers. A lovely free spirit and single mother of two, Annie has a physical challenge of her own—she's been completely deaf since childhood.

Finn and Annie find themselves tested and growing in ways they never imagined. Join this unlikely duo as they investigate their way through murder, arson, theft, embezzlement, and maybe even love, seeking to distinguish between truth and lies, scammers and victims.

This FREE special collection of mysteries by *Wall Street Journal* bestselling author CHRISTOPHER GREYSON is available EXCLUSIVELY to loyal readers. Get your FREE first installment ONLY at ChristopherGreyson.com. Become a Preferred Reader to enjoy additional FREE *Adventures of Finn and Annie*, advanced notifications of book releases, and more.

Don't miss out, visit ChristopherGreyson.com and JOIN TODAY!

You could win a brand new
HD KINDLE FIRE TABLET
when you go to
ChristopherGreyson.com
Enter as many times as you'd like.
No purchase necessary.
It's just my way of thanking my loyal readers.

Looking for a mystery series mixed with romantic suspense?
Be sure to check out Katherine Greyson's bestselling series:
EVERYONE KEEPS SECRETS

ACKNOWLEDGMENTS

I would like to personally THANK YOU for taking the time to read this story and coming along for the ride with me and Jack and his friends and family. I am so grateful for all the words of encouragement I have received. Thank you for spreading the word via social media on Facebook or Twitter and taking the time to go back and write a great review. Word-of-mouth is crucial for any author to succeed. If you enjoyed *Girl Jacked*, please consider letting others know; it would make all the difference and I would appreciate it very much. Your efforts give me the encouragement and time to keep writing. I can't thank YOU enough.

I would also like to thank my wife. She's the best wife, mother, and my partner in crime. She is an invaluable content editor and I could not do this without her!

My thanks also go out to: my two awesome kids, my dear mother, my family; my fantastic editors—David Gatewood of Lone Trout Editing, Faith Williams of The Atwater Group, and Karen Lawson and Janet Hitchcock of The Proof is in the Reading; to my fabulous proofreader, Charlie Wilson of Landmark Editorial; to my unbelievably helpful beta readers; and to Stuart and Rachel.

ABOUT THE AUTHOR

My name is Christopher Greyson, and I am a storyteller.

Since I was a little boy, I have dreamt of what mystery was around the next corner, or what quest lay over the hill. If I couldn't find an adventure, one usually found me, and now I weave those tales into my stories. I am blessed to have written the bestselling Detective Jack Stratton Mystery-Thriller Series. The collection includes *And Then She Was GONE, Girl Jacked, Jack Knifed, Jacks Are Wild, Jack and the Giant Killer, Data Jack, Jack of Hearts, Jack Frost*, with *Jack of Diamonds* due later this year. I have also penned the bestselling psychological thriller, *The Girl Who Lived* and a special collection of mysteries, *The Adventures of Finn and Annie*.

My background is an eclectic mix of degrees in theatre, communications, and computer science. Currently I reside in Massachusetts with my lovely wife and two fantastic children. My wife, Katherine Greyson, who is my chief content editor, is an author of her own romance series, *Everyone Keeps Secrets*.

My love for tales of mystery and adventure began with my grandfather, a decorated World War I hero. I will never forget being introduced to his friend, a WWI pilot who flew across the skies at the same time as the feared, legendary Red Baron. My love of reading and storytelling eventually led me to write *Pure of Heart*, a young adult fantasy that I released in 2014.

I love to hear from my readers. Please visit ChristopherGreyson.com, where you can become a preferred reader and enjoy additional FREE *Adventures of Finn and Annie*, advanced notifications of book releases and more! Thank you for reading my novels. I hope my stories have brightened your day.

Sincerely,